The Man from Kinvara

Other Books by Tess Gallagher

POETRY

Dear Ghosts,
My Black Horse: New and Selected Poems
Moon Crossing Bridge
Portable Kisses
Amplitude: New and Selected Poems
Willingly
Under Stars
Instructions to the Double

ESSAYS

Against Forgetting (edited by Holly Hughes, preface by Tess Gallagher)
Sawdust Mountain (with photographs by Eirik Johnson; introduction,
        "After the Chainsaws," by Tess Gallagher)
Distant Rain (a conversation between Tess Gallagher and Jakucho Setouchi)
Soul Barnacles: Ten More Years with Ray (edited by Greg Simon)
A Concert of Tenses: Essays on Poetry
Carver Country (photographs by Bob Adelman, introduction by Tess Gallagher)
A New Path to the Waterfall (Raymond Carver, introduction by Tess Gallagher)
All of Us (Raymond Carver, introduction by Tess Gallagher)

FICTION

Barnacle Soup: Stories from the West of Ireland (with Josie Gray)
At the Owl Woman Saloon
The Lover of Horses and Other Stories

TRANSLATION

The Sky Behind the Forest: Selected Poems by Liliana Ursu (with Adam J. Sorkin
        and the poet)
A New Path to the Sea: Poems by Liliana Ursu (with Adam J. Sorkin and the poet)

The Man from Kinvara

Selected Stories

Tess Gallagher

[signature]

Graywolf Press

Excerpt from "My Father's Love Letters" copyright 1987 by Tess Gallagher. Reprinted from *A Concert of Tenses* with the permission of the University of Michigan Press.

Publication of this volume is made possible in part by a grant provided by the Minnesota State Arts Board, through an appropriation by the Minnesota State Legislature; a grant from the Wells Fargo Foundation Minnesota; and a grant from the National Endowment for the Arts, which believes that a great nation deserves great art. Significant support has also been provided by the Bush Foundation; Target; the McKnight Foundation; and other generous contributions from foundations, corporations, and individuals. To these organizations and individuals we offer our heartfelt thanks.

Published by Graywolf Press
250 Third Avenue North, Suite 600
Minneapolis, Minnesota 55401
All rights reserved.

www.graywolfpress.org

Published in the United States of America

Printed in Canada

ISBN 978-1-55597-537-1

2 4 6 8 9 7 5 3 1
First Graywolf Printing, 2009

Library of Congress Control Number: 2009926847

Cover design: Christa Schoenbrodt, Studio Haus

Cover art: Josie Gray, *Near Kinvara*

For Ray, always; for my stalwarts Josie, Dorothy and Dick, Greg and Helle, Alice and Bruce, Bill and Maureen, Nita and John, and Ted. Also my Irish and American families, especially Sheila and the young ones who read or love a good story: Tiernan most of all, Caleb, Rijl, Devin, Hayden, and Brian Questa. And remembering my mother who gave me several of these stories and is my heart's companion.

Contents

Introduction: A Letter Mailed

*Fiction is . . . its own memory. It is now a thing apart
from the writer; like a letter mailed, it is nearer by now
to its reader.*

—Eudora Welty

While reading and choosing from all my stories for this volume I also reread "My Father's Love Letters," an essay in which I tell the story of my favorite uncle's murder in Missouri. His loss, one of the central stories of my family, was something none of us ever got over—the sacrifice of the good man to the sudden, eruptive violence of America. I go back to this true story as the root of my impulse to carry in prose and poetry those elements of our lives that break us open to hard truths and to the daily mysteries and quandaries that continue to haunt us.

Here are the elements of that story as I wrote them in my book of essays, *A Concert of Tenses*:

Children sometimes adopt a second father or mother when they are cut off from the natural parent. Porter Morris, my uncle, was the father I could speak with. He lived with my grandparents on the farm in Windyville, Missouri, where I spent many of my childhood summers. He never married but stayed with the farm even after my grandparents died. He'd been a mule trainer during the Second World War, the only time he had ever left home. He loved horses and raised and gentled one for me, which he named Angel Foot because she was black except for one white foot.

I continued to visit my grandfather and my uncle during the five years of my first marriage. My husband was a jet pilot in the Marine Corps. We were stationed in the South, so I would go to cook for my uncle during the haying and I would also help stack the hay in the barn. My uncle and I took salt to the cattle. We sowed a field with barley and went to market in Springfield with a truckload of pigs. There were visits with neighbors, Cleydeth and Joe Stefter or Jule Elliot, when we sat for hours telling stories and gossiping. Many images from my uncle's stories and from these visits to the farm got into my writing, both the poetry and the stories.

My uncle lived alone at the farm after my grandfather's death, but soon he met a woman who lived with her elderly parents. He began to remodel an old house on the farm. There was talk of marriage. One day my mother called to say there had been a fire at the farm. The house had burned to the ground and my uncle could not be found. She returned to the farm, what remained of her childhood home. After the ashes had cooled, she searched with the sheriff and found my uncle's skeleton where it had burned into the mattress springs of the bed.

My mother would not accept the coroner's verdict that the fire had been caused by an electrical short circuit, or a fire in the chimney. It was summer and no fire would have been laid. She combed the ashes, looking for the shotgun my uncle always kept near his bed, and the other gun, a rifle, with which he hunted. They were not to be found. My mother believed her brother had been murdered and she set about proving it. She offered a reward and soon after, a young boy walking along the roadside picked my uncle's billfold out of the ditch, his name stamped in gold on the flap.

Three men were eventually brought to trial. I journeyed to Bolivar, Missouri, to meet my parents for the trial. We watched as the accused killer was released and the other two men, who had confessed to being his accomplices, were sentenced to five years in the penitentiary for manslaughter. Parole would be possible for them in two to three years. The motive had been money— although one of the men had held a grudge against my uncle for having been ordered to move out of a house he'd been renting from my uncle some three years before. They had taken forty dollars from my uncle, then shot him when he could not give them more. My parents and I came away from the trial stunned with disbelief and anger.

I tried to write this out, to investigate the nature of vengeance, to disarm myself of the anger I carried. I wrote two poems about this event: "Two Stories" and "The Absence." Images from my uncle's death also appeared in "Stepping Outside," the title poem of my first, limited-edition poetry collection. I began to see poems as a way of settling scores with the self. I felt I had reached the only possible justice for my uncle in the writing out of my anger and the honoring of the life that had been taken so brutally. The *In Cold Blood* aspect of my uncle's murder has caused violence to haunt my vision of what it is to live in America. Sometimes, with my eyes wide open, I still see the wall behind my grandfather's empty bed, and on it the fiery angels and Jacob burning.

My storytelling began then as a process of unburdening and search-ing, of trying to see why ordinary people do the things they do and what consequences they must live out accordingly. The early stories owe much to Raymond Carver, who encouraged me and who read and remarked on all the stories of *The Lover of Horses*. When the book was published he gathered all our friends at our favorite restaurant in Syracuse, New York, and paid for our meal together to celebrate. I have a photo on my desk of him sitting next to me, my arms full of roses he had given me on that day. His belief in my ability to tell stories has been sustaining nourishment.

After his death I missed greatly helping Ray with his stories as they were written, the pure excitement of each of us showing the other our work, whether poems or stories, or even at times our letters. The only way to get stories back into my half-empty house was to begin to write them myself. The result was *At the Owl Woman Saloon,* its stories often centered in the Pacific Northwest where I was born and raised.

My storytelling impulse, whether it manifests itself in poetry or prose, provides a deep window into the struggle, heartbreak, and tenderness of the lives these stories have allowed me to witness in that inner space of the imagination, which is so important to remaking our sense of what can matter in our lives and in those lives beside ours.

Tess Gallagher
November 18, 2008

The Man from Kinvara

At the beheading of the statue
the laurel parted from
the garter, and what they did
with King Billy's head I do not know,
for in 1763 the statue stood at
the Boyle bridge, near the Royal Hotel.

But bridges come and go, as this one did
and when rebuilt in 1834, Viscount Lorton
had Billy hefted to the Pleasure Grounds,
complete with picnics and strollers.
But pleasure seekers, as a residue
of the early 1920s "troubles,"
beheaded the statue among sycamore
and ash—the headless remains later
removed, as an assault on order. Arms
and torso, feet and waistcoat
bludgeoned down. Now the spot

is simply: "the pedestal where King Billy
stood," for it is the pedestal-makers
who win the day as that young boy
strikes a pose, then leaps like a jaguar
onto the back of his unsuspecting
friend. Double portrait of heads rolling

through grass, dew cool to their cheeks:
gleeful cries of predator and victor unravel
below the Curlew Mountains,
named for birds we seldom see.

Still, there will always be witnesses; I am waiting
for the man from Kinvara. He is mild
for someone having attended
a beheading. Like me he was a visitor
to the event. But having held on to one's head
while another's falls, rearranges
notions of a body. May he let
some detail slip to enlighten me, such as
what they did with a head so dislodged, so
beyond its danger.

The man from Kinvara is taking his time.
I think, like me, he often walks headless under stars,
above the child combatants
rolling across the lawns of the world.
One might yet encounter such a man
with his headless moment, his freedom-glee,
his vacant stare.

Let me up on your back, oh man from Kinvara.
I've a spare head with a girlish sheen
gazing out across Lough Arrow
where daily the swans are shedding a lake
and taking up a sky.

from
The Lover of Horses

The Lover of Horses

 They say my great-grandfather was a gypsy, but the most popular explanation for his behavior was that he was a drunk. How else could the women have kept up the scourge of his memory all these years, had they not had the usual malady of our family to blame? Probably he was both, a gypsy and a drunk.

Still, I have reason to believe the gypsy in him had more to do with the turn his life took than his drinking. I used to argue with my mother about this, even though most of the information I have about my great-grandfather came from my mother, who got it from her mother. A drunk, I kept telling her, would have had no initiative. He would simply have gone down with his failures and had nothing to show for it. But my great-grandfather had eleven children, surely a sign of industry, and he was a lover of horses. He had so many horses he was what people called "horse poor."

I did not learn, until I traveled to where my family originated at Collenamore in the west of Ireland, that my great-grandfather had most likely been a "whisperer," a breed of men among the gypsies who were said to possess the power of talking sense into horses. These men had no fear of even the most malicious and dangerous horses. In fact, they would often take the wild animal into a closed stall in order to perform their skills.

Whether a certain intimacy was needed or whether the whisperers simply wanted to protect their secret conversations with horses is not known. One thing was certain—such men gained power over horses by whispering. What they whispered no one knew. But the effectiveness

5

of their methods was renowned, and anyone for counties around who had an unruly horse could send for a whisperer and be sure that the horse would take to heart whatever was said and reform his behavior from that day forth.

By all accounts, my great-grandfather was like a huge stallion himself, and when he went into a field where a herd of horses was grazing, the horses would suddenly lift their heads and call to him. Then his bearded mouth would move, and though he was making sounds that could have been words, which no horse would have had reason to understand, the horses would want to hear; and one by one they would move toward him across the open space of the field. He could turn his back and walk down the road, and they would follow him. He was probably drunk, my mother said, because he was swaying and mumbling all the while. Sometimes he would stop dead-still in the road and the horses would press up against him and raise and lower their heads as he moved his lips. But because these things were only seen from a distance, and because they have eroded in the telling, it is now impossible to know whether my great-grandfather said anything of importance to the horses. Or even if it was his whispering that had brought about their good behavior. Nor was it clear, when he left them in some barnyard as suddenly as he'd come to them, whether they had arrived at some new understanding of the difficult and complex relationship between men and horses.

Only the aberrations of my great-grandfather's relationship with horses have survived—as when he would bathe in the river with his favorite horse or when, as my grandmother told my mother, he insisted on conceiving his ninth child in the stall of a bay mare named Redwing. Not until I was grown and going through the family Bible did I discover that my grandmother had been this ninth child, and so must have known something about the matter.

These oddities in behavior lead me to believe that when my great-grandfather, at the age of fifty-two, abandoned his wife and family to join a circus that was passing through the area, it was not simply drunken

bravado, nor even the understandable wish to escape family obliga-
tions. I believe the gypsy in him finally got the upper hand, and it led
to such a remarkable happening that no one in the family has so far
been willing to admit it: not the obvious transgression—that he had
run away to join the circus—but that he was, in all likelihood, a man
who had been stolen by a horse.

This is not an easy view to sustain in the society we live in. But
I have not come to it frivolously, and have some basis for my belief.
For although I have heard the story of my great-grandfather's defec-
tion time and again since childhood, the one image that prevails in all
versions is of a dappled gray stallion that had been trained to dance a
variation of the mazurka. So impressive was this animal that he mes-
merized crowds with his sliding step-and-hop to the side through the
complicated figures of the dance, which he performed, not in the way
of Lipizzaners—with other horses and their riders—but riderless and
with the men of the circus company as his partners.

It is known that my great-grandfather became one of these dancers.
After that he was reputed, in my mother's words, to have gone "completely to ruin." The fact that he walked from the house with only the
clothes on his back, leaving behind his own beloved horses (twenty-
nine of them to be exact), further supports my idea that a powerful
force must have held sway over him, something more profound than
the miseries of drink or the harsh imaginings of his abandoned wife.

Not even the fact that seven years later he returned and knocked
on his wife's door, asking to be taken back, could exonerate him from
what he had done, even though his wife did take him in and looked
after him until he died some years later. But the detail in the account
that no one takes note of is that when my great-grandfather returned, he
was carrying a saddle blanket and the black plumes from the headgear
of one of the circus horses. This passes by even my mother as simply a
sign of the ridiculousness of my great-grandfather's plight—for after all,
he was homeless and heading for old age as a "good-for-nothing drunk"
and a "fool for horses."

No one has bothered to conjecture what these curious emblems—saddle blanket and plumes—must have meant to my great-grandfather. But he hung them over the foot of his bed—"like a fool," my mother said. And sometimes when he got very drunk he would take up the blanket and, wrapping it like a shawl over his shoulders, he would grasp the plumes. Then he would dance the mazurka. He did not dance in the living room but took himself out into the field, where the horses stood at attention and watched as if suddenly experiencing the smell of the sea or a change of wind in the valley. "Drunks don't care what they do," my mother would say as she finished her story about my great-grandfather. "Talking to a drunk is like talking to a stump."

Ever since my great-grandfather's outbreaks of gypsy-necessity, members of my family have been stolen by things—by mad ambitions, by musical instruments, by otherwise harmless pursuits from mushroom hunting to childbearing or, as was my father's case, by the more easily recognized and popular obsession with card playing. To some extent, I still think it was failure of imagination in this respect that brought about his diminished prospects in the life of our family.

But even my mother had been powerless against the attraction of a man so convincingly driven. When she met him at a birthday dance held at the country house of one of her young friends, she asked him what he did for a living. My father pointed to a deck of cards in his shirt pocket and said, "I play cards." But love is such as it is, and although my mother was otherwise a deadly practical woman, it seemed she could fall in love with no man but my father.

So it is possible that the propensity to be stolen is somewhat contagious when ordinary people come into contact with people such as my father. Though my mother loved him at the time of the marriage, she soon began to behave as if she had been stolen from a more fruitful and upright life that otherwise might have been hers.

My father's card playing was accompanied, to no one's surprise, by bouts of drinking. The only thing that may have saved our family from a life of poverty was the fact that my father seldom gambled with money.

Such were his charm and powers of persuasion that he was able to convince other players to accept his notes on everything from the fish he intended to catch next season to the sale of his daughter's hair.

I know about this last wager because I remember the day he came to me with a pair of scissors and said it was time to cut my hair. Two snips and it was done. I cannot forget the way he wept onto the backs of his hands and held the braids together like a broken noose from which a life had suddenly slipped. I was thirteen at the time and my hair had never been cut. It was his pride and joy that I had such hair. But for me it was only a burdensome difference between me and my classmates, so I was glad to be rid of it. What anyone else could have wanted with my long shiny braids is still a mystery to me.

When my father was seventy-three he fell ill and the doctors gave him only a few weeks to live. My father was convinced that his illness had come on him because he'd hit a particularly bad losing streak at cards. He had lost heavily the previous month, and items of value, mostly belonging to my mother, had disappeared from the house. He developed the strange idea that if he could win at cards he could cheat the prediction of the doctors and live at least into his eighties.

By this time I had moved away from home and made a life for myself in an attempt to follow the reasonable dictates of my mother, who had counseled her children severely against all manner of rash ambition and foolhardiness. Her entreaties were leveled especially in my direction since I had shown a suspect enthusiasm for a certain pony at around the age of five. And it is true I felt I had lost a dear friend when my mother saw to it that the neighbors who owned this pony moved it to pasture elsewhere.

But there were other signs that I might wander off into unpredictable pursuits. The most telling of these was that I refused to speak aloud to anyone until the age of eleven. I whispered everything, as if my mind were a repository of secrets to be divulged only in this intimate manner. If anyone asked me a question, I was always polite about answering, but I had to place my mouth near the head of my inquisitor and, using only my breath and lips, make my reply.

My teachers put my whispering down to shyness and made special accommodations for me. When it came time for recitations I would accompany the teacher into the cloakroom and there whisper to her the memorized verses or the speech I was to have prepared. God knows, I might have continued on like this into the present if my mother hadn't plotted with some neighborhood boys to put burrs into my long hair. She knew by other signs that I had a terrible temper, and she was counting on that to deliver me into the world where people shouted and railed at one another and talked in an audible fashion about things both common and sacred.

When the boys shut me into a shed, according to plan, there was nothing for me to do but cry out for help and curse them in a torrent of words I had only heard used by adults. When my mother heard this she rejoiced, thinking that at last she had broken the treacherous hold of the past over me, of my great-grandfather's gypsy blood and the fear that against all her efforts I might be stolen away, as she had been, and as my father had, by some as yet unforeseen predilection. Had I not already experienced the consequences of such a life in our household, I doubt she would have been successful, but the advantages of an ordinary existence among people of a less volatile nature had begun to appeal to me.

It was strange, then, that after all the care my mother had taken for me in this regard, when my father's illness came on him, my mother brought her appeal to me. "Can you do something?" she wrote, in her cramped, left-handed scrawl. "He's been drinking and playing cards for three days and nights. I am at my wit's end. Come home at once!"

Somehow I knew this message was addressed to the very part of me that most baffled and frightened my mother—the part that belonged exclusively to my father and his family's inexplicable manias.

When I arrived home my father was not there.

"He's at the tavern. In the back room," my mother said. "He hasn't eaten for days. And if he's slept, he hasn't done it here."

I made up a strong broth, and as I poured the steaming liquid into a thermos I heard myself utter syllables and other vestiges of language I could not reproduce if I wanted to. "What do you mean by that?" my mother demanded, as if a demon had leapt out of me. "What did you say?" I didn't—I couldn't—answer her. But suddenly I felt that an unsuspected network of sympathies and distant connections had begun to reveal itself to me on my father's behalf.

There is a saying that when lovers have need of moonlight, it is there. So it seemed, as I made my way through the deserted town toward the tavern and card room, that all nature had been given notice of my father's predicament, and that the response I was waiting for would not be far off.

But when I arrived at the tavern and had talked my way past the barman and into the card room itself, I saw my father with an enormous pile of blue chips at his elbow. Several players had fallen out to watch, heavy-lidded and smoking their cigarettes like weary gangsters. Others slumped on folding chairs near the coffee urn with its empty "Pay Here" Styrofoam cup.

My father's cap was pushed to the back of his head so his forehead shone in the dim light, and he grinned over his cigarette at me with the serious preoccupation of a child who has no intention of obeying anyone. And why should he, I thought, as I sat down just behind him and loosened the stopper on the thermos. The five or six players still at the table casually appraised my presence to see if it had tipped the scales of their luck in an even more unfavorable direction. Then they tossed their cards aside, drew fresh ones, or folded.

In the center of the table were more blue chips, and poking out from my father's coat pocket I recognized the promissory slips he must have redeemed, for he leaned to me and in a low voice, without taking his eyes from his cards, said, "I'm having a hell of a good time. The time of my life."

He was winning. His face seemed ravaged by the effort, but he was clearly playing on a level that had carried the game far beyond the realm of mere card playing and everyone seemed to know it. The dealer cocked an eyebrow as I poured broth into the plastic thermos cup and handed it to my father, who slurped from it noisily, then set it down.

"Tell the old kettle she's got to put up with me a few more years," he said, and lit up a fresh cigarette. His eyes as he looked at me, however, seemed over-brilliant, as if doubt, despite all his efforts, had gained a permanent seat at his table. I squeezed his shoulder and kissed him hurriedly on his forehead. The men kept their eyes down, and as I paused at the door, there was a shifting of chairs and a clearing of throats. Just outside the room I nearly collided with the barman, who was carrying in a fresh round of beer. His heavy jowls waggled as he recovered himself and looked hard at me over the icy bottles. Then he disappeared into the card room with his provisions.

I took the long way home, finding pleasure in the fact that at this hour all the stoplights had switched to a flashing-yellow caution cycle. Even the teenagers who usually cruised the town had gone home or to more secluded spots. *Doubt,* I kept thinking as I drove with my father's face before me, that's the real thief. And I knew my mother had brought me home because of it, because she knew that once again a member of our family was about to be stolen.

Two more days and nights I ministered to my father at the card room. I would never stay long because I had the fear myself that I might spoil his luck. But many unspoken tendernesses passed between us in those brief appearances as he accepted the nourishment I offered, or when he looked up and handed me his beer bottle to take a swig from—a ritual we'd shared since my childhood.

My father continued to win—to the amazement of the local barflies who poked their faces in and out of the card room and gave the dwindling three or four stalwarts at the table a commiserating shake of their heads. There had never been a winning streak like it in the history of the tavern, and indeed, we heard later that the man who owned the card room and tavern had to sell out and open a fruit stand on the edge of town as a result of my father's extraordinary good luck.

Twice during this period my mother urged the doctor to order my father home. She was sure he would, at some fateful moment, risk the entire winnings in some mad rush toward oblivion. But his doctor spoke of a new "gaming therapy" for the terminally ill, based on my father's surge of energies in the pursuit of gambling. Little did he know that my father was, by that stage, oblivious to even his winning, he had gone so far into exhaustion.

Luckily for my father, the hour came when, for lack of players, the game folded. Two old friends drove him home and helped him down from the pickup. They paused in the driveway, one either side of him, letting him steady himself. When the card playing had ended there had been nothing for my father to do but get drunk.

My mother and I watched from the window as the men steered my father toward the hydrangea bush at the side of the house, where he re- lieved himself with perfect precision on one mammoth blossom. Then they hoisted him up the stairs and into the entryway. My mother and I took over from there.

"Give 'em hell, boys," my father shouted after the men, concluding some conversation he was having with himself.

"You betcha," the driver called back, laughing. Then he climbed with his companion into the cab of his truck and roared away.

Tied around my father's waist was a cloth sack full of bills and coins, which flapped and jingled against his knees as we bore his weight be- tween us up the next flight of stairs and into the living room. There we deposited him on the couch, where he took up residence, refusing to sleep in his bed—for fear, my mother claimed, that death would know where to find him. But I preferred to think he enjoyed the rhythms of the household; from where he lay at the center of the house, he could overhear all conversations that took place and add his opinions when he felt like it.

My mother was so stricken by the signs of his further decline that she did everything he asked, instead of arguing with him or simply refusing. Instead of taking his winnings straight to the bank so as not to miss a day's interest, she washed an old goldfish bowl and dumped all the money into it, most of it in twenty-dollar bills. Then she placed it on the coffee table near his head so he could run his hands through it at will, or let his visitors do the same.

"Money feels good on your elbow," he would say to them. "I played them under the table for that. Yes sir, take a feel of that!" Then he would lean back on his pillows and tell my mother to bring his guests a shot of whiskey. "Make sure she fills my glass up," he'd say to me so my mother was certain to overhear. And my mother, who'd never allowed a bottle of whiskey into her house before now, would look at me as if the two of us were more than any woman should have to bear.

"If only you'd brought him home from that card room," she said again and again. "Maybe it wouldn't have come to this."

This included the fact that my father had radically altered his diet. He lived only on greens. If it was green he would eat it. By my mother's reckoning, the reason for his change of diet was that if he stopped eating what he usually ate, death would think it wasn't him and go look for somebody else.

Another request my father made was asking my mother to sweep the doorway after anyone came in or went out.

"To make sure death wasn't on their heels; to make sure death didn't slip in as they left." This was my mother's reasoning. But my father didn't give any reasons. Nor did he tell us why he wanted all the furniture moved out of the room except for the couch where he lay. And the money, they could take that away too.

But soon his strength began to ebb, and more and more family and friends crowded into the vacant room to pass the time with him, to laugh about stories remembered from his childhood or from his nights as a young man at the country dances when he and his older brother would work all day in the cotton fields, hop a freight train to town, and dance all night. Then they would have to walk home, getting there just at daybreak in time to go straight to work again in the cotton fields.

"We were like bulls then," my father would say in a burst of the old vigor, then close his eyes suddenly as if he hadn't said anything at all.

As long as he spoke to us, the inevitability of his condition seemed easier to bear. But when, at the last, he simply opened his mouth for food or stared silently toward the far wall, no one knew what to do with themselves.

My own part in that uncertain time came to me accidentally. I found myself in the yard sitting on a stone bench under a little cedar tree my father loved because he liked to sit there and stare at the ocean. The tree whispered, he said. He said it had a way of knowing what your troubles were. Suddenly a craving came over me. I wanted a cigarette, even though I don't smoke, hate smoking, in fact. I was sitting where my father had sat, and to smoke seemed a part of some rightness that had begun to work its way within me. I went into the house and bummed a pack of cigarettes from my brother. For the rest of the morning I sat under the cedar tree and smoked. My thoughts drifted with its shiftings and murmurings, and it struck me what a wonderful thing nature is because it knows the value of silence, the innuendos of silence and what they could mean for a word-bound creature like myself.

I passed the rest of the day in a trance of silences, moving from place to place, revisiting the sites I knew my father loved—the "dragon tree," a hemlock at the far end of the orchard, so named for its wind-tossed triangular head; the rose arbor where he and my mother had courted; the little marina where I sat in his fishing boat and dutifully smoked the hated cigarettes, flinging them one by one into the brackish water.

I was waiting to know what to do for him, he who would soon be a piece of useless matter, of no more consequence than the cigarette butts that floated and washed against the side of his boat. I could feel some action accumulating in me through the steadiness of water raising and lowering the boat, through the sad petal-fall of roses in the arbor and the tossing of the dragon tree.

That night when I walked from the house I was full of purpose. I headed toward the little cedar tree. Without stopping to question the necessity of what I was doing, I began to break off the boughs I could reach and to pile them on the ground.

"What are you doing?" my brother's children wanted to know, crowding around as if I might be inventing some new game.

"What does it look like?" I said.

"Pulling limbs off the tree," the oldest said. Then they dashed away in a pack under the orchard trees, giggling and shrieking.

As I pulled the boughs from the trunk I felt a painful permission, as when two silences, tired of holding back, give over to each other some shared regret. I made my bed on the boughs and resolved to spend the night there in the yard, under the stars, with the hiss of the ocean in my ear, and the maimed cedar tree standing over me like a gift torn out of its wrappings.

My brothers, their wives, and my sister had now begun their nightly vigil near my father, taking turns at staying awake. The windows were open for the breeze and I heard my mother trying to answer the question of why I was sleeping outside on the ground—"like a damned fool" I knew they wanted to add.

"She doesn't want to be here when death comes for him," my mother said, with an air of clairvoyance she had developed from a lifetime with my father. "They're too much alike," she said.

The ritual of night games played by the children went on long past their bedtimes. Inside the house, the kerosene lantern, saved from my father's childhood home, had been lit—another of his strange requests during the time before his silence. He liked the shadows it made and the sweet smell of kerosene. I watched the darkness as the shapes of my brothers and sister passed near it, gigantic and misshapen where they bent or raised themselves or crossed the room.

Out on the water the wind had come up. In the orchard the children were spinning in a circle, faster and faster, giddy and reeling with speed and darkness. Then they would stop, rest a moment, taking quick ecstatic breaths before plunging again in the opposite direction, swirling round and round until the excitement could rise no higher, their laughter and cries brimming over, then scattering as they flung one another by the arms or chased each other toward the house as if their lives depended on it.

I lay awake for a long while after their footsteps had died away and the car doors had slammed over the good-byes of the children being taken home to bed. The last of the others had been bedded down in the house while the adults went on waiting.

It was important to be out there alone and close to the ground. The pungent smell of the cedar boughs was around me, rising up in the crisp night air toward the tree, whose turnings and swayings had altered, as they had to, in order to accompany the changes about to overtake my father and me. I thought of my great-grandfather bathing with his horse in the river, and of my father who had just passed through the longest period in his life without the clean feel of cards falling through his hands as he shuffled or dealt them. He was too weak now even to hold a cigarette; there was a burn mark on the hardwood floor where his last cigarette had fallen. His winnings were safely in the bank and the luck that was to have saved him had gone back to that place luck goes to when it is finished with us.

So this is what it comes to, I thought, and listened to the wind as it mixed gradually with the memory of children's voices, which still seemed to rise and fall in the orchard. There was a soft crooning of syllables that was satisfying to my ears, but ultimately useless and absurd. Then it came to me that I was the author of those unwieldy sounds, and that my lips had begun to work of themselves.

In a raw pulsing of language I could not account for, I lay awake through the long night and spoke to my father as one might speak to an ocean or the wind, letting him know by that threadbare accompaniment that the vastness he was about to enter had its rhythms also in me. And that he was not forsaken. And that I was letting him go. That so far I had denied the disreputable world of dancers and drunkards, gamblers and lovers of horses to which I most surely belonged. But from that night forward I vowed to be filled with the first unsavory desire that would have me. To plunge myself into the heart of my life and be ruthlessly lost forever.

King Death

It was five-thirty and the sun just coming up when I heard Dan brace his ladder outside against the bedroom wall. His paint bucket clanged against the rungs. I'd been dreaming. Something about dressing myself, then finding later that I hadn't dressed myself. Nobody in the dream minded that I was half-dressed, but I minded. Leonard was on his side, with his hands near his chest. He was grinding his teeth. I gave him a nudge with my knee and he stopped.

I got up, put my robe on, and went to make the coffee. Dan passed the kitchen window on his way to get something from his truck. We waved good morning and smiled. I liked having him around. He was a hard worker; he had just gotten married and was doing odd jobs in addition to his regular one with the city parks department.

I let Leonard sleep. I knew the light falling across the bed would wake him soon enough. I took a glass of juice out to Dan.

"Going to get hot," he said. "I should start at midnight and work till daylight."

"Then you'd have to fight the bugs," I said.

"I don't mind bugs," he said. "You can kill a few bugs and feel better, but you can't kill sun. It's going to get hot as Hades pretty soon." Dan was a Mormon, so he was always careful about what he said. He used "darn" and "shucks" a lot.

Dan was helping me get the house ready to sell. Leonard designed heating and air-conditioning systems for industrial buildings, and was due to be transferred to Dallas in the next couple of months. The transfer meant a promotion, so he was glad about it. If every move we'd made had meant a promotion, Leonard would have been president of the company. But most of the time the bosses were just shifting personnel here and there to cover themselves.

I met Dan a year ago, when we first moved to Tucson. Leonard and I had closed on the house, then driven to Sacramento to pack things up for the move. But before the movers could get our things to Tucson, the house was vandalized—the living room carpet slashed, light fixtures broken, cabinet doors yanked off, handprints smeared on the walls. The neighbors said it must have been the gang of young men who'd rented the house before we bought it. They'd had wild parties. Sometimes as many as fifty cars and motorcycles would be parked along the street.

"We weren't about to mess with them," the man across the street told me. "We saw all kinds of things. Thugs like that run in a pack. They wouldn't think twice about cutting your throat. I got kids and a wife and a home to think about. No, they made their music day and night, and we put up with it."

Leonard wanted to sell the house immediately. He was spooked that it had been broken into. But I didn't want to be run out of a house before I'd even lived in it. I said I'd take charge of fixing the place up again. It was going to be a nice place, I told him. I got Dan's name from a man at the hardware store, and he came to paint the inside of the house. Leonard and I stayed in a motel for two weeks, eating restaurant food and watching TV in bed at night. It wasn't so bad. Now, a year later, Dan was painting the outside. The house was starting to look so good I wanted to forget about having to move again.

"You got yourself a new neighbor," Dan said to me. He was resting his glass on a rung of the ladder.

"What do you mean?"

"There's somebody in the alleyway between your house and the next," Dan said. "I saw him from the ladder while I was painting."

There was a high board fence around the house. It was over my head and nearly over Dan's, too. The property had been fenced to leave a wide fire lane between our house and the house of a neighbor who called himself the Mad Hatter. He was a middle-aged disc jockey. He probably had a real name, but on the radio he called himself the Mad Hatter and that's all we ever knew him by. His mailbox had recently been vandalized, and he told me he was going to shoot the next kids he caught messing with it. He didn't care if they were in diapers, he said; he was going to plug them.

Dan motioned toward the fence and shook his head. "He's comfortable as a king," he said. "He's laying over there sleeping on his back, this old guy."

"On the ground?" I said. "With no covers?"

"Just his clothes," Dan said. "It's nobody I know," he added, and laughed. He drank down the last of his juice.

"You hold the ladder," I said. I cinched my robe around my waist and went up the ladder just far enough to see over the fence. There in the tall grass a man was lying face up with his eyes closed. One big-knuckled hand was outstretched in the grass. The other lay across his chest. He was using a flattened cardboard box for a bed. Paper wrappers and some wine bottles lay near him. I looked down at Dan and lowered my voice. "Maybe he's dead," I said.

"No, he moved," Dan said. "I just saw him move."

"He could die over there and not be found for days," I said. "He's probably been smoking in that high grass." I remembered how when I was a child the railroad bums had come up to our back fence and my mother had gone into the house and gotten slices of bread for them. She was superstitious about beggars. She believed that if you turned them away they'd put a curse on you. But instead my father cursed at her, and said he didn't buy bread so she could hand it away to every down-and-outer who passed the fence.

I went inside and woke Leonard. It was time for him to get ready for work anyway. I followed him into the bathroom and talked to him while he splashed water on his face. "There's a bum sleeping on the other side of our fence," I said. "I want you to go out there before you leave and tell him he can't sleep there. He can't make a bedroom out of our yard."

"Maybe he's just passing through," Leonard said. "I need a clean towel." He turned to me, his eyes squinted shut and water dripping onto his chest.

I handed him a towel from the cupboard near the medicine cabinet. "He'll tell his bum pals about this place," I said. "I don't want him out there. We'll never sell the house. Can you imagine showing people around and saying, 'Oh and the fellow over the fence—that's our resident bum'?"

"I'll take care of it," Leonard said.

I went back into the kitchen to fix scrambled eggs and toast. Leonard came in, smelling of shaving lotion. "Some neighborhood we landed in," he said. He pulled out his chair and sat down at the table. "We should never have moved into this house. You'll listen to me now."

"It's like this all over," I said. "Jeana, right next to the university, she told me that little nurse next door to her woke up with a man standing over her bed. It was the middle of the night. The nurse asked him what he wanted. She stayed calm the whole time. He said he was looking for his friend John. 'John doesn't live here,' the nurse told him. 'I think you better leave.' So the man left, all right—with her stereo, her hair dryer, some eggs, and a pair of fingernail clippers. She was lucky she wasn't killed. He'd cut a hole in a screen on one of the living room windows and crawled in."

"We may as well live in Alaska," Leonard said. "It's worse than Alaska. It's lawless here. It's like the Old West. Like the Gold Rush all over again. Two thousand people a month moving into this place. It's a wonder they don't put tents on our lawn."

"Some of them don't have tents," I said. I pointed my spatula toward the alley.

"I know, I know. I'll take care of it," he said.

In a little while he picked his car keys off the counter, gave me a kiss

on the cheek, and headed outside. I went into the bedroom and opened
the blinds. Leonard was at the fence. He'd taken a cigarette out and was
lighting it. Then a head came up on the other side of the fence.

The bum had short white hair, and his face was tanned and wrin-
kled. I could see a white stubble of beard. The bum was squinting at
Leonard. Then one of his hands came up over the fence and took a
cigarette from the pack Leonard held out to him. Leonard steadied
the bum's hand until he could get the cigarette lit. The window was
up, so I could hear through the screen some of what they were saying.
Something about the VA hospital, the bum saying he was going to have
to go there. Leonard was smoking and listening. Then he nodded and
said yes, he knew what it was to be hooked on booze.

"I was a practicing alcoholic for fifteen years," I heard my husband
say. It was a history he gave every now and then—mostly when he
heard somebody was having trouble with drinking. It made me mad
sometimes to hear him say he was an alcoholic, as if it were a kind of
reverse status. But I knew it was serious business—that he'd got out
of the drinking and managed to stay out. His recovery happened a few
years before we met, and this made it hard for me to appreciate how
much he'd changed. I believed it, but only because he told me he'd
been another person then. If he hadn't kept telling me about it—what
an awful drunk he used to be—I would have forgotten. I guess that's
what I wanted.

"I'd do anything for a drink," the bum said. "Oh, it's the Devil's juice,
don't I know it. But I tell you, I'd kill for a drink. There's times I want
it that bad."

"Well, you get yourself in there to the hospital and let them help
you," Leonard said. Then he took some money from his billfold and gave
it to the bum, along with the pack of cigarettes.

"What's your name?" the bum asked.

"Leonard."

"Put her there, Leonard," he said. Leonard took his hand. "I won't
forget this," the bum said. "I used to be somebody myself once," he said.

"I might pull out of this yet. You know what it is, don't you, to be drowned alive like this? I can tell you do. It's in your eyes. You know about it. I thank you," he said. "I thank you."

About noon Dan came into the house. He'd been painting the trim on the shady side of the house. "Is he gone?" I asked.

"Yes," Dan said. "He went off toward the boulevard. But he'll be back."

"How do you know?" I said.

"If you give them money they always come back," he said. "Give them anything but money." He went over to the sink and drew himself a glass of water. When he got ready to go back to work I walked outside with him and went over to the fence. I lined up my eye with a knothole. In the fire lane I could see the flattened cardboard. The grass was crushed, and I counted four empty wine bottles.

"You know that doughnut stand over by the park?" Dan asked. "Well, it's open twenty-four hours. That's where these transients—we call them blanket people—that's where they go to stay warm in winter. They must be feeding them doughnut holes over there," he said. He laughed, and pulled the bill of his blue work cap.

When Leonard came home from work, I asked him what the bum had said.

"I told him he'd have to move on," Leonard said. "I told him he should get some help for his drinking. He said he was a vet, was in Korea. He's only fifty-five, but he looks like King Death himself. I'd say seventy if I had to guess."

"Did he say anything else?" I asked. I was at the kitchen table shelling peas into an aluminum bowl.

"Just that he used to have a house, kids, a wife—the whole works."

"I heard him say he'd kill for a drink," I said. I tossed an empty pod onto a newspaper on the floor.

"That was a figure of speech," Leonard said. "I don't think he'd hurt anybody. He just wants enough to drink, and maybe some cigarettes."

"Dan says he'll be back. He says if you give them money they come back."

"I could be where he is, but for the grace of God," Leonard said.

"You were never that bad," I said.

"In a way, I was worse," he said. "I blamed it all on somebody else. I made anybody who loved me pay and pay hard."

"I'm glad I didn't know you then," I said.

"I'm glad, too," he said.

I bundled the empty pods in the newspaper and stuffed them into a garbage bag near the back door. I was thinking that I wouldn't have stuck with Leonard in those days. I would have let him down and I was ashamed, realizing that. But it was true.

I was drying my hands on the towel near the sink. Leonard came over to me at the sink and turned me toward him. He put his arms around me and held me in close under his chin. I kept my eyes closed. We stood still and hugged each other.

One morning we'd just finished breakfast and Leonard was on the phone talking long-distance when someone knocked on the door. I pulled the curtain back and saw the bum. He hadn't been around for at least a week. I'd kept checking the fire lane to make sure. I opened the door a crack.

"Is Leonard here?" the bum asked. His eyes were the bluest blue I'd ever seen—two caves of blue. I shut the door and went into the kitchen.

"Leonard," I said. "It's him. King Death."

Leonard put his hand on the receiver. "Tell him just a minute," he said.

I went to the door and opened it. "Just a minute," I said. Then I shut it and sat down near the window, where I could see him standing on the porch. He looked vacant like one of those dogs you see tied to a parking meter, waiting for somebody to come back.

Leonard came out of the kitchen. He opened the door and stepped onto the porch. "Here," Leonard said. He handed the bum some money. "Take this and don't come back," he said.

"You're God's own," the bum said.

"Don't come back, now," Leonard said. "You understand me?"

"I got you, friend. Don't you worry," the bum said. I stood up, so I could see through the open door. The bum was walking backward toward the street. "You touched my heart," he called out to Leonard. "Yes, you did."

Leonard shook his head and reached for a cigarette from a pack on the counter. "He's like a piece of the past that nearly happened," he said. "It hunts you down and tries to move in."

"Don't give him any more money," I said. "I like your goodness. I admire it. But you can't really do anything for him. Not in the long run."

"No, nothing that lasts," Leonard said. "He'll cash it in out there. He'll just lie down with his bottle, and some morning he won't wake up."

Leonard's company needed him a month early, so the transfer went through before I'd sold the house. Leonard drove to Dallas and I stayed behind to supervise the last of the repairs. Dan was doing the work. With Leonard gone, it was good to have him around. I told him he should bring his new wife over for me to meet, and he joked with me, saying he didn't want to do that. She'd be too jealous. He'd never get in a day's work for me again.

One day I asked Dan to help me pick up all the papers and bottles in the fire lane. It was a mess.

"Shameful for any human being to live like this," Dan said. "You'd think salvation cost a million dollars, when it's free." That was the one thing about Dan that made me uncomfortable—how absolutely convinced he was about his salvation and about salvation being within everybody's reach. I'd given up talking to him about anything resembling religious matters. But once in a while I couldn't resist saying what I thought.

"It's a shame, all right," I said. "But maybe he's got to pay for his sal-

vation in ways we can't even imagine. Or maybe he asked to be quits
with drink but God turned him down."

"God's not like that," Dan said. "Ask, and ye shall receive."

"But he doesn't say *what* ye shall receive," I said. I'd carried a rake
along and was scraping some broken glass into a pile. I noticed how
even the smallest pieces glittered in the bright sunlight. "You might
have to earn your salvation," I said. "You might have to go through some
things before God would even turn his face in your direction."

"If he can save little children, he can save anybody anytime," Dan
said. He was pulling a large box full of trash along the fence. He stopped
and folded up the bum's cardboard bed and stuffed it into the box.
Then he climbed in himself and jumped. He raised each foot up and
brought it down hard.

"I don't believe salvation is something you get once when you're a
kid, like the chicken pox, and then you're bound for heaven," I said.
"There are times you fail. Times nobody may know about. You've got
to set yourself straight again and again." I looked up and saw that the
Mad Hatter had come out of his house and was pacing along a row of
pineapple palms he'd planted to let us know where his property line
was. He walked over to the fire lane and stood with his hands on his
hips, looking at the trash we were piling up.

"I'm going to get this grass mowed," I told him.

"Those hoodlum kids use this fire lane as a footpath," he said. "I've
warned them. I told them I'll pull the trigger on them without batting
an eye if they so much as set their big toe on my property." His face was
puffy and he didn't stand still when he talked; he moved sideways, as
if he were working up to something.

"You can't shoot to maim anymore," the Mad Hatter said. "You got
to shoot to kill. Then you're okay. If you just maim, they'll sue you for
everything you've got. You have to kill them outright to stay within the
law." Then he recited the findings of some court case he'd read about
in the newspaper. Somebody who'd shot a robber in the arm and had
to pay the hospital bill.

I never said anything when I heard him go into his tirades. I just nodded and got away from him as fast as I could. His wife locked him out of the house sometimes. I'd been woken up more than once when he was drunk and pounding on his own door to get in. One time I heard glass breaking over there.

Dan and I carried the trash to the front of the lot. The Mad Hatter was striding along the fire lane with his eyes on the ground. I watched him cross onto his property and make the rounds of his palms, checking with the toe of his shoe to see if they were still tamped into the ground firmly.

I felt better once the fire lane had been cleared. Dan had a friend with a big mower, and I hired him to cut the grass. Then I had Dan stretch barbed-wire fencing along the back of the property. Several people came to look at the house, and one young couple seemed particularly interested. Leonard and I talked on the phone, making plans for me to pack and call the movers as soon as the house sold. I began sorting clothes, getting rid of winter things we'd kept in case we should ever get sent back to upstate New York. I packed the clothes in paper sacks—Leonard's wool trousers, neck scarves, several hand-knitted vests, odds and ends—and I was planning to take them to Goodwill.

Dan had just one more job to do. He was going to replace some bathroom tiles. I was making jam on the morning he was supposed to come, when I heard a knock at the front door. I turned the burner off and went into the front room. I opened the door and there he was—King Death himself. But he was clean shaven now, and he had on a white shirt with a spangled vest over it. He looked like a rich gypsy. His eyes hadn't changed, though. They were the only young thing about him. They sizzled with energy. I took a step back and pulled the door closed to a narrow opening for my eyes and mouth.

"Your husband, Leonard," he said. "Is he here?"

Before I could think, I'd said it—that Leonard didn't live here anymore. "He's moved away," I said. "He won't be back."

The man looked down at his feet as though he were embarrassed. I was panicky, thinking now he'd know I was alone. I tried to figure how to put Leonard back in the picture.

"Tell him for me—tell Leonard when you see him—that I didn't want anything," he said. "Tell him I just stopped by to see him."

"Just a minute," I said. I closed the door and locked it. Then I went into the bedroom and got one of the sacks of clothes. There were some of my things in it and some of Leonard's, but I didn't take time to sort anything. I went to the door, unlocked it, and pushed the sack through until I felt the man take it. "You might get some use out of these," I said. I was afraid and glad at the same time, but I was trying to keep from showing how I felt.

The man made a little bow with the sack in one arm. His eyes snapped down. "Thank you, ma'am. I thank you."

Then he turned and started down the walk. I watched him pass along the street a little way, then I shut the door and went to heat the jam again. I sat down at the kitchen table. The house seemed very quiet. Soon there was the soft burbling of the jam beginning to boil, but that was all. I thought of the man going somewhere behind a building or into the park and taking our clothes out of the sack, holding them up to himself, trying them on but having no mirror to look into. If Leonard had been there, I'd never have given the man anything.

The young couple finally decided to buy the house. The man was about twenty-five. He climbed onto the roof and said he thought the house should have a new roof. I said if he wanted a new roof he could put it on himself. "This house is for sale *as is*," I said. When he saw he couldn't bully me, he went ahead and offered what we were asking.

I'd backed the car to the end of the driveway and was about to head for the real-estate office to sign the papers when I spotted the bum again. He was knocking at the Mad Hatter's door, gazing across to our oleander bushes while he waited. He had on Leonard's wool slacks. It was ninety-degree weather. The slacks were drawn up around his waist with a length of white cord. He was wearing my black knit vest over Leonard's blue shirt.

I scooted over to the passenger side and rolled the window down. I sat there a minute waiting to see if anyone would answer the Mad Hatter's door. I hoped no one was home. I could hear the dogs barking inside the house, and then the door opened and the Mad Hatter appeared. "You want to get shot?" he said. "You know where you're standing?"

"I need a little help," the bum said.

"Just a minute," the Mad Hatter said. He shut the door. I heard the dogs start up again.

The bum looked up at the sky. Then he clasped his hands behind his back and waited. His having our clothes on made him seem somehow familiar, as if I ought to know his name and be able to call out to him. I thought of Leonard, the Leonard I had never known.

The Mad Hatter opened the door again. "You see this?" he said. "This is a Smith and Wesson .38. It's loaded. I'm going to count to ten and on the count of ten I'm going to fire it directly at you."

The bum did not move. He did not say anything, either. I couldn't see his face, but I could see the Mad Hatter's mouth counting. I got out of the car when he reached six. I walked into my driveway on seven and eight. I could see both their faces then. I knew there wasn't time to call anyone. I kept remembering what the Mad Hatter had said earlier about not maiming, but shooting to kill. I could see the gun pointing at the bum's chest. He was looking straight at the Mad Hatter. The Mad Hatter had said *nine* some time ago.

"Ten," said King Death.

Then he held there a minute, looking past the Mad Hatter. It was as if he were looking right through the house and out the back. Finally, he turned and began to walk toward the street. The Mad Hatter stood in the doorway holding the gun. He took a step forward onto the porch. The gun was aimed at the man's back. I thought of the bullet going through my vest and through Leonard's blue shirt, knocking the man down. Then the Mad Hatter turned and the gun began to drift slowly toward me. I stood still. I could feel my strength slipping from me. It was as though I were there and not there at the same time. The gun was trained on me. I had nothing, was nothing. I wanted to call out, "It's me! It's me, your neighbor." But I couldn't make any words. The Mad Hatter raised the gun over his head. A bullet cracked out of it. I looked up into the sky where the bullet must have gone. There were no clouds. There was nothing to see.

"It's loaded!" he called. "You better believe it's loaded. All of you!"

I was still looking up at the sky. I heard the door close and it was quiet a minute. Then I heard the yipping and whining of the dogs.

I stood a moment in the driveway, trying to think what to do with myself. I saw my car sitting near the street, where I'd left it. I made my way slowly toward it. I got inside and sat behind the wheel. The seat was hot. I closed my eyes. I put my hands on the wheel and turned it as I sat there. I felt like I'd died and come to life in the front seat of a car in a strange city. I opened my eyes and looked up at my house. It seemed far away and nowhere I'd ever lived.

Recourse

Jewel Kirk, my neighbor, was sleeping nights on my couch while she tried to find a buyer for her tavern. I was having my own sale—a garage sale. Word had spread and there were only a few odds and ends left, most of it from my married life with Velda.

Velda had been dead six years so this was something I'd needed to do for a long time. It was hard, but it had to be done. Jewel had been my employer. I'd worked for her while she was running the tavern. But events during the past weeks had changed our lives considerably.

Three years before, Jewel had moved into her father's place next door—she and her husband, Burt. It was a surprise to both Jewel and me to find ourselves neighbors after forty-five years. When we were kids we never guessed we'd grow up, go away, and eventually come back to live alongside each other on the Little Niangua River. Anyway, there we were, farmland on either side of us and the nearest house a half mile away.

Now, three years later, Jewel was sleeping nights on my couch, and we were going to do something even further from anything we'd imagined. When all our affairs were settled, we were going to California! Jewel had already settled more things than anyone in the county had been ready to witness. I'd overheard a number of views on her recent actions down at the coffee shop. The coffee drinkers were taking sides on what Jewel had done to her wayward husband, Burt. They'd shake their heads and take a sip of their coffee. "She's a chip off the old block, that Jewel," they'd say. The "old block" they were talking about was Jewel's father, Ed Kirk. He had the distinction of being remembered as the meanest man in Dallas County. The theory down at the coffee shop was that this explained a lot about Jewel Kirk.

But I had another view of Jewel, though I kept it to myself. What was the point of trying to tell these coffee drinkers anything when they'd already made up their minds? Jewel was somebody I trusted and understood to a good degree, even when she went out of bounds, which had happened fairly often of late. On the other hand, Burt and I had drawn the line almost from the minute we laid eyes on each other.

We'd first met up near the trash barrels out back after he and Jewel moved into the house next door. I noticed he was wearing gloves. Not workman's gloves, but leather gloves with little machine-made holes in them—driving gloves, he called them. This was enough for me, those gloves, and the way he went around day in and day out in a flat cap like you see Frenchmen wearing in the movies. He didn't improve on things when he opened his mouth, either. Once he'd come over and complained to me about my dandelions. I had a few that I regularly missed when I mowed because the lawn rose sharply around back of the house where it bordered on a field, and it was hard to lift the mower up there. Besides, dandelions are pretty. Next to the fields and pastureland they didn't look out of place. I'd just finished mowing one day when Burt knocked on my door.

"Those dandelions are blowing onto my lawn," he said. "I'm getting dandelions at the side of my house." I knew it was Jewel's lawn and Jewel's house so what he said hit me wrong. So did the fact that Burt never did anything around there but mow the damn lawn and empty the trash in his leather gloves. His driving gloves—which was pretty funny since neither he nor Jewel owned a car. I told Burt those dandelions must have blown in from the Davidsons' field since I always mowed everything down to the nub. He just shook his head, turned, and walked back the way he'd come.

All in all I felt I'd made a good decision when I'd sold the place Velda and I had in Lebanon and bought this house next to the old Kirk place in the area where I'd grown up. I had lots of memories about this land along the Little Niangua River. Things like fording the river on my horse to visit Jewel and her sisters. (I was especially interested in the sister nicknamed Pebble.) I also prowled the Indian caves around here, hunting for arrowheads. Things like that. My own father had shoed horses. He'd gotten along with everybody, even Jewel's father. I used to go with him to steady the horses while he worked.

"There's a curse on that family," my father would say after we'd leave from doing a day's work for Ed Kirk. He was referring to the fact that all the Kirk children, excepting Jewel, had this bone disease that caused their joints to freeze up. There were six girls, counting Jewel, and one boy, Grover. The girls, all of them except Pebble, had been lucky enough to find someone. After they got married, they all lived in and around Dallas County. Pebble was different in every way, and she'd managed to make it on her own. She worked as a teller in a bank and learned to save her money. That's how she eventually moved to California. Grover had died when he was twenty, and the girls, who were women now, still suffered various degrees of disability as a result of the bone disease. Two of them were in wheelchairs and one had been in Kansas City for some time in a hospital. In the days when we'd been children, Jewel's father had rounded the kids up and loaded them into the wagon. He'd driven them fifty miles to Kansas City to a clinic. I remember they stopped at our house to get my dad to mend the harness before they started out. "He must have cared about those kids," my father said afterward.

When a story was told by one of the neighbors about terrible Ed Kirk, my father would remind the person of that trip to the clinic with a wagonload of crippled children. But it was the only evidence I ever heard offered in Ed Kirk's defense. He quarreled with neighbors on all sides of him. He'd been known to kill the prize cow of one of his neighbors. Once he'd even dammed the Little Niangua River with staves until it flooded another neighbor's barnyard.

But these were small offenses compared to the time he outright shot a man in town after the man made an indecent overture to one of his

daughters, then turned around the next minute and called her a hopeless cripple. The insult to his daughter had happened several years before, but Ed Kirk hadn't forgotten. He met the man in an alleyway and
shot him without so much as a how-do-you-do. There'd been a trial in
Bolivar over in the next county. But the dead man had been carrying
a gun, and since nobody had actually witnessed the shooting, Ed Kirk
went free.

Pebble was Jewel's youngest sister. I always had an eye out for her
in those days. I guess that's what made those trips to the Kirk place so
memorable. Pebble would drag and hop her way out from the house
to bring my father and me lunch while my father was there shoeing
horses. She'd sit with us under a big walnut tree while we ate. She had
nice features and a sweet disposition. Her arms and legs were contorted
but, for all that, she seemed to manage okay.

"She's like this tree I saw once," my father said. "It's when I was back
East that time, and they took me to the ocean. There was this tree on a
bluff. The wind shaped that tree. You looked at it and you knew something. You knew that tree didn't have a choice in the way it grew. If I
ever get back East again, I'd like to go take another look at that tree."

After Pebble had saved enough money to make her move to California, Jewel used to send me news about her. She knew Pebble and
I'd been sweet on each other. This was after I was married and had my
own life. Velda and I were living in Lebanon then. But Jewel was a great
one to keep in touch. Every year she'd send a card on my birthday, in
addition to her other cards and letters. She wrote me that Pebble lived
in Huntington Beach, California, and that she worked assembling elec-
tronic parts of some sort. People she worked with picked her up and
drove her to the job and afterward drove her home again. Then, my
wife and I went to Leadmine for Decoration Day services. These services were held at the church I'd gone to as a kid. I saw Jewel during
the course of the activities. She told me that Pebble had been banished
from the family by their father. Before the old man died, he struck out
at everybody who'd given help to his wife after the two had split up.

Pebble was living in California at the time, had been for twenty years. She paid her mother's way to California and nursed her right to the end. The mother was a great hulk of a woman and I often wondered how Pebble, a small thing and with that bone disease, ever managed to take care of the old woman. It would have made more sense for Jewel to have taken it on. Jewel was a big woman. But Jewel was her father's favorite because, some said, she was the only one of the children who wasn't cursed with the bone disease.

Pebble was nobody's favorite but mine. I'd tried to court her, in my own way, back there in my teens. "Oh Johnny," she'd say to me when I brought her some toilet water, or a bunch of daisies, the least little thing. "You shouldn't have done it," she'd say. She had big green eyes. Her eyes were the color of a pond where I used to take her catfishing. "I love your eyes," I told her one day, before I could stop myself. She just smiled, like she knew everything good and bad in the world and then some.

"You mean my bullfrog eyes?" she said, and laughed. I threw a rock into the pond and tried to pretend I hadn't said anything.

Pebble's father caught on to me, the way I kept finding excuses to come around for first one thing, then another. The last time I was allowed on the place I'd come over with a baby squirrel some dogs had mauled. It was just the sort of creature Pebble loved to fuss over.

"What you got in that cage?" he asked me.

"A baby squirrel, for Pebble," I said.

"Well, you can turn right around with it," he said. He shot a stream of tobacco into the bushes next to the porch. He stood there glaring at me. "Pebble's got work to do. You keep to home from now on," he said.

I took the long way home that day, following the river, carrying the squirrel. About halfway home I just couldn't bear the cries of the thing and turned it loose. It half rolled, half scuttled into the bushes.

After Velda died, and Jewel came to live in her family's home next door, we used to sit out on the porch of her house. Burt would be inside watching television. "I don't know how we lived through it," Jewel would say, talking about her childhood. Then she'd tell stories about her father making her and Pebble and the rest of them carry staves on their backs to build fences. "And remember," she'd say, "these children were crippled."

I reminded Jewel of how she'd bring notes on horseback from Pebble to me. When I got married, Velda made me get rid of all those scraps of paper with Pebble's wobbly writing on them. Pebble never said much in the notes, just a few sentences. But she drew plenty of flowers and hearts at the bottom of the page and put her own two eyes into the drawings, like she was watching me as I read. There was a connection between us, Pebble and me, that seemed to survive in spite of the fact that we seldom saw each other. It was like that right up until the time Pebble left for California, and I met Velda, in that order. After that, Jewel more or less took over giving me the news on Pebble. I still felt affection for Pebble, but she was like somebody I wished well, but couldn't do anything for. How could I? I was a married man. Anyway, she seemed to be doing fine on her own.

At the time Jewel moved in next door with Burt, I was at loose ends. When I'd relocated back alongside the Little Niangua I'd brought a lot of Velda's things with me. I'd boxed them and stored them in the garage at the side of the house. I couldn't think what else to do with them. I had to climb over those boxes to plug in my power tools. When Velda was alive, I was always cursing these boxes of junk. But the thing that hit me after she died was how much pleasure she'd had from going to rummage sales, collecting everything from broken-down treadle sewing machines to fifteen yards of clothesline I'd never gotten around to stringing up. It was, I saw then, maybe her greatest pleasure. I gave a few items to Jewel, but the rest just stayed in the garage.

"You got to get busy," Jewel said to me one day when we met at the side of the road near the mailboxes. I noticed her hair had only a little black left in the white, and it hit me that we were old, both of us. I remembered her long black pigtails. But they'd been cut ages ago, and those little flecks of black were all that was left of them. "You come down and help me at the tavern," Jewel said. "I'll put you to work."

I said, "I'll think about it."

I suppose people wondered why Jewel didn't put her husband to work. But he never showed his face at the tavern, and Jewel insisted it be that way. She'd had one alcoholic husband, she said, and she didn't want another. Her first husband had fallen by the wayside early on, up in Kansas. Jewel had packed her bag and skipped out, the story went.

I thought it over and then told Jewel I'd work for her. The routine went like this. I'd get up at 5 AM and go with her to clean up the tavern from the night before. There was a little grocery store addition to one side of it that had to be opened for business at 8 AM. Jewel kicked everybody out of the tavern at closing time, then went home herself. But the place was always in a hell of a shape when we got there the next morning. I'd open the door and walk into the stale beer and cigarette smell like somebody coming out onto a battlefield at dawn. Everything was in there but dead bodies. Sometimes I'd find items of clothing that made me think people had used the place for a dressing room. Those mornings it would occur to me to wonder about Burt, what he was doing while Jewel and I slaved away at the tavern and the store. He looked able enough to do clean-up work. But it was none of my business.

"He looks for work," Jewel would say, "but he can't find anything. He drives as far away as Liberty looking for work, but so far nothing." When she talked like that I knew she was worried, in spite of the face she put on things. I tried to do as much as I could to help her with the tavern, because there wasn't a thing I could do about Burt.

When he had worked, Burt had driven heavy equipment, cats and shovels, graders—that sort of thing. He didn't want to have to do anything else, Jewel said. She said she could understand that. She loved running her tavern and grocery, and she wouldn't like to have to stop and become, say, a beautician or a telephone operator—especially at her age. She thought Burt would get something, what he wanted, eventually.

But during this "eventually," a lot of things were going on behind her back. A friend of mine in a town twenty miles away told me he'd seen my neighbor drinking in a bar there. At first I thought he meant

Jewel. She'd been known to take a drink or two in other establishments, though she never drank in her own. But the neighbor in question was Burt. My friend said Burt had been in the company of a woman, and the description of the woman bore no resemblance to Jewel.

I began to feel even more uneasy about Jewel's married life when I looked over at her house in the middle of the day once, while Jewel was working, and saw a woman waiting in a car. The woman honked the horn. That's how I happened to look out. Burt came hopping down the steps, all spruced up, slid into the driver's seat, and drove off with her. I was working that night with Jewel at the tavern, so I don't know how or when or even *if* Burt got back. I do know there were no lights in their house when I drove into my driveway and Jewel got out and walked next door. Of course I didn't mention what I'd seen to Jewel. She'd find out soon enough.

The next day Jewel and I were carrying in some cases of beer from a delivery truck parked behind the tavern, and she said to me, out of the blue, "Nobody ever wanted to go with me except some old drunk. And if they weren't a drunk to start with, they ended up that way." She was talking like she was closing a chapter on something. She was my friend and I was ready to listen. But that's all she said. She had a case of beer on her shoulder and I had one on mine too. We were walking with our free shoulders side by side.

"Jewel," I said, "you got your name for a reason. You're a jewel in my book." She gave me a stiff little grin, and I knew that too much had happened to her for that kind of remark to go far, but I think she appreciated it anyway. She just hoisted the beer onto the stack in the storage room and went to the truck for more.

It got to be general knowledge before long that Burt had a woman over in Jefferson County. He was drinking with her in public places. But his carousing time was seriously limited when he finally got a job with the highway department. That must have made him careless or desperate, trying to find time to meet the woman and also hold down a job—not to mention the fact that he was married.

One night it was so slow at the tavern I said to Jewel, "Why don't you take the night off? I'll close up." So she went home and caught the two of them, her husband and his new woman, on the premises. When Jewel told me about it, she said she'd thrown a kettle of spaghetti over the two of them. It was cold spaghetti, she said, but it did her heart good anyway. Burt, knowing Jewel's temper, must have imagined she'd be standing by the front door with a butcher knife, because while he and his woman were cleaning spaghetti off themselves, Jewel could hear a squabble going on. Burt was telling the woman they'd have to climb out the bedroom window and the woman was saying it would ruin her dress. Jewel went around to the back next to the window. Pretty soon the woman was hanging from the windowsill with Jewel cussing and throwing things at her. Burt got his share too when he jumped down. Somehow the two of them made it away in the woman's car.

Two weeks after Burt cooked his goose with Jewel, nothing appeared to have changed over there—though it had. Burt was gone, but his heavy equipment was still sitting in front of the house. Jewel had called the highway department to come and move it. The equipment belonged to them. But the machines were still sitting there like a couple of dinosaurs. Jewel would look at that equipment and make threats. Another week passed and the equipment still hadn't been moved.

It was about this time that Pebble came home from California. Jewel had told her about the entire mess, and Pebble had taken her vacation early and come out to give her sister some support. She still had those green bullfrog eyes, but of course she'd aged, like the rest of us. Her limbs were even more crooked than I'd remembered. Still, she had a good strong manner—something I'd loved about her from the beginning.

We were glad to see each other. I squeezed her hand and she smiled at me in a way that made me remember those hearts and flowers at the bottom of her notes. But we didn't have much time to talk. I was doing

the biggest share of work at the tavern while Jewel tried to get herself
right side up. She'd hired a lawyer and was trying to undo a bad situation. And I don't just mean the marriage to Burt, though that was the
heart of her trouble. It seems Jewel had signed over the house to Burt
in order to avoid paying inheritance tax on the place. Since the marriage had gone to hell, Burt informed Jewel he intended to move into
the house with his new sweetheart, once he got Jewel out. Legally, he
said, it was his. Pebble was doing her best to calm Jewel, but without
much success. And who could blame Jewel? It wasn't the kind of thing
you could take lying down. It hurt her self-respect, and it threatened to
put her out on the street.

One night I was lying in bed when I heard an ungodly racket. It was
nearly three o'clock. I knew the tavern was closed and that Jewel must
be hearing the noise too. I looked out the window. I could see somebody holding a flashlight and somebody else up on one of those big
graders. I could see the beam of light skipping around over the huge
tires of the thing. Then I heard glass breaking and the sound of metal
being hammered. Finally, I could make out that it was Jewel doing the
hammering. She was up on the machine near the controls, pounding
the living daylights out of it with a sledgehammer. The fury of that
noise was awful. I was glad there was nobody else close enough to hear
it. When Jewel finished with that machine, she went on to a big dozer
with a shovel on the front. Whoever held the flashlight was nervous—
the light was jumping all over the place. But every now and then I'd
get a glimpse of Jewel's arm on the hammer. It came down again and
again onto the machine. This time it was headlights I heard breaking. I
walked onto my porch to get a better look, but then the flashlight went
out. I stood there listening. I could hear Pebble's voice pleading with
Jewel. The lights in Jewel's house were off and so were mine. I felt I'd
seen enough, though there was lots more to hear. I went back in and
got into bed. After a while, the hammering stopped and I fell asleep.

The next morning I was almost afraid to look out. When I did, I had to marvel. The heavy equipment in Jewel's yard was pretty well demolished. I went out into the yard to get a better view.

I saw a pickup truck pull into Jewel's drive. It had a highway department insignia on the door. Two men got out of the cab with clipboards and moved toward the remains of the equipment. They shook their heads as they circled the machines, from time to time making notations on their clipboards. One of the men saw me wrestling the water hose over to some flowers. He called and waved, then started to walk in my direction. I acted senile, like I couldn't make out what the guy wanted. I turned and headed into the house.

Around noon Pebble limped over and said she needed me to drive her somewhere.

"I can't tell you where," she said. "You won't do it if I tell you. You'll just have to go this one blind, Johnny." Her green eyes looked tired, but there was enough mischief in them to get me to agree. I said I was having my coffee first, so she came into the kitchen and sat down.

"Somebody went to work on that machinery," I said. I poured her a cup of coffee and set it in front of her. "I guess you must have heard it all," I said. I was playing dumb and Pebble knew it.

"I called the highway department and the sheriff," Pebble said. "I told them it was vandals. That it must have happened while we were at the tavern. Jewel was going to tell them she'd done it. She said she didn't give a tinker's damn. It's terrible how this divorce thing is working on her." Pebble brushed her face with one of her crippled arms. "I couldn't stop her last night, Johnny. She feels she's got no recourse." Pebble folded her crooked arms and stared into her coffee cup. I was starting to fall in love with her all over again, right there in my kitchen. We finished our coffee, and I locked the back door. We went out the front, and I locked that door too. "Vandals," I said to Pebble and winked. Pebble shook her head. She situated herself in the front seat. I made sure she was comfortable, then shut the car door, went around, and got in under the wheel.

"Now where?" I said. Pebble had an address scribbled on a piece of paper. She read it to me. It was an address in town, over near the municipal swimming pool. We saw herds of kids carrying towels and swimming suits as we got into the neighborhood.

"That's the house," I said, and Pebble leaned across me to check it out. It was a little shoebox of a house. Probably built after the war, sometime in the late forties.

"Doesn't look like a honeymoon cottage," Pebble said. Then I understood where we were. I expected Burt to step onto the porch any minute with his new woman. We crept along in the car.

"Keep going," Pebble ordered. "Now, pull into that alley." We turned off the street and drove until we got within a house or two of Burt's new residence.

"This'll do," Pebble said. I left the engine running and took a glance around the alley. A lot of garbage cans and brambles. There were kids' toys scattered in some of the yards. We could see a clothesline in Burt's yard, and on it were some of Burt's clothes I'd seen hanging on the line out behind Jewel's house. But there was a short white nightie next to one of his denim work shirts. It was not part of Burt's regular wardrobe. Pebble had spotted the nightie too, and down the line there were items of clothing that didn't bear speculating on.

"I'm glad Jewel can't see this," Pebble said. "She'd put a torch to that house before you could say Jack Robinson—whoever he was."

We sat there a while longer, watching a breeze ruffle the clothes on the line. The white nightie billowed and fluttered against Burt's shirt-sleeve, then went slack. I was nervous and looking for something to do. I saw the ashtray was full of Jewel's cigarette butts. I unhooked the thing and dumped the mess out the window into the alley.

"Would you mind telling me what we're doing?" I said to Pebble as I worked the ashtray back under the dashboard.

"We're kidnapping a dog," Pebble said, as if it were the most normal thing in the world. I was sorry I'd asked. Pebble looked over at me and said, "It isn't what you think." She had on a green pullover that matched her eyes, and I felt that connection from our childhood at work again, as if we had an invisible hookup to each other's feelings.

The back door to Burt's house opened and his new woman stepped onto the porch in a housedress with big daisies on it. Right at her heels we could see a white toy poodle. The woman came off the porch and disappeared behind a bedsheet in the middle of the clothesline. The poodle was nosing the ground, frantically circling the woman's legs where they came down behind the sheet. The legs walked along the sheet and then the woman's head appeared above the white nightie. She was blond and had tight little curls all around her face. The rest of the hair puffed out like she still had to deal with it—spray it or whatever. Then Burt's woman unpinned the nightie and a few of Burt's things, turned, and went back into the house.

The poodle was still in the yard, so I had the feeling the woman would be making more trips to the clothesline. Without a word, Pebble climbed out of the car. "Pebble," I said in a low voice. I saw her carry herself a few feet in front of the car and stop. Then she bent and patted her hip. I saw the poodle prick up its ears. Then I heard Pebble make a noise with her lips. The dog ran right into Pebble's arms. When she straightened and hobbled back to the car, it looked like she was carrying a stuffed animal. She let the dog into the car. It started to yip and show its little teeth the minute it laid eyes on me. Then it set those teeth into my arm just below the elbow. "God," Pebble said. I shook at the thing until it had mostly shirtsleeve. The car was elbows and fur for a few minutes. Finally, Pebble got the dog off me and under control. It rooted itself into her lap and sat down facing me. Then Pebble went and kissed the dirty thing right on its nose. It kept up an intermittent *erring* sound as we drove back to my house. "That's a good dog," she said every so often and cradled the poodle in her bent arms.

At my place Pebble let herself out of the car and carried the dog inside. The yipping noise the dog kept up was nothing anybody'd ever want to live with.

"It can't stay here," I said. "I don't have any use for this breed of dog." I was holding my elbow and wondering how deep its teeth had gone. Pebble was still cradling the menace. I wanted to fling the poodle into the yard and take her in my own arms—but now one of my arms was disabled. I pulled my shirtsleeve past the teeth marks. Pebble gave a little cry when she saw the bite. She carried the poodle into my bedroom and shut the door. The poodle didn't like this one bit and yipped away some more.

Pebble attended to me. Her hands seemed to know everything about gentleness. The bone disease had skipped right over those sweet hands. Just as she finished swabbing my arm with disinfectant I grabbed up one of those hands and gave it a kiss. Pebble acted like it wasn't anything out of the ordinary, as if it was something I'd always been in the habit of doing. She rolled my sleeve down and I let her button the cuff for me. But right then, with that crazy dog yipping and those wrecked machines over in Jewel's yard, I felt like picking up my life again. I mean having somebody to love and to be with. But I didn't want to say anything right then.

"Jewel was going to poison that poor pup," Pebble said. "She set the poison out on the kitchen table this morning. She meant to do it. All because the dog belonged to that woman, and the woman loved it more than anything—more even than Burt," Pebble said and laughed. She put the stopper into the bottle of disinfectant. I rubbed my arm. The bite was stinging but somehow it wasn't entirely unpleasant. I thought I should be feeling something out of the ordinary to go along with what I was thinking.

That night I slept on the couch and let the dog have the bedroom. I hoped it liked table scraps because that's all there was for it to eat. I put together an odd assortment of baloney and string beans and sprinkled it with bacon drippings. It didn't look half bad. Then I stuck my arm into the bedroom, set the dish down, and jerked the door shut. Jewel had closed the tavern down for a week, so I had no place I needed to be. "Renovation," she'd written on the sign, but she didn't mean the tavern. I settled myself onto the couch, and the last thought I had was that maybe in the morning I'd scramble some eggs for the dog and myself.

When Pebble came over the next day, she was all dressed up. She looks cute enough to take on a honeymoon, I thought, but I just said, "That dog is driving me nuts."

"Can you take us to the airport?" she said. For a crazy minute I thought she was asking me to run off with her. I passed my hand over where there used to be hair during the days I'd been a young buck hanging around her door. Then, without letting me answer, Pebble walked toward the bedroom. The dog started to yip, and I understood I'd slipped off the track a considerable way.

In the car the dog behaved itself. It sighed and laid its nose across Pebble's arm.

"It's not good, Johnny," Pebble said. "Jewel could lose everything. I'm afraid for her peace of mind, but what can I do? I've got to go back to my job."

"Don't worry," I said, and patted her arm. "I'll stick by her." Pebble turned her big green eyes on me. She seemed to be thinking about something. I felt that a lot of unsaid things were getting said.

At the airport I helped her arrange for the dog, then saw it caged and wheeled away. Good! I thought. After we checked Pebble's luggage I was glad to have a few minutes alone with her. She leaned on my arm as we walked slowly to the gate area. I had her traveling case in the other hand.

"You call me, Johnny, when you hear what's happening," Pebble said. "In about a week there'll be a hearing to decide who gets the house. That's going to be rough," Pebble said. She started to take her traveling case from me. Then I reached out for her. I held her stiff body with its damaged bones close to me. Then I let go. Pebble suddenly gave a quick jerk of her head and landed a kiss on the highest point she could reach on my neck. "Will you write me, Johnny, or else call?" she said.

"You can count on it, Pebble," I said. "I've got some things to talk over with you." She gave my hand a squeeze. She stood like that with my hand a few moments, looking worried. Then she smiled. I watched her turn and move toward the gate. She moved quickly for somebody with her physical troubles. The other passengers stood aside for her like she was some kind of dignitary. And maybe she was.

When I got home I went into the bedroom to see what effect the dog's night in there'd had. My windup alarm clock was on its side with the hands stopped. I stepped over a puddle and noticed another puddle under the bed. I patted the bed with both hands to make sure that was dry. It was. My socks were scattered on the floor, but other than that, unless the dog had fleas, the place was going to be habitable again. I considered the likelihood of fleas and thought of buying some spray and giving the room a good going over.

During the week that followed, I called Pebble once to tell her that Jewel's hearing was set for 11 AM Friday. She asked me some questions about Jewel's state of mind. Then she told me about sanding down a little chest of drawers she'd bought at a lawn sale. I could hear the dog yipping in the background.

"I hope that poodle's not going to be a permanent resident," I said. But I didn't have any way to tell her what I really intended. I said I'd call her and let her know when the legal ownership of the house had been decided. It didn't help that the judge for the case was a brother to the manager of the division Burt worked for at the highway department.

The morning of the hearing I drove Jewel into town and dropped her off at the courthouse. I told her I'd pick her up when she called. But she never called. About noon, somebody brought her home. I saw her steam into the house and slam the door, and I could tell she was in no mood to see anyone. I guessed the outcome of the hearing and decided to wait awhile before going over to hear the whole story.

I sat at the kitchen table and folded and unfolded my hands. I got to thinking about Pebble and what a long detour it had been to find her again. She'd been on her own for so long it made me afraid she wouldn't have me. We were old now, and we each had our ways of doing things.

Suddenly I heard glass breaking outside. I looked out the window in time to see a chair sticking through the glass at one of Jewel's side windows. Then I heard glass breaking around to the far side of her house. I saw Jewel come outside and head for her garage. She came back carrying two paint buckets. I had an idea what she intended to do.

By the time I went over there, the damage had been done. Jewel was standing in the ruination of her house, the very place she'd grown up in. She was holding an empty paint can. She had paint all over herself and over the floors and walls. She stared at me like she wanted to paint me too. For a minute we just stood there looking at each other. Then she started to cry and wipe at her face, still holding the paint can.

"Let him have the damn house now," she said. "Let her have it too." She started to walk toward me like a blind person. I stepped up to her and put my arm around her shoulders. I shook the paint can out of her hand and then I walked her, like that, with my arm around her shoulders, over to my place.

When we got inside I sat her down in the kitchen. I went to the cupboard and brought down some whiskey and two glasses. We sat there working on the bottle, talking over what to do next. All the anger had gone out of her, and she wanted me to understand she was sane again and able to go on now. But *on to where?* she wanted to know. I said Pebble seemed to like it fine in California. And then I proposed something.

"Why don't we go out to California?" I said. "We'll start a tavern there." Maybe I was a little drunk by then.

She shook her head. Then she said, "We'll see." She passed her hand over the table top, as if she were wiping at something. She looked at me. "Things are finally working out for you and Pebble? I'm glad, Johnny."

"Nothing's been said one way or the other," I said. "No promises or questions yet. Just hopes."

Jewel held her whiskey up and gave it a little nod, a kind of toast, before she drank it. I remembered then what she'd said that morning earlier in the summer—how nobody could love her but old drunks. I knew Jewel deserved better than she was ever going to get. I noticed she was still flecked with paint. Also, there was a long white streak down the underside of one arm. I got up and found some turpentine under the sink. I handed it to her along with an old towel. She got up from the table and went into the bathroom to clean up.

Meanwhile, I looked around in the cupboards for something to fix for supper. I took down two cans of chili, found a pan, and went to work. When the chili was hot, I put two bowls on the table and dished it up. Jewel still had paint in her hair and in the creases of her skin, but she looked better. Her cheeks were pink where she'd rubbed the paint off.

After we'd eaten I left Jewel at the kitchen table. "Help yourself to that whiskey," I said. I went to the living room and made up a bed for her on the couch. Then I got ready for bed myself. In a few minutes I thought I heard Jewel open the front door and go out. I supposed she was stepping over to her house to get her night things.

I went out to the kitchen and drew a glass of water. It was then I glanced out the kitchen window to see if the lights were on over at Jewel's—but there was more than lights on. The entire back of the house was aflame. I could hear crackling and see angry spurts of fire darting through the windows. I dressed in a hurry and went out the back door. I started calling for Jewel. I was afraid she might not have been able to get herself out. Then I saw someone huddled where my dandelion patch is, on the slope behind the house. The light from the flames brightened and flickered against the sky. It was Jewel all right. She was sitting with her arms around her legs, watching. I didn't say anything, just dropped down beside her and began to snap off the heads of a few dandelions. Jewel was rocking slightly, not taking her eyes off the burning house.

"I decided to finish it off," she said without looking at me. "I didn't do it mad, Johnny. I was right at the heart of calm when I did it."

I patted her on the knee, stood up, and offered my hand to her. She took it and raised herself up. By then there were neighbors driving down the road to park and watch. Someone had seen the flames and phoned others. In the distance I could hear the yowling of fire engines as they turned off the main road and headed toward us. Jewel and I moved around to the front of my place and went inside. I gave her my jacket and she went out to stand near my car and watch the firefighters go to work on saving what was left of her house. I couldn't think of it as Burt's house, no matter what the law had decided, and I guessed nobody else who knew the situation would either.

The noise of water hoses spraying and men calling to each other kept up for hours. I stayed inside the house. After a long while Jewel came inside. We sat at the kitchen table with our coffee cups and watched until the last of the ladders had been taken away. There was nothing but the shell of a house with smoke leaking out here and there. Jewel was still wearing my jacket.

"I didn't know it would hurt so much, watching this," she said. "Daddy would have done the same thing though. There's nothing left now except California," she said. She roused herself and laughed.

I laughed too. Then I got up and rinsed out my coffee cup. A few birds were starting to chirp and a dawn half-light was coming into the window. I remembered I hadn't called Pebble. I wondered how she was going to take the news that the house was gone. I knew she was going to worry that Jewel would be arrested, but I was the only witness and I wasn't saying anything. Let them investigate till hell freezes over, I thought.

"We'll call Pebble after we've had some sleep," I said. "We'll talk to her about California, and the possibilities for us out there." I found an old flannel shirt and a pair of my own pajama bottoms for Jewel, then went about putting on my pajamas in the bedroom. When I was ready to turn off the light I called, "Good night." After a minute she said, "Good night." But her voice was muffled, and I think she was crying.

I pulled the covers over me and lay there. After a while I thought I felt something biting me. Damn fleas, I thought. I lay there with my mind empty awhile. Then I thought of the river, of leaving it behind, and I felt something that had nothing to do with California or anywhere else I might ever be. I was getting close to sleep, but I seemed to be moving through images of my young days on the Little Niangua River, of Pebble as a girl and then of Pebble's father, and how, like Jewel, I was soon to have the final word.

Turpentine

I was in the basement in my rain boots when Tom called down that there was someone to see me. I was sloshing around in water that had a pink tinge to it. It didn't take a plumber to know lint from some red bath mats had plugged the drain.

By the time I opened the door to the kitchen, Tom had gone back upstairs to his study. From where I stood, I could look through the kitchen and see a young woman sitting on the couch. She was staring at something out the window. She stood up when she saw me. While we were shaking hands she looked at my rain boots. They were causing a puddle on the hardwood floor. I knew the kitchen tiles would be glistening with welts of water where I'd passed.

"A little crisis of the lower regions," I said. She squeezed my hand lightly, then took her hand back. It left a waxy feeling. "I'm Ginny Skoyles," I said.

"I'm your Avon Lady," the woman said. She was smiling now. I could see why Tom had let her in, even though he didn't like door-to-door people.

"So you really exist," I said. "I thought they'd just made you up, like Mr. Clean. Do you have a name of your own?"

"Mary," she said. "Mary Leinhart."

She turned and moved back toward the couch, then sat down on the edge of the cushion. I pulled off my boots. I looked at her more closely then. She had large dark eyes and her skin was so white it was almost translucent. I thought of the word "alabaster."

"I live in the neighborhood," she said, "so I thought I'd stop in and show you a few things." She had a camel-colored sample case. She opened it across her lap and took out two catalogues. She was wearing a powder blue nylon parka. It had zippers every which way on it, and I wondered what she might be keeping inside the pockets. She had on beige slacks and blue-striped sneakers.

"Maybe you'd like to look through these," she said. "There are some good sale items in soaps and talcs."

I looked at the top catalogue. The cover showed a red-nailed hand reaching out of the sky to set a box of talcum powder onto a crimson expanse of water. In the background were violet blue mountains. The sky behind the mountains had the same tortured look as the water. The hand was wearing a gold initialed ring with the letter *J*. The cover resembled a religious tract, like pamphlets I remembered seeing around the house in my childhood.

"Thank you," I said. I began to flip through the book, glancing at the models whose eyes stared out seductively as they held cream-softened hands near their faces or suggestively touched an ear lobe.

"I've brought some things to show you," Mary Leinhart said. She took out a pearl ring and handed it to me. I could see that she was wearing the identical ring herself and, although I had no intention of buying it, I slipped it onto the index finger of my right hand. The fit was exact. I took it off quickly and gave it back.

"I do a lot of rough work," I said. "It wouldn't make it through a day with me. Tom, that's my husband, he doesn't know how to screw a lid on a mustard jar so I have to do everything that gets done around here." The floor was creaking over our heads so I knew he was in his study, pacing and smoking, passing from the files to the desk to the window. Walking, he said, helped him think, but he hated the out-of-doors, so he walked his room as other men might have walked the city.

Mary Leinhart put the ring back into its bed of cotton in a tiny box that bore a diamond design. "It's very simple and pure looking, don't you think? I kept wondering myself how that pearl stayed on there, so I asked a jeweler. He said there's a steel pin that runs right up through the middle of the pearl. That holds it on. Now I wish he hadn't told me. I thought it was magic."

Her fingers were long, the nails shapely. They reminded me of the ads in the brochure. But she wore no nail polish and if she was wearing makeup, there was no way to tell by looking.

"These perfumes are on special this week," she said, digging into the sample case. She came up with a tray of small bottles filled with varying amounts of amber liquid. "This one's called 'Timeless.' It's my favorite." She took the cap off the bottle and handed it to me. I sniffed it, then dabbed a little onto my wrist.

"Smells like nasturtiums," I said and handed it back. It was not a smell I liked. She didn't seem to mind, just tipped the bottle between her thumb and index finger and touched herself behind each ear. I asked to smell some others and to be told their names. I settled on one called 'Moonwind.'"

"Do you want the perfume or the cologne?" Mary Leinhart asked.

"Perfume lasts longer, doesn't it?" I said. "I'll take the perfume."

I'd run out of places on my hands and wrists to try on more perfumes, yet I felt I should buy one more item. I pointed to a delicate necklace with three stars on it. I asked her the price, then said I'd take it.

"These face creams are very nice," she said, lifting a fat white jar with a pink label. "I have oily skin and can't use oil-based creams. This has no oil and it prevents lines. That's what my information says," she added.

I had trouble understanding why she was telling me about preventing lines. Surely she could see the time for that had long passed. Her own face was as line-free as a plaster-of-Paris madonna. I took the jar and dipped my fingers into it. Then I rubbed the cream onto my throat. I could feel the loose skin as I rubbed. I had what the beauty books called "turkey neck."

"Very nice," I said. I worked a little more of the cream into my forehead and remembered how it had been my sister, ten years younger than me, who had first begun to worry about my face. She'd given me an entire face-salvage kit when I was about thirty-five—complete with mud packs and eye balms. I'd even used it for a while. But it didn't take long to see that no matter what I did, a lot of things were happening anyway.

"I damaged my skin when I was in high school," Mary Leinhart said. She brushed the back of her hand across her forehead. "I had such bad acne, so I bought this lotion they were advertising. I'd try anything in those days. I rubbed it on and left it, like the directions said. When I washed it off, my skin was raw. Something in the formula had penetrated several layers of skin and scorched me. I had to have treatments. It left pockmarks on my forehead so I've had to put makeup there ever since. It's terrible what they'll try to sell you, what you'll do when you're desperate. Teenagers are always desperate about their looks. At least I was." She mused a moment, her eyes away from me.

Her word "scorched" stuck in my mind. She gathered up her samples, but she left some catalogues on the coffee table for me to look over. We set a delivery time for the following Saturday, and I saw her as far as the front door.

I was rinsing my good teacups when Tom came into the kitchen. He was helping himself to a glass of milk and wanted to know what all I'd bought from the Avon Lady and wasn't I glad I'd been home when she came, because, ha, ha, you know the stories about door-to-door saleswomen.

"Don't make fun of her," I said. "She's struggling. She's a nice young woman. She's had an awful time with her complexion," I said. "Someone sold her dangerous face cream when she was a kid and it scarred her face."

"I didn't see any scars," Tom said. I realized I hadn't seen any either, but I remembered feeling as though I had.

"There must have been some at one time," I said. "She covers them with makeup. She told me a terrible story."

"Why are these people always coming in off the street to tell you their life stories?" he said.

"How should I know!" I said. But he was right. A chimney sweep had come to our house not long ago. He'd learned his trade in Germany, where the sweeps go to weddings and kiss all the women on their cheeks for luck. He'd told an incredible story about falling into a well at the age of twelve. He'd had to be rescued by his father, who'd lowered himself on a rope so the boy could grab onto his father's ankles and be pulled up. His affection for chimneys, he thought, was entirely due to the excitement and danger of his having fallen into a well when he was twelve.

Just yesterday a neighbor had come over to borrow a loaf pan and ended up telling me how their Siamese cat had rushed in behind the burning logs in the back of the fireplace, then stared back at the family through the flames. They'd had to douse the fire and the cat.

Whatever anyone said to me, I listened. Sometimes I told them back one of the stories someone else had told me. And once in a while I told it back as though it had happened to me. It was harmless enough and it gave me something to say.

We hadn't lived here long. Tom supervises the installation of computer systems in universities. We generally buy a place somewhere in the area near where he'll be working and he travels short distances, two or three days out at a time. I work on the houses, and we sell them at a profit a year or so later when we're ready to move on.

A long time back I'd decided there was no use making friends when you had to pack up and leave every year. So I keep to myself. I usually get to know the guys at the local hardware store pretty well because I'm always buying insulation or paint or wiring materials from them. They give me a lot of advice and make their share of jokes, I suppose, about the old gal who's "fixing up her place." I never tell them I'm married, so they kid me, say I ought to keep an eye out for a rich widower, someone who could handle the repairs and take me on long winter vacations to Florida. I don't let on that I need anybody.

My project for the week was the repair and installation of the ground-floor storm windows. Some had panes of glass missing, others needed brackets, and still others gave no clue as to which window they belonged. There were codes to be broken. For instance, what was I to make of KBPW? Or LRME? My success depended finally on not believing my eyes. The P of KBPW was actually an eroded R. The M of LRME was an augmented N, which gave me North East. If I'd been charting our course by the stars I couldn't have been more baffled.

As Saturday approached, I began to realize I was anticipating my visit from the Avon Lady. So much so that I was disappointed to find a message Tom had left near the phone during one of my absences in search of tools or materials. "Avon Lady sick. Please call to set new time."

On the phone she sounded as if she barely had enough strength to lift the receiver. Her voice was high and girlish.

"I've got the flu. I'm running a temperature," she said. "I'll have to see you next week, if that's all right." We arranged to meet the following Saturday.

But on Saturday Tom said he needed me to drive him to a meeting in Albany. He wanted the time during the drive to review some new data before the meeting. There was no time to call Mary Leinhart. I tacked a note to the front door, saying unexpected business had come up. I felt sorry when I thought about her walking up to the door, taking down the note, reading it, then turning and walking back down the steps.

Tom was wearing his blue suit. He smoked while he read the reports. I kept my eyes on the road and wished I could turn on the radio. It had started to rain, which seemed to make everything happen faster. Even the scenery seemed to be rushing ahead. I looked over at Tom as he turned the pages in the report. He must have felt me looking at him because he shut the folder and began to stare out the window. We were passing a truck that cut us off from the farmhouses. When we got even with the truck we could see, in modest blue lettering, "Karp's Casket Co."

"Jesus," Tom said. "Pass this guy, will you."

I tried to step on it and pull away, but we stayed even until the highway took us up a steep incline and the truck finally began to fall away behind us.

"You forget they have to make those things somewhere," he said. "Imagine, a factory where they make nothing but caskets. And the guys that work there, they have kids and when these kids get asked what their dad does they have to say, 'My dad makes caskets.'"

"And their wives," I said, "they have to say they're married to a casket maker."

"It gives me the willies," Tom said. He lit a fresh cigarette. His brother was three years older. He'd died of a heart attack at fifty-nine just two months before. I knew Tom thought about it. He had tried to quit smoking and he tried to stop eating eggs, but he couldn't. Still, he looked trim and he liked to dress well, so that he always seemed much younger than he was. I could see the casket truck getting smaller and smaller behind us in the rearview mirror until it was a black nub in the distance.

A few days later I called the number Mary Leinhart had left with Tom and a man answered the phone. A young man. For some reason it gave me a start to hear this man's voice. I hadn't associated her with a man. I gave him the message and hung up. From time to time during the week I found myself wondering who this man was, and when Mary and I did meet that following Saturday, I said, "A man answered when I called you."

"That was my brother," she said. She unzipped one of her zippers and took out a tube of ChapStick, which she rubbed across her lips. Then she zipped it into the same slot and folded her hands on her lap. "My brother's just back from California. He's around on weekends."

"I hope you're feeling better," I said. I was sitting in the same chair as before and it seemed no time had passed since our last meeting.

"I'm better," she said. "But I've fallen behind in my school work."

"You're in school?" I said. "At the university?"

"No. The junior college," she said. "Bookkeeping. I'm not far from finishing, but I don't know if I'll ever get a chance to use what I've learned."

"Why not?" I said. I wondered if she was about to get married. Maybe there was some family problem or a terminal illness.

"It started with my brother suggesting I have my tea leaves read," she said, raising the back of her hand to brush her forehead. "An idea he must have gotten in California. I don't usually listen to him, but he said it might be fun for me. I'd been sick. I was so far behind at school I just decided to have some fun and forget it."

She took out the purchases I'd made and set them on the coffee table in a white sack with the bill neatly stapled to it. On the sack was a face, a perfect heart-shaped face of a woman representing Beauty. Under her chin was written, in slender blue script, "Open up to Beauty." It reminded me again of the urgent religious teachings of my childhood—the fundamentalist preacher at my parents' church who stood behind the altar each Sunday and said, "Open up your hearts to Jesus."

"I didn't want to go alone," Mary Leinhart said, "so I asked my sister-in-law to come with me." She took her hands out of her coat pockets. "Is it all right if I take my coat off?" she said.

"Please do," I said. It rustled as she slipped it from her shoulders and she lifted herself slightly so she could take it from behind her. She folded it once and laid it beside her, then clasped her white hands on her knees. She seemed even paler than I remembered. This made her dark eyes so prominent I found myself staring into them. I felt I'd never looked at anyone quite in this way.

"Well, the woman told me I should develop my psychic powers," she said. She smiled, a little embarrassed to be saying such a thing. "She said I shouldn't hold back energy from these powers." There was a trace of humor in her retelling of this, but I could see she was troubled too. Suddenly she asked if I had any tea. She could use a cup of tea, she said, though she hated to put me to the trouble.

"I must still be a little weak from that flu," she said and shivered. "I was even hallucinating in the worst of it."

I said it was no trouble. I went out to the kitchen to boil the water. Tom was at a meeting with some computer hotshots from Pennsylvania and I was hoping he wouldn't get back early. It seemed important for the house to be quiet, for there to be no floor creaking above us, no other presence in the house. I fixed a little tray with napkins and took down my silver creamer and sugar bowl. I put just enough water in the kettle for two cups. When I went back into the living room with the tea I saw that she had draped her coat over her shoulders. I put the tray down in front of her and pulled my chair nearer the coffee table.

She let her tea bag stay at the bottom of her cup a long time, then danced it up and down a couple of times and took it out. She placed it on her saucer and lifted the cup to her knees, where she balanced it while she talked. They were my good china cups and they seemed exactly right for her pale, calm hands.

"The first thing the psychic said to me was: 'Who's been praying to the Virgin Mary?' Well, I'm a lapsed Catholic. I think of the Virgin sometimes but I don't pray to her, not consciously anymore. Then my sister-in-law spoke up. She said she'd been praying to the Virgin. She's very religious, so the psychic explained that's how it got into my reading. The psychic discourages anyone from sitting in on the readings. But I wouldn't have gone alone. Patty said she'd just step into the front room if she was bothering things, but I said no, if she went I went."

She was not drinking her tea. Just warming her hands on the cup. Then she went on.

"So after we got the Virgin Mary business settled, the psychic wanted to know if I'd ever seen lights. 'What kind of lights?' I asked her. 'Blue lights or sudden flashes of white lights,' she said. It's odd, but you know, I have seen lights like that off and on. When it happened I'd just been afraid, and hadn't told anyone. But once I was with someone who saw the same light. I told the psychic and she wanted to hear about it."

"Then you really believe in communications and the like?" I took a sip of my tea and waited.

"Not really," she said. She opened and closed her fingers around the

cup. "This was a lark, you know, visiting the tea-leaf reader. I did want
to tell her about those lights though. I admit I wanted to ask her about
that."

Then she began to tell me about one particular time when she'd
seen an unusual light.

"It was spring and we were looking for a place to walk that night. We
wanted to be outside under the trees. I remember the trees were just
getting their leaves. There were three carloads of us. Someone thought
of the cemetery, the Old Bernard Jacobs Cemetery on Nottingham Road."

As she spoke I thought I could hear people talking. The voices seemed
to come from outside the house. I looked out the window behind her
but I couldn't tell where the sound was coming from.

"There's a hill," Mary Leinhart said, "then a little bridge you pass
over and to the right of that there's a parking area. The gate's never
locked."

Then I saw where the noise was coming from. People were walking by outside, carrying their blankets and thermos bottles. They were
on the way to the basketball game. Mary Leinhart sat facing into my
kitchen. She seemed to be looking into a place not in the room or even
in the house.

"As I say, if I'd been the only one to see this light, I'd have been scared
enough, but there was another girl—Jeannie, not someone I was especially friends with. But she saw it too. I'd gone about ten yards down
the slope toward the gate when this light flashed up. It was so strong
it nearly knocked me down." She drew herself back on the couch, remembering. "I turned and ran back to the car. The others came back a
while later. They were laughing over near the other cars. Kind of wild.
Then I noticed that Jeannie had come back ahead of them. She was
inside and her face was against the car window. She looked terrible. I
didn't know until later that we'd seen exactly the same light."

"Are you still cold?" I said. "Did that tea warm you or should I turn
the heat on?"

"Oh, don't turn it on for me," she said. "I'll be all right. I can always put my coat back on."

"I'll just turn on the furnace to take the chill off," I said.

I turned the thermostat and in a minute or two the furnace started up. Mary Leinhart had not taken anything out of her sample case. It lay on its side under the coffee table. She was still cradling her teacup in her white fingers.

"How long did that light last?" I said.

"I don't know. Several seconds. But it seemed a long time, you know. It was blinding. It seemed to be everywhere at once. It was so strong I just stood still in it and thought, 'I'm alone. I've come here alone.' That's all I remember."

"Who were these people? These people you were with?" I asked. It seemed important that she go on.

"They were friends of my ex-husband's," she said. I wanted to hear more about this husband in her past, but she quickly continued her story.

"And then the psychic told me there was a baby in my future," she said. "She asked me if I was married and when I said no, she said then that's why I was going to be so unhappy about having the baby."

I was listening, but I couldn't avoid seeing my neighbor walking her white Samoyed out on the street. I was glad to see her. It made me feel sure I was in my house, on my street. Now she was bringing the dog up onto my lawn. She was wearing her short white gloves as usual, and high heels. They went out of sight behind a portion of wall, but I knew what was happening.

"Strangely enough, I'd been thinking sometime I might adopt a baby. By myself," Mary Leinhart continued. "That's getting easier to do now, you know. I wasn't going to do it anytime soon. 'Maybe it's my sister who's going to have a baby,' I said. Then the woman, the psychic, got angry. She stood up and threw down her shawl. 'Why does everyone want to blame things on their sisters? No, it's you, it's *your* baby,' she said."

I could see Mary was upset about the baby—that the psychic had predicted she would have it. She had to wonder how this could be so. Still, her face was as calm as the faces etched on cameos, and I had to tell from her voice what she felt. She took up her coat and began un-zipping the openings, looking for something.

"I have the woman's card with me," she said. "I could leave it with you if you wanted." She took out an eyebrow pencil and a circle of vio-let eye shadow from one pocket. From another pocket she brought out a small white stone. "There's my lucky stone!" she said. She transferred these things into her sample case.

"That's all right," I said. "If you can't find it."

I couldn't sit still. I got up and went into the kitchen. I looked around and then I brought back a plate of butterscotch cookies. I felt hungry and I thought she might be too. She took a cookie, had a small bite, then laid it next to her teacup. She had found the psychic's card and she handed it to me as I settled myself again in my chair.

"One thing the psychic said did come true," she began again. I leaned toward her and waited to hear. She took another bite of her cookie.

"The woman said I was going to be contacted. An investigator was going to come to me. She asked could I think of any instance in which this might happen. I couldn't, of course. Then last week the Board of Labor Relations sent me a letter about my last job. Some of us had filed a complaint against the boss. We'd been having to work double shifts with no breaks and the pay was below minimum. They said they were sending an investigator to talk with me. I'd forgotten all about it."

"Where had you been working?" I asked, just to keep her going.

"A place called The Blue Robin," she said. "But *there* was my 'inves-tigator.' Just like the woman said."

I noticed the little sack with the face of Beauty and remembered I'd ordered these things weeks before. I couldn't remember what I'd bought. I wrote out the check for the amount, and opened the sack. I took out a box. Inside was the necklace with three tiny gold stars. I wanted to try it on right away. But I had on one of Tom's old shirts because I'd been painting the back steps when Mary Leinhart had arrived. I decided to wait until I was alone.

"It's just beautiful," I said. "Really, it's beautiful. It's very delicate looking."

Mary put on her coat. She smiled at me as she buttoned it, as if we had been friends a long time.

"I'm glad you like it," she said. "Your cookies are great." She was about to leave without asking me if I wanted anything more. I picked up her catalogue and said I would take three bars of white ginger soap and a butterfly stick pin. A gift for my sister, I said.

She sat down on the edge of the couch again and got out her order blanks, then noted the catalogue prices for the soap. She apologized for having taken up so much of my day.

"I don't believe all that stuff, you know, about psychic powers," she said. "But ever since the labor investigator's letter arrived, it's been hard not to look for the other things, to wonder if they would be coming true. The baby is the one thing I can't figure. The woman said I wouldn't like it at first, but it would turn out to be the best thing in my life. I don't even have a man I care about."

I could see the idea of the baby had got hold of her. I understood how you could wish for it and not want it at the same time. I took the slip from her and walked her to the front door. Then I opened the door and let her out. "Good-bye," I said. I watched her walk down the steps to the sidewalk. After a while I could see her blue parka and the sun striking its many zippers until she turned the corner toward James Street. I shut the door and locked it.

I went out to finish painting the back steps. I managed to pour too much turpentine into the bucket so the paint drizzled from the brush across my knee and dripped from the edges of the steps. I somehow got the paint down my arms and into my hair. I saw I'd missed the undersides of the steps. I bent down and worked my way under the steps. There were places where the paint had dripped into the dirt. It was so dark under the steps I just painted by guess at first. It was like being a child, always crawling under things to see what was there. Crawling to see what it felt like to be lost, to have lost yourself from everyone.

Gradually I could see my hand above me and the paint coming out of my brush. I could see a strip of light between one step and the next.

My skin felt stiff where the paint had dropped on it. I stayed still a moment and looked out. The world was like a thought I might suddenly stop having. I closed my eyes and felt the eyelids sticking to themselves. Then I opened them when I heard someone come into the house.

I could hear footsteps in the kitchen, then the back door opening, the boards creaking on the porch. Then nothing.

"Ginny?" The voice was muffled but it was Tom's.

"Ginny?" he said again, and then the slat of light between the steps was blotted out as his foot came down on the wet steps. I wondered if he would see my legs. I could feel him think a moment about where I might be. I liked the smell of dirt and the darkness. By raising up on my elbow I could see the grass scuffed with white paint where he had stood, turned, then walked toward the garage. I didn't hear my name anymore. I would have to stop him before he tracked paint back into the house. The daylight made me blind a few moments as I raised myself from under the porch. When I could see again, Tom was staring at me from the side gate.

"Ginny," he said, but he wasn't calling me. "Jesus, Ginny," he said.

I knew the white paint was all over my face and arms. My eyelids were thick with it, and even though it would come off with turpentine, I could feel him hating how I looked.

"You'll have to take off your shoes," I said.

"Why didn't you answer me?" he said. He bent to untie his shoes. I held my forearm against my brow so I could see him better. The shoes were black with white on the rims of the soles. "Didn't you hear me calling you?" he said. He held the shoes away from his suit as he walked in his socks back toward the house.

I didn't go in right away. I took a little turpentine from the can and rubbed it along my arms. I did the same to my face, holding my eyes and mouth closed. It scalded as if I'd been slapped. The smell of turpentine made me light-headed. It gave little shocks to the air as I walked around to the front porch. I knocked on the door and waited to be let in.

Tom still had his shoes off. He let me in and walked ahead of me into the living room.

"I found this on the table," he said, and handed me the psychic's card. "What's this about?"

I went past him into the kitchen and drew a glass of water. It was cool, but I thought I tasted turpentine. I put the glass aside and rubbed my mouth with the back of my hand.

"Just stick the card up on the mantel, okay?" I said. But he had followed me into the kitchen.

"Madame Zeller," he read aloud. "Answers your questions. Sees into your future." He tossed it onto the counter and leaned back, waiting.

"She happens to be the real thing," I said.

"I didn't know you put much stock in con artists like that," Tom said. "What do you mean, the real thing?"

"I mean she knows things. She knew things about me I haven't told anyone, not even you," I heard myself say. He was looking at me as if I had suddenly grown strange to him, let him see something that surprised him.

"And I suppose she told you the future, too," he said.

I soaked the end of a hand towel under the kitchen tap and began to rub at my neck. I felt as if I didn't know what I might say next.

"Yes," I said. "She did. She said there would be an investigator soon. Someone checking into things." I carried the towel with me into the hall bathroom, where I got a bar of soap. My face in the mirror was smeared with a residue of white paint. I looked pale and calm.

"Investigating what?" Tom called after me.

I carried the soap with me and stood at the hall mirror, where the natural light was good.

"Just an investigation. I don't know about what. She said she could tell me, but she wouldn't. There are some things best left to the future, she said."

"It doesn't sound like you got your money's worth," he said. He was standing now in such a way that I could see him behind me in the mirror. My face was red and raw looking in the places where I'd rubbed. He kept watching me clean myself. He wanted to question me, to find out the things that might be about to happen.

A Pair of Glasses

Her grandmother would put on glasses to read labels on cans when the girl went to the market with her. She would read the brand names and the prices out loud to the girl. The girl could not read much yet herself, but sometimes she pretended she could. The grandmother would read a word, and the girl would say it to herself and stare at the word—trying to hold it in her mind. They would go down the aisles this way, the girl pushing the cart and saying the brand names and prices. At the counter the grandmother would take her billfold out of her purse, hand the purse to the girl, and take off the glasses.

"Here, put these away for me, honey," she'd say, and the eyeglasses would come into the girl's hands. It was always an important moment, to be holding the glasses. Under the lenses the girl's fingers seemed larger, and as if they had a life of their own. When she looked down, her shoes leapt up at her from the floor. Once when her grandmother had to leave the counter for a moment, the girl had put the purse in the shopping basket and opened up the eyeglasses. She set them on the bridge of her nose and held them there, looking around at the blurred faces of the other shoppers. It was a wonderful, dizzying feeling and it gave her the idea that the wearing of glasses was a way of seeing that only a few people were privileged to have. When the grandmother returned with the missing grocery item, she took the eyeglasses from the girl.

"You're going to break those, honey. Here, let's put them away." Then the glasses had gone back inside the purse until the next shopping trip.

Neither the girl's father nor her mother wore eyeglasses. The nearest

69

thing to glasses in the house was a pair of field glasses her father kept in the corner cabinet. He used these when he went deer hunting and also to watch ships passing through the inlet of water their house over-looked. Once the girl had stood in a chair at the window and her father had stood behind her holding the field glasses to her eyes. The glasses were heavy.

"Can you see now?" he asked her. He twisted the lenses and the girl stared into the glasses until she could begin to see an object taking shape. When she could tell what it was, she jumped up in the chair until her nose knocked against the metal bridge of the glasses.

"A boat! A boat with a man in it," she reported. Then her father said sternly, "Now you're getting silly. Stand still or I'll put them away." Then the girl stood still and watched the waves lapping the side of the boat. The man stood up and turned sideways so the girl could see he was reeling on a fishing pole.

"He's got a fish!" the girl said, pressing her eyes into the metal rims of the field glasses.

"Let me see," her father said, and lifted the glasses from her. Then she could see only a far black speck on the blue-gray water.

"I don't think he's got anything," her father said after he'd held the glasses on the speck a long time. "If he did, he lost it." Finally her father put the glasses back into their leather case.

The girl liked the smell of the leather case. Sometimes she would beg to be allowed to put the field glasses away, just for the pleasure of how perfectly the lenses slid into the darkness of the case. Then she snapped the case shut and her father swung the glasses up to the top of the corner cabinet, until the next time he wanted to watch something on the water.

No one in the girl's class at school wore eyeglasses, but on the playground she saw several children who wore them. This set them apart from the others—as if they might be smarter or able to see things she couldn't. She began to yearn for the company of those who wore glasses.

At recess the girl played jump rope with an older girl who wore glasses. The other girl's name was Brenda, and Brenda loved to jump double Dutch. The girl was especially good at turning the ropes for double Dutch, so Brenda often asked her to get a partner and turn the ropes while she jumped. Besides the glasses, which had blue plastic rims, Brenda had pigtails that her mother often tied with blue ribbons. The girl thought the sight of Brenda jumping double Dutch with her blue-rimmed glasses and the blue hair ribbons bouncing on her pigtails between the whipping sound of the ropes was the most wonderful sight she could imagine.

Then one day while the girl was turning the ropes, one of Brenda's pigtails caught in them and the blue-rimmed glasses went flying. The girl dropped her end of the ropes and ran over to the glasses before anyone else could reach them. She picked them up. But when she saw the crack across one lens she started to cry. Brenda was upset too and the girls wept into each other's hair with the eyeglasses pressed between them. The next day Brenda came to school without the glasses and she seemed then, to the girl, to have passed back into the ranks of the ordinary.

It was late October and leaves covered the sidewalk. The girl walked to school in the crisp morning air. On her way she gathered a bouquet of the brightest orange and red leaves she could find. She gave these to her teacher, Miss Binki. Miss Binki was very tall and slender, but one feature of her appearance held the girl's amazement, and she supposed that all the other students were similarly fascinated. Miss Binki had pointed breasts that pushed her sweater out. The girl stared with her mouth open as the breasts moved around the schoolroom, hovering over her classmates' shoulders when Miss Binki stooped beside them to help with their work. Some days the breasts seemed more prominent than others. These were days when Miss Binki apparently felt like setting a good example for her students. It was then she would show them how to stand tall and straight with their shoulders back and chests out.

Good posture was important, Miss Binki said, and she saw to it that they practiced it by walking around the room with encyclopedias balanced on their heads.

The girl carried the volume *Bu-Cz* on her head. When she passed Miss Binki's desk the woman smiled at her. It was at this minute the girl lost her balance and the book tumbled from her head across Miss Binki's desk and into her lap. Miss Binki very calmly picked up the book, walked around the desk, and placed it back on the girl's head. After a moment, the girl continued walking.

Once, before leaving for school in the morning, the girl asked her mother if there wasn't something she could take to Miss Binki as a present. Her mother went into the fruit cellar and brought up a jar of raspberry jam. The girl carried the jam to school and placed it on Miss Binki's desk before the teacher arrived.

"Who brought me this nice jar of jam?" Miss Binki asked the class once they were all seated at their desks. The girl was too shy to answer. Then one of the boys who'd seen the girl put the jam on the desk began to point his finger and call, "She did, she did!" Later, on the playground, this same boy called her "teacher's pet" and chanted this until the girl left the playground.

It was about this time that the girl, in the presence of grown-ups, began to rub at her eyes with the heel of her hand and to blink when grown-ups talked to her. At school the children were cutting out pilgrims— men in their tall black hats, women in bonnets. The girl preferred to draw. She drew a turkey with a tail showing all the colors in the rainbow. She drew a pilgrim holding the turkey by the feet, and she added a pair of spectacles to the pilgrim. She told Miss Binki that this was so he could see all the beautiful colors of the tail feathers. But in the girl's reading group she complained that she couldn't see the letters plainly, and she asked to be moved closer to the blackboard.

Miss Binki sent a note home with the girl in a sealed envelope. Not long after that, the girl's father and mother dressed up in their good clothes and drove the girl to an eye doctor for an examination. At first the girl thought this doctor must be a kind of dentist and that he intended to pull her eyes out. She put her fists over her eyes and braced against the wall of the office. She wouldn't go into the examination room. But finally she took her father's hand and went into the room, which held various machines and charts.

After a short while, the doctor came in. The girl noticed that he was wearing spectacles, and then that he was wearing a white jacket with several pens clipped to his pocket. The doctor turned off the lights in the room and positioned himself in front of the girl. He began to flash sharp pinpoints of light into her open eyes. Then he asked her if she knew the alphabet. The girl said she did. The doctor began to project different-sized letters of the alphabet onto a large screen on one wall of the examination room. The girl knew something serious was taking place. Her parents were worried about her eyesight. They had brought her to a man who gave out eyeglasses to those with poor eyesight. The girl hoped more than anything that her eyesight would be found poor enough so the doctor would prescribe a pair of eyeglasses for her.

When the letter *C* flashed onto the screen the girl knew it was *C*, but she said *"O."* An *h* appeared and she said it was a *b*. If there was an open space to the letter, she closed it and made another letter out of it. Sometimes she couldn't think what to do, so she just said she couldn't see what the letter was. She was certain she'd demonstrated that she had terrible eyesight. Leaving the examination room, she bumped into things as the bright daylight streamed down on her.

She sat with her mother in the waiting room while the doctor talked to her father. Finally her father came out.

"You talk to him," her father said to her mother.

Then the girl sat with her father until her mother reappeared. Her mother was nodding to what the doctor was saying. "We'll talk it over," her mother told the doctor. "We'll see."

The girl felt worried and happy at the same time. She got into the car with her parents and stared out the window as they passed the familiar stores and houses of the town. When they arrived home her parents went inside and into the kitchen, where they made coffee and sat at the kitchen table. They were quiet and the girl supposed they were thinking of what to do about her bad eyes. She wondered why they hadn't had her fitted for eyeglasses right then and there at the doctor's office—why she was being allowed to walk around in such a condition. Then her father called her over to the table and told her to sit with them.

"The doctor says you've got an eye disease," her father said. "It could get worse, and it could get better. But there are treatments, and if that doesn't work there's an operation they can do." Her father looked at her mother and then took a sip from his coffee. "But it costs a lot of money," he said. "There's no way we can pay for such things," her father said.

"Here, honey," her mother said. "Here's a glass of milk. Sit over here next to me and drink it." The girl moved over next to her mother, took the glass of milk, and looked into it as if it had betrayed her. She felt too sad to drink anything, but she took several large gulps of milk.

"We'll just have to hope the trouble isn't as serious as the doctor thinks," her mother said. "Maybe it will clear up."

In the days and weeks that followed, the girl tried to remember that she had bad eyes, but she often forgot and became perfectly able to see words on the blackboard. Miss Binki praised her and several times said how glad she was that the girl's eyesight was improving. This forgetfulness did not mean that the girl had given up the idea of getting her own pair of glasses.

On a trip to the dimestore with her grandmother to buy hair ribbons, the girl had spotted rows and rows of eyeglasses between the handkerchief and yarn displays. When she picked up a pair and peered through them, the shelves in the store had loomed up around her until the pit of her stomach ached. She begged her grandmother to buy her a pair.

"Those glasses are for old people like me," her grandmother said. "Those are reading glasses for very weak, tired eyes."

A few days before Christmas the girl's father asked her to name a few things she might like to find under the Christmas tree when she opened her gifts.

"A pair of glasses," the girl said. "Like those in the dimestore."

"Oh, I don't know about that," her father said and laughed. Then he looked at her and said, "Is that what you really want?"

"Yes," the girl said. "A pair of eyeglasses."

On Christmas Eve the girl opened her gifts with her parents and grandmother watching. She got a pair of rain boots, more hair ribbons, and a bag of peppermint candies. But no eyeglasses. Then her father left the room and came back with a small package.

"Here," he said. "Maybe this will cheer you up."

Inside the wrapping paper was a pair of eyeglasses from the dimestore. The girl was so happy she forgot all her other gifts. She unfolded the eyeglasses and tried them on.

"They're a little big," her mother said. "Maybe we should take them back and get a smaller pair."

"No, no," the girl cried. "They fit me. They fit fine." She got up from the chair she'd been sitting in and took a few steps into the room. The glasses wiggled on her nose as she walked, and the room seemed to tilt back and forth. The Christmas tree lights blurred into each other and blazed against her face as she stared at them. The faces of her parents and her grandmother seemed odd to her, like masks, and she drew back from this vision. But mostly she was pleased with what she saw through the eyeglasses. She felt as if she had grown larger, and although she knew this wasn't so, she loved the feeling because she thought it made her seem older.

The next day she wore the glasses all day. She was disappointed that there were no children in the neighborhood she could show them to. School would begin again in a few days, she knew, but in the meantime she was the only one except her family who knew she had a pair of eyeglasses. That evening, her mother came in to say good night and discovered the girl in bed with her glasses on.

"What do you expect to see while you're asleep?" her mother asked, and took the glasses from her. But the next day her mother gave them back. The girl put them on when the mailman came. She met him on the porch.

"Are you the doctor of the house?" he asked. "Oh no, you're the professor. Here's some mail to answer," he said. The girl came back into the house carrying the mail and feeling very proud because the mailman had noticed that she had her own pair of eyeglasses.

School was starting again after the Christmas vacation, and the girl's father said to her that morning, "Now have a little sense, honey. Don't take those glasses to school." So the girl had been all day at school without her eyeglasses. She ran home after school and hurried into the house. She found the eyeglasses in the drawer of her nightstand where she'd put them for safekeeping. She spit onto each of the lenses, then polished them with the hem of her skirt. She put the glasses on and went out into the yard to lie on her back and stare up at the clouds. But the sky was so bright she closed her eyes and daydreamed instead.

The next day she slipped the eyeglasses into her lunch bucket and took them to school. She sat in her seat in Miss Binki's class and put them on. She felt very special and different from the other children as she sat with her glasses on. It did not matter that she could hardly see to write her name at the top of her paper. She was happy and proud to be wearing eyeglasses.

Miss Binki kept looking in the girl's direction, and the girl supposed that Miss Binki was admiring her glasses. Then Miss Binki came up beside the girl's desk and spoke to her.

"Did you get a new pair of glasses?" Miss Binki asked. "Are your eyes bothering you again, dear?"

"Yes," the girl said. "I got some glasses for Christmas."

"May I see them?" Miss Binki asked.

The girl did not hesitate. She wanted Miss Binki to admire her glasses. She handed them up to her and watched Miss Binki try them on.

"Oh my! Oh dear," Miss Binki said. "Your eyes can't be *this* bad. You're going to ruin your eyes, dear, wearing these glasses." Miss Binki removed the brown-rimmed glasses from her nose and slipped them into her dress pocket. Then she took a step away. The girl could not believe what was happening. She sat gazing at the pocket into which her glasses had disappeared.

"I'll save them for you," Miss Binki said. "You can have them back at the end of the year." She walked to her desk and the girl saw her take the eyeglasses out and place them into her desk drawer and turn a key. It was a drawer into which the girl had seen many forbidden items disappear. Things of an altogether different nature from her eyeglasses—a succession of slingshots, marbles, toys, candy bars—all to be collected by their owners at the end of the school year.

The girl went home in tears. She told her mother and father what had happened. She thought surely they would go to Miss Binki and get her eyeglasses back. But the girl's father only shook his head and said, "It's good enough for you. I guess you'll learn to listen now."

After that the girl had periods where she forgot entirely about the glasses. But there were other times when she would fasten her attention on them there in Miss Binki's desk drawer, and she would be unable to think of anything else. She knew that the end of school was months away.

The girl's opinion of Miss Binki began to change. She no longer seemed the beautiful young woman all the children loved for her pointed breasts and bright red lipstick. The girl had noticed something decidedly sharp, even harsh, about the woman's features. There were lines under her eyes. Miss Binki called for quiet more and more often. Several times a day children were banished to the cloakroom for misbehaving. But the girl continued to conduct herself quietly and patiently in the hope that she would do nothing further to bring disfavor to herself.

Finally it had come, the last day of school, and the children were told to form a line at Miss Binki's desk. She was handing back the last of their schoolwork. It was also the moment at which the children who'd had their belongings appropriated would have them returned. The girl was fully prepared to forgive Miss Binki when her eyeglasses were returned to her. She was thinking this, that she would apologize, when suddenly her turn came and she found herself standing before Miss Binki. The teacher had put on her best posture for these final moments with her students. Her head was erect, her back straight.

"Here you are, dear," Miss Binki said, handing the girl the bundle of drawings and scribblings. She smiled at the girl. "Have a good summer."

"My glasses," the girl said.

"I knew there was something," Miss Binki said. "I almost forgot." She reached into her desk drawer and brought out the eyeglasses. "Yes, here are your glasses. I don't think they'll hurt your eyes now. You have a good summer, dear."

The girl took the glasses and ran with them out into the school yard. She dropped her papers and fitted the eyeglasses to her head. But something was wrong. The world stayed the same. There was no miraculous fuzziness and the girl felt the same as she'd always felt—too small and too young. Her stomach did not leap and swerve with each step she took. Her glasses had somehow lost their magic in Miss Binki's desk drawer. The girl put her hand up to touch the lenses and was surprised when her finger went through the frame into her eye. She gave a little cry and took off the glasses. Then she saw that the lenses had been removed from the frames. The girl held the glasses and stuck her finger through the frame into one of the eye spaces and twirled the eyeglasses in disbelief. Then she put the glasses back on to make sure. She could see other children coming gaily in little groups out of the school building. She saw her papers blowing crazily across the school yard. She was seeing with her own good eyes through the plastic rims.

There was a tight feeling in her chest as she walked slowly home wearing the empty frames. There were moments when her eyes welled up, and it seemed that the lenses had miraculously returned to the glasses. But when she reached her fingers up through the rims and wiped her eyes, she found she could see quite normally. She thought of Miss Binki bent over her eyeglasses, purposely removing the lenses. As she imagined this, a hot feeling came up in her. It was a feeling so terrible that the girl stopped where she was on the sidewalk and shouted, "I hate her! I hate her!" A man who was sitting with his dog on his front porch looked at her and the girl felt the awful feeling pour out of her until she became afraid and began to run as fast as she could, holding the eyeglass frames to her face with one hand.

When the girl reached home she didn't go into the house but went instead around to the backyard and sat in the swing. She kicked herself high into the air, then higher, until she felt she might fly out over the rooftops. Gradually the feeling of hatred left her. After a while she climbed down from the swing and went into the house for supper.

"What did I tell you," her father said at the supper table. The empty frames lay near her plate. "I guess that serves you right, doesn't it."

"Even if the teacher meant well—and I'm sure she did," her mother said, "it was a mean thing to do." The girl's mother went to the stove and took up the rest of the fried potatoes. But the girl knew her mother couldn't understand.

The girl didn't say anything. She chewed her food slowly and felt she had fallen into the company of people who hated eyeglasses. She didn't know why this was so. She squinted at her plate. It seemed a great effort to lift food to her mouth. She was glad when at last her plate was empty.

Bad Company

Mrs. Herbert drove into the cemetery, parked near the mausoleum, and got out with her flowers. The next day was Memorial Day, and the cemetery would be thronged with people. Entire families would arrive to bring flowers to the graves of their loved ones. Tiny American flags would decorate the graves of the veterans. But today the cemetery was still and deserted.

When she reached her husband's grave she saw that someone had been there before her. The little metal vase affixed to the headstone was crammed with daffodils and dandelions. Whoever had put them there hadn't known the difference between a flower and a weed. She set her flowers down on the flat gravestone and stared at the unsightly display. Only a man could have thrown together such a bouquet, she thought.

She raised her hand to her brow and looked around. A short distance away she saw a girl stretched out next to a grave. She hadn't seen her at first because the girl had not been standing. She lay propped on one elbow so she could look down at the gravestone next to her. When Mrs. Herbert walked toward her, the girl did not lift her head or move. Then she saw the girl pluck a blade of grass and touch it to her lips before letting it fall. Mrs. Herbert's shadow fell across the girl, and the girl looked up.

"Did you happen to see anyone at that grave yonder?" Mrs. Herbert asked.

The girl raised herself into a sitting position. She looked at the woman, but didn't say anything.

She's crazy, Mrs. Herbert thought, or else she can't talk. She regretted

81

having spoken to her at all. Then the girl stood up and touched her hands together.

"There was a man. About an hour ago," the girl said. "He could have been to that grave."

"It's my husband," Mrs. Herbert said. "His grave. But I don't know who could have left those flowers." She noticed that the grave next to the girl had no flowers. She wondered at this, that anyone would come to a grave and then leave nothing behind. At this time of day the shadows of the evergreens at the near end of the graveyard crept gradually across the grass. This sent a chill through her shoulders. She drew her sweater together at the neck and folded her arms.

"He didn't stay long," the girl volunteered. And then she smiled.

Mrs. Herbert thought it was a nice thing after all to speak to this stranger and to be answered courteously in this sorrowful place.

"He was over at the mausoleum too," the girl said.

Mrs. Herbert thought hard about who it might be. She only knew one person buried in the mausoleum. He had been dead ten years and only one member of his family still survived. "It must have been Lloyd Medly," she said. "His brother, Homer, is over there in the mausoleum. His ashes, anyway. They grew up with my husband and me, those boys." She had spoken to Lloyd just last week on the telephone. He was in the habit of calling up every few weeks to see how she was. "Homer's on my mind a lot," he'd said to her when they last talked.

"I don't know anybody in the mausoleum," the girl said.

Mrs. Herbert looked down and saw a little white cross engraved over the name on the stone. There were some military designations she didn't understand and, below the name, the dates 1914–1967. "Nineteen-fourteen! That's the year I was born," she said, as if surprised that anyone born in that year had already passed on. For a moment it seemed as if she and the one lying there in the ground had briefly touched lives.

"I can barely remember him," the girl said. "But when I stay here awhile, things come back." She was a pretty girl with high Indian cheekbones. Mrs. Herbert noticed the way her hips went straight down from her waist. She had slow, black eyes, and appeared to be in her late twenties.

"I can't remember what Homer looked like," Mrs. Herbert said. "But he could yodel like nobody's business. Yodeling had just come in." She thought of Lloyd and how he said he and Arby, another brother, had been lucky to get out of California alive after they'd gone there to bring Homer's body back. Homer had been found dead in a fleabag hotel with Lloyd's phone number in his shirt pocket. "They'd as soon knock you in the head in them places as to look at you," Lloyd said afterward.

"He was a street wino," she told the girl. "But he was a beautiful yodeler. And he could play the guitar too."

"I think my dad used to whistle," the girl said. "I think I remember him whistling." She gazed toward the grove of trees, then across the street to the elementary school building. No one was coming in or going out of the building. It occurred to Mrs. Herbert that she had been to the cemetery hundreds of times and had never once seen any children coming or going from the school. But she knew they did, as surely as she knew that the people buried under the ground had once walked the earth, eaten meals, and answered to their names. She knew this as surely as she knew Homer Medly had been a beautiful yodeler.

"If I died tomorrow, I wonder what my little girls would remember," the girl said suddenly. Mrs. Herbert didn't know what to say to this so she didn't say anything. After a moment the girl said, "I'd like to start bringing my girls with me out here, but I hate to see kids run over the graves."

"I know what you mean," Mrs. Herbert said. But then she thought of her own father. Something he had said when he'd refused to be buried in the big county cemetery back home in Arkansas. "I want to be close enough to home that my grandkids can trample on my grave if they want to." But, as it turned out, everyone had moved away, and it hadn't mattered where he was buried.

"I always try to walk at the foot of the graves," the girl said. "But sometimes I forget." She put her hands into the hip pockets of her jeans and looked toward the mausoleum. "Those ones that are ashes, they don't have to worry," she said. She took her hands out of her pockets and sat down again on the grass next to the grave. "Nobody walks over them," she said. "I guess they just sit forever in those little cups."

Mrs. Herbert considered the idea of Homer's remains being contained in a little cup. She was glad she'd never have to see it. Then she remembered that Lloyd had said he and his brother had wanted to bring Homer's body back, but there was too much red tape. And the expense. So they'd had him cremated and, between them, they'd taken turns on the train holding the box with his ashes in it until they got home. Remembering this made her want to say a few words about Homer. She'd met Homer in her girlhood at nearly the same time she'd met her husband. For a moment, the thought came to her that Homer could have been her husband. But just as quickly she dismissed the thought. What had happened to Homer had made a deep, unsettling impression on her. She and Lloyd had talked about it once when they'd spoken in the supermarket. Lloyd had shaken his head and said, "Homer could've been something. He just fell in with the wrong company." And then he hadn't said anything else.

The girl brushed at something on the headstone. "My father was killed in an accident," she said. "We'd all been in swimming and then we kids went to the cabin to nap. My mother woke us up, crying. 'Your daddy's drowned,' she said. This drunk tried to swim the river and, when my father tried to save him, the man pulled him down. 'Your daddy's drowned,' my mother kept saying. But you don't understand things when you're a kid," the girl said. "And you don't understand things later either."

Mrs. Herbert was struck by this. She touched her teeth against her bottom lip, then ran her tongue over the lip. She didn't know what to say, so she said: "There's Homer that lived through the Second World War and then died in California a pure alcoholic." She shook her head. She didn't understand any of it.

The girl stretched out on the ground once more and made herself comfortable. She looked up and nodded once. Mrs. Herbert felt the girl slipping into reverie, into a place she couldn't follow, and she wanted to say something to hold her back. But all she could think of was Homer Medly. She couldn't feature why she couldn't get Homer off her mind. She wanted to tell the girl everything that was important to know about him. How he'd fallen into bad company in the person of Lester Yates, a boy who had molested a young girl and been sent to the penitentiary. How Beulah Looney had gone to the horse races in Santa Rosa, California, in 1935, and brought back word that Homer was married, and to a fine-looking woman! But the woman didn't live very long with Homer. He got drunk and hammered out the headlights of their car, then threatened to bite off her nose.

But she didn't tell the girl any of this. She couldn't. Besides, the girl looked to be half-asleep. Mrs. Herbert thought it seemed the most natural thing in the world for the girl to be lying there alongside her father's grave. Then the girl raised up on one elbow.

"I came out here the day of my divorce," the girl said. "And then I kept coming out here. One time I lay down and fell asleep," she said. "The caretaker came over and asked me was I all right. Sure, I said. I'm all right." The girl laughed softly and tossed her black hair over her shoulder. "Fact is, I don't know if I was all right. I been coming here trying to figure things out. If my dad was alive I'd ask him what was going to become of me and my girls. There's another man ready to step in and take up where my husband left off. But even if a man runs out on you it's no comfort just to pick up with the next one that comes around. I got to do better," the girl said. "I got to think of my girls, but I got to think of me too."

Mrs. Herbert felt she'd listened in on something important, and she wished she knew what to say to the girl for comfort. She and her husband hadn't been able to have children and, like so much of her life, she'd reconciled herself to it and never looked back. But now she could imagine having a daughter to talk with and to advise. Someone she could help in a difficult time. She felt she'd missed something precious and that she had nothing to offer the girl except to stand there and listen. Since her husband's death nearly a year ago it seemed she seldom did more than exchange a few words with people. And here she was telling a stranger about Homer and listening to the girl tell her things back. Her memory of Homer seemed to insist on being told, and though she didn't understand why this should be, she didn't want this meeting to end until she'd said what she had to say.

The shadows from the stand of trees had darkened the portion of the cemetery that lay in front of the school building. The girl tilted her head toward the place her father was lying, and Mrs. Herbert thought she might be praying—or about to pray.

"Well, I've got peonies to put out," Mrs. Herbert said, and she moved back a few steps. But the girl did not acknowledge her leaving. Mrs. Herbert waited a minute, then turned and headed back across the graves. The ground felt softer than it had when she'd approached the girl, and she couldn't help thinking, each time she put her foot down, that she had stepped on someone.

She felt relieved when she reached her husband's grave. She stood on the grave as if there at least she had a right to do as she pleased. The grave was like a green island in the midst of other green islands. Then she heard a car start up. She turned to look for the girl, but she was no longer there. Just then Mrs. Herbert saw a little red car pass out of the cemetery.

She took hold of her flowers and began to fit them into a vase next to the flowers she guessed must be from Lloyd. Once, a few weeks earlier, Lloyd had stopped at her house on the way to the cemetery and she'd given him some flowers to take to Homer and some for her husband. "They were roarers, those two," Lloyd had said as she'd made up the bouquets. She thought of her husband again. He'd been a drinker like Homer and, except for having married her, he might have fallen in with bad company and ended the way Homer had.

She took her watering can and walked toward the spigot that stood near the mausoleum. She bent down and ran water into the can as she gazed at the mausoleum. Bad company, she thought. And it occurred to her that her husband had been *her* bad company all those years. And when he hadn't been bad company, he'd been no company at all. She listened to water run into the metal can and wondered what had saved her from being pulled down by the likes of such a man, even as Lester Yates had pulled down Homer Medly.

She let herself recall the time her husband had flown into a rage after a drinking bout and accused her of sleeping around, even though every night of their married life she'd slept nowhere but in the same bed with him. He'd taken her set of china cups out onto the sidewalk and smashed them with the whole neighborhood looking on. From then on they'd passed their evenings in silence. She would knit and he would look after the fire and smoke cigarettes. God knows it wasn't the way she'd wanted things. She'd thought she'd done the best she could. But the memory of those long, silent evenings struck at her heart now, and she wished she could go back to that time and speak to her husband.

She knew there were old couples who lived differently, couples who took walks together or played checkers or cards in the evenings. And then it came to her, the thought that she had been bad company to him, had even denied him her company, going and coming from the house with barely a nod in his direction, putting his meals on the table out of duty alone, keeping house like a jailer. The idea startled and pained her, especially when she remembered how his illness had come on him until, in the last months, he was docile and then finally helpless near the end. What had she given him? What had she done for him? She could answer only that she had been there—like an implement, a shovel or a hoe. A lifetime of robbery! she thought. Then she understood that it was herself she had robbed as much as her husband. And there was no way now to get back their life together.

The water was running over the sides of the can, and she turned off the spigot. She picked up the watering can and stood next to the mausoleum and stared at it as if someone had suddenly thrown an obstacle in her pathway. She couldn't understand why anyone would want to be put into such a place when they died. The front was faced with rough stones and one wall was mostly glass so visitors could peer inside. She had tried the door to this place once, but it was locked. She supposed the relatives had keys, or else they were let in by the caretaker. Homer was situated along the wall on the outside of the mausoleum. Thinking of Homer made her glad her husband hadn't ended up on the wall of the mausoleum as a pile of ashes. There was that to be thankful for.

When she reached his grave she poured water into the vase, then stared at the bronze nameplate where enough space had been left for her own name and dates.

She remembered the day she and her husband had quarreled about where to buy their burial plots. Her husband had said he wasn't about to be buried anyplace that was likely to cave into the ocean. There were two cemeteries in their town—this one just off the main highway near the elementary school, and the other, located at the edge of a cliff over-looking the ocean. He did not want to be near the ocean. He had said this several times. Then he had gone down and purchased two plots side by side across from the school and near the mausoleum. She hadn't said much. Then he had shown her the papers with the location of the graves marked with little *X*'s on a map of the cemetery. The more she thought about it, though, the more she set her mind on buying her own plot in the cemetery overlooking the ocean. Then one day she arranged to go there, and she paid for a gravesite that very day.

She hadn't meant to tell her husband about her purchase, but one night they'd quarreled bitterly, and she'd flung the news at him. She had *two* gravesites, she said—one with him and one away from him; and she would do as she pleased when the time came. "Take your old bones and throw them in the ocean for all I care," he told her.

They'd left it like that. Right up until he died, her husband hadn't known where his wife was going to be buried. But what a thing to have done to him! To have denied him even that small comfort. She realized now that if anyone had told her about a woman who had done such a thing to a dying husband she would have been shocked and ashamed for her. But this was the story of herself she was considering, and she was the one who'd sent her life's company lonely to the grave. This thought was so painful she felt her body go rigid.

She'd taken comfort in the idea of the second grave, even when she couldn't make up her mind where she would finally lie. She had prolonged her decision and she saw this clearly now for what it was, a way to deny this man with whom she had spent her life. Even when she came to the cemetery where her husband lay, she would still be thinking, as she was now, about the cemetery near the ocean—how when she went there she could gaze out at the little fishing boats on the water or listen to gulls as they wheeled over the bluff. An oil tanker or a freighter might appear and slide serenely across the horizon. She loved how slowly the ships passed, and how she could follow them with her eyes until they were lost in the distance.

She gave the watering can a shake. There was water left in it, and she raised the can to her lips and drank deeply and thought again of the ocean. What she also loved about that view was the thought that those who walked in a cemetery, any cemetery, ought to be able to forget the dead for a moment and gaze out at something larger than themselves. Something mysterious. The ocean tantalized her even as she felt a kind of foreboding when she looked on it with her own death in mind. She could imagine children galloping over the graves, then coming to a stop at the sharp cliff edge to stare down at the waves far below. Her visits to the cemetery near the ocean gave her pleasure even after her grave there was no longer a secret. When her husband asked, "Have you been out there?" she knew what he meant. "I have," she said. And that was the extent of it. She thought she understood those who committed adultery and then returned home—unfaithful and divided. Yet she'd done nothing to change the situation. Then he had died, and some of the pleasure in her visits to the other grave seemed to have gone with him. As Mrs. Herbert's life alone had settled into its own routine, weeks might go by until, with a start, she would realize she hadn't been to either cemetery. The fact of her two graves became a mystery to her.

The shadows of the evergreens had reached where she was standing. She saw that the school building across the street was entirely in shadow now. She gathered up the containers she'd used to carry flowers to the grave and picked up her garden shears. On her way to the car she turned and looked at the flowers on her husband's grave. They seemed to accuse her of some neglect, some falsehood. She had decorated his grave, but there was no comfort in it for her. No comfort, she thought, and she knew she had simply been dutiful toward her husband in death as she had been in life. The thought quickened her step away from there. She reached her car and got in. For a moment she could not think where it was she meant to go next.

A month passed after her visit to the cemetery. Daisies and carnations were in bloom, but Mrs. Herbert made no visit to her husband's grave. It was early on a Sunday when she finally decided to go again. She expected the cemetery to be empty at that time of morning, but no sooner had she arrived than a little red car drove into the narrow roadway through the cemetery and parked near the mausoleum. Then the driver got out. Mrs. Herbert was not surprised to see that it was the young woman she'd met before Memorial Day. She felt glad when the girl raised her hand in greeting as she passed on her way to her father's grave.

The girl stood by the grave with her head down, thinking. She had on a short red coat and a dress this time, like she might be on her way to church. Mrs. Herbert approved of this—that the girl was dressed up and might go on to church. This caused another kind of respect to come into the visit. But what she felt most of all was that this was a wonderful coincidence. She had met the girl twice now in the cemetery and she wondered at this. She thought it must mean something, but she couldn't think what.

Mrs. Herbert took the dead flowers from the vases and emptied the acrid water. There was a stench as if the water itself had a body that could decay and rot. She remembered a time in her girlhood when she and Homer and her husband had been driving to a dance in the next county. The car radiator had boiled over and they'd walked to a farm and asked for water. The farmer had given them some in a big glass jug. "It's fine for your car, but I wouldn't drink it," the man said. But the day was hot and after they'd filled the radiator each of them lifted the jug and took a drink. The water tasted like something had died in it. "Jesus save me from water like that!" Homer had said. "They invented whiskey to cover up water like that." Her husband had agreed that the water tasted bad, but he took another drink anyway.

Mrs. Herbert straightened and glanced again toward the girl. She seemed deep in thought as she stood beside the grave. Mrs. Herbert saw that once again the girl had brought no flowers.

"Would you like some flowers for your grave?" Mrs. Herbert called to her. The girl looked startled, as if the idea had never occurred to her. She waited a moment. Then she smiled and nodded. Mrs. Herbert busied herself choosing stems from her own bunch to make a modest bouquet. Then she stepped carefully over the graves toward the girl. The girl took the flowers and pressed them to her face to smell them, as if these were the first flowers she'd held in a long time.

"I love carnations," she said. Then, before Mrs. Herbert could stop her, the girl began to dig a hole with her fingers at the side of her father's headstone.

"Wait! Just a minute," Mrs. Herbert said. She walked to her car and found a jar in the trunk. She returned with this and the girl walked with her toward the mausoleum to draw water to fill the container. The water spigot was near the corner of the mausoleum where Homer's ashes lay, and she remembered having told the girl about his death.

"There's Homer," Mrs. Herbert said, and pointed to the wall of the mausoleum. There were four nameplates on each marble block, and near each name a small fluted vase was attached to the stone. Most

of the vases had faded plastic flowers in them, but Homer's vase was
empty. The girl opened and closed her black eyes, then lifted her flowers and poured a little of the fresh water into the container fastened to
Homer's stone. Then she took two carnations and fitted them into the
vase. It was the right thing to do and Mrs. Herbert felt as if she'd done
it herself.

As they walked back toward the graves, Mrs. Herbert had the impulse to tell the girl about her gravesite near the ocean. But before
she could say anything, the girl said, "I've got what I came for. I been
coming here asking what I'm supposed to do with my life. Well, I'm
not for sale. That's what he let me know. I'm free now and I'm going to
stay free," the girl said. Mrs. Herbert heard the word "free" as if from a
great distance. *Free,* she thought, but the word was meaningless to her.
It came to her that in all her visits to her husband's grave she'd gotten
nothing she needed. She'd just as well go and stand in her own backyard for all she got here. But she didn't let on to the girl she was feeling
any of this, and when they set the container of carnations on the grave
she said only, "That's better, isn't it."

"Yes," the girl said. "Yes, it is." She seemed then to want to be alone,
so Mrs. Herbert made her way back to her husband's grave. But after a
few minutes she saw that instead of staying around to enjoy the flowers, the girl was leaving. She waved and Mrs. Herbert thought, *I'll never
see her again.* Before she could bring herself to lift her hand to wave
good-bye, the girl got into her car. Then the motor started, and she
watched the car drive out of the cemetery.

A week later the widow drove to the cemetery again. She looked around
as she got out of the car, half expecting to see the little red car drive up
and the girl get out. But she knew this wouldn't happen. At her husband's grave she cleared away the dead flowers from her last visit.

She had brought no flowers and didn't quite know what to do with
herself. She looked past the mausoleum and saw that a new field was
being cleared to make room for additional graves. The sight brought a

feeling of desolation. She felt more alone than she had ever felt in her life. For the first time she realized she would continue on this way to the end. Her whole body took on the dull hopelessness of it. She felt that if she had to speak she would have no voice. She was glad the girl wasn't there, that she would not have to speak to anyone in this place of regret and loneliness. Suddenly the caretaker came out of a shed in the trees, turned on a sprinkler, and disappeared back into the shed. Then there was no one.

She waited a minute, then lowered herself onto the grave. The water from the sprinkler whirled and looped over the graves, but did not reach as far as her husband's grave. She looked around her, but saw no one. She leaned back on the gravestone and stretched out her legs. She put her head on the ground and closed her eyes. The sun was warm on her face and arms and she began to feel drowsy.

As she lay there she thought she heard children running and laughing somewhere in the cemetery. But she couldn't separate this sound from the sound of the water, and she did not open her eyes to see if there really were children. The sprinkler made a *whit-whit* noise like a scythe going through a field of tall grass.

"I'm going to rest here a moment," she said out loud without opening her eyes. Then she said, "I've decided. You bought a place for me here, and that's what you wanted. And that's what I want too."

She opened her eyes then and with awful certainty knew that her husband had heard nothing of what she had said. And not in all of time would he hear her. She'd cut herself off from him as someone too good, too proud to do anything but injury to the likes of him. And this was her reward, that it would not matter to anyone on the face of the earth what she did. This, she thought, was eternity—to be left so utterly alone and to know that even her choice to be buried next to him would never reach her husband. Was she any better than the meanest wino who died in some fleabag hotel and was eventually reduced to ashes? No, she understood, no better. She had been no better than her husband all those years, and if she had saved him from a death like

Homer's, it was only to die disowned at her own hearth. The enormity of this settled on her as she struggled to raise herself up.

A light mist from the sprinkler touched her face, and when she looked around her, she saw a vastness like that of the ocean. Headstones marked off the grass as far as she could see. She saw plainly a silent and fixed company set out there, a company she had not chosen.

She looked and saw the caretaker in the doorway of the shed. He drew on his cigarette as he stood watching her. She raised her hand and then brought it down to let him know she had seen him. He inclined his head and went on smoking.

Girls

Ada had invited herself along on the four-hour drive to Corvallis with her daughter, Billie, for one reason: she intended to see if her girlhood friend, Esther Cox, was still living. When Billie had let drop she was going to Corvallis, Ada had decided. "I'm coming too," she said. Billie frowned, but didn't say no.

"Should I wear my red coat or my black one?" she'd asked Billie. "Why don't I pack a few sandwiches." Billie had told her to wear the red coat and not to bother about sandwiches; she didn't like to eat and drive. Ada packed sandwiches anyway.

Billie had on the leather gloves she used when she drove her Mercedes. When she wasn't smoking cigarettes, she was fiddling with the radio, trying to find a station. Finally, she settled on some flute music. This sounded fine to Ada. "Keep it there, honey," she said.

"Esther was like a sister to me, an older sister," Ada said. "I don't know anyone I was closer to. We did the cooking and housekeeping for two cousins who owned mansions next door to one another—the Conants was their name. Esther and I saw each other every day. We even spent our evenings together. It was like that for nearly four years." Ada leaned back in her seat and stole a look at the speedometer: seventy-five miles an hour.

"It's like a soap opera," Billie said. "I can't keep the names straight or who did what when." She brought her eyes up to the rearview mirror as if she were afraid someone was going to overtake her.

Ada wished she could make her stories interesting for Billie and make it clear who the people were and how they had fit into her life. But it was a big effort and sometimes it drove her to silence. "Never mind," she'd say. "Those people are dead and gone. I don't know why I brought them up." But Esther was different. Esther was important.

Billie pushed in the lighter and took a cigarette from the pack on the dash. "What are you going to talk to this person about after all these years?" she said.

Ada considered this for a minute. "One thing I want to know is what happened to Florita White and Georgie Ganz," Ada said. "They worked up the street from us and they were from Mansfield, where Esther and I were from. We were all farm girls trying to make a go of it in the city." Ada remembered a story about Florita. Florita, who was unmarried, had been living with a man, something just not done in those days. When she washed and dried her panties she said she always put a towel over them on the line so Basil, her man, couldn't see them. But that was all Ada could remember Florita saying. There had to be more to the story, but Ada couldn't remember. She was glad she hadn't said anything to Billie.

"You might just end up staring at each other," Billie said.

"Don't you worry," Ada said. "We'll have plenty to say." That was the trouble with Billie, Ada thought. Since she'd gone into business, if you weren't *talking* business you weren't talking. Billie owned thirty llamas—ugly creatures, Ada thought. She could smell the llama wool Billie had brought along in the backseat for her demonstration. Ada had already heard Billie's spiel on llamas. There were a lot of advantages to llamas, according to Billie. For one thing, llamas always did their job in the same place. For another, someone wanting to go into the backcountry could break a llama in two hours to lead and carry a load. Ada was half-inclined to think Billie cared more about llamas than she did about people. But then Billie had never gotten much out of people, and she *had* made it on llamas.

"Esther worked like a mule to raise three children," Ada said.

"Why are you telling me about this woman?" Billie said, as if she'd suddenly been accused of something. She lit another cigarette and turned on her signal light. Then she moved over into the passing lane. The car sped effortlessly down the freeway.

Ada straightened herself in the seat and took out a handkerchief to fan the smoke away from her face. What could she say? That she had never had a friend like Esther in all the years since? Billie would say something like: *if she was so important then why haven't you seen her in forty-three years?* That was true enough, too; Ada couldn't explain it. She tried to stop the conversation right where it was.

"Anyway, I doubt if she's still living," Ada said, trying to sound unconcerned. But even as she said this Ada wanted more than ever to find Esther Cox alive. How had they lost track? She'd last heard from Esther after Ada's youngest son had been killed in a car crash, twenty years ago. Twenty years. Then she thought of one more thing about Esther, and she said it.

"The last time I saw Esther she made fudge for me," Ada said. "You'll see, Billie. She'll whip up a batch this time too. She always made good fudge." She caught Billie looking at her, maybe wondering for a moment who her mother had been and what fudge had to do with anything. But Ada didn't care. She was remembering how she and Esther had bobbed each other's hair one night, and then gone to the town square to stroll and admire themselves in the store windows.

In the hotel room, Ada hunted up the phone book.

"Mother, take off your coat and stay awhile," Billie said as she sat down in a chair and put her feet up on the bed.

Ada was going through the *C*'s, her heart rushing with hope and dread as she skimmed the columns of names. "She's here! My God, Esther's in the book." She got up, then sat back down on the bed. "Esther. She's in the book!"

"Why don't you call her and get it over with," Billie said. She was flossing her teeth, still wearing her gloves.

"You dial," Ada said. "I'm shaking too much."

Billie dropped the floss into a wastebasket and pulled off her gloves. Then she took Ada's place on the bed next to the phone and dialed the number her mother read to her. Someone answered and Billie asked to speak to Esther Cox. Ada braced herself. Maybe Esther was dead after all. She kept her eyes on Billie's face, looking for signs. Finally Billie began to speak into the phone. "Esther? Esther Cox?" she said. "There's someone here who wants to talk to you." Billie handed Ada the phone and Ada sat on the bed next to her daughter.

"Honey?" Ada said. "Esther? This is Ada Gilman."

"Do I know you?" said the voice on the other end of the line.

Ada was stunned for a moment. It *had* been a very long time, yes. Ada's children were grown. Her husband was dead. Her hair had turned white. "We used to work in Springfield, Missouri, when we were girls," Ada said. "I came to see you after my first baby was born, in 1943." She waited a moment and when Esther still did not say anything, Ada felt a stab of panic. "Is this Esther Cox?" she asked.

"Yes it is," the voice dreamily said. Then it said, "Why don't you come over, why don't you? I'm sorry I can't remember you right off. Maybe if I saw you."

"I'll be right over, honey," Ada said. But as she gave the phone to Billie she felt her excitement swerving toward disappointment. There had been no welcome—no recognition, really, at all. Ada felt as if something had been stolen from her. She listened dully as Billie took down directions to Esther's house. When Billie hung up, Ada made a show of good spirits.

"I'll help you carry things in from the car," she said. She could see Billie wasn't happy about having to drive her anywhere. After all, they'd just gotten out of the car.

Billie shook her head. She was checking her schedule with one hand and reaching for her cigarettes with the other. "We don't have much time. We'll have to go right now."

The street they turned onto had campers parked in the front yards, and boats on trailers drawn up beside the carports. Dogs began to bark and pull on their chains as they drove down the street.

"Chartreuse. What kind of a color is that to paint a house?" Billie said, as they pulled to the curb and she turned off the ignition. They didn't say anything for a minute. Then Billie said, "Maybe I should wait in the car."

The house had a dirty canvas over the garage opening, and an accumulation of junk reached from the porch onto the lawn. There were sheets instead of curtains across some of the windows. A pickup truck sat in the driveway with its rear axles on blocks. Esther's picture window looked out onto this. Ada stared at the house, wondering what had brought her friend to such a desperate-looking place.

"She'll want to see how you turned out," Ada told Billie. "You can't stay in the car." She was nearly floored by Billie's suggestion. She was trying to keep up her good spirits, but she was worried about what she might find inside.

They walked up to the front door. Ada rang the bell and, in a minute, when no one answered, she rang it again. Then the door opened and an elderly, small woman wearing pink slacks and a green sweater looked out.

"I was lying down, girls. Come in, come in," the woman said. Despite the woman's age and appearance, Ada knew it was Esther. She wanted to hug her, but she didn't know if she should. Esther had barely looked at her when she let them in. This was an awful situation, Ada thought. To have come this far and then to be greeted as if she were just anyone. As if she were a stranger.

A rust-colored couch faced the picture window. Esther sat down on it and patted the place beside her. "Sit down here and tell me where I knew you," she said. "Who did you say you were again?"

"God, woman, don't you know me?" Ada said, bending down and taking Esther's hand in hers. She was standing in front of the couch. "I can't believe it. Esther, it's me. It's Ada." She held her face before the woman and waited. Why wouldn't Esther embrace her? Why was she just sitting there? Esther simply stared at her.

"Kid, I wish I did, but I just don't remember you," Esther said. "I don't have a glimmer." She looked down, seemingly ashamed and bewildered by some failure she couldn't account for.

Billie hovered near the door as if she might have to leave for the car at any moment. Ada dropped the woman's hand and sat down next to her on the couch. She felt as if she had tumbled over a cliff and that there was nothing left now but to fall. How could she have been so insignificant as to have been forgotten? She was angry and hurt and she wished Billie *had* stayed in the car and not been witness to this humiliation.

"I had a stroke," Esther said and looked at Ada. There was such apology in her voice that Ada immediately felt ashamed of herself for her thoughts. "It happened better than a year ago," she said. Then she said, "I don't know everything, but I still know a lot." She laughed, as if she'd had to laugh at herself often lately. There was an awkward silence as Ada tried to take this in. Strokes happened often enough at their age, so she shouldn't be surprised at this turn of events. Still, it was something she hadn't considered; she felt better and worse at the same time.

"Is this your girl? Sit down, honey," Esther said and indicated a chair by the window stacked with magazines and newspapers. "Push that stuff onto the floor and sit down."

"This is my baby," Ada said, trying to show some enthusiasm. "This is Billie."

Billie let loose a tight smile in Esther's direction and cleared a place to sit. Then she took off her gloves and put them on the window sill next to a candle holder. She crossed her legs, lit a cigarette, and gazed out the window in the direction of her Mercedes. "We can't stay too long," she said.

"Billie's giving a talk on business," Ada explained, leaving out just what kind of business it was. "She was coming to Corvallis, so I rode along. I wanted to see you."

"I raise llamas," Billie said, and turned back into the room to see what effect this would have.

"That's nice. That's real nice," Esther said. But Ada doubted she knew a llama from a goat.

"Now don't tell me you can't remember the Conants—those cousins in Springfield we worked for," Ada said.

"Oh, I surely do remember them," Esther said. She was wearing glasses that she held to her face by tilting her head up. From time to time she pushed the bridge of the glasses with her finger. "I've still got a letter in my scrapbook. A recommendation from Mrs. Conant."

"Then you must remember Coley Starber and how we loaned him Mrs. Leslie Conant's sterling silver," Ada said, her hopes rising, as if she'd located the scent and now meant to follow it until she discovered herself lodged in Esther's mind. Billie had picked up a magazine and was leafing through it. From time to time she pursed her lips and let out a stream of smoke.

"Coley," Esther said and stared a moment. "Oh, yes, I remember when he gave the silver *back*. I counted it to see if it was all there. But, honey, I don't remember you." She shook her head helplessly. "I'm sorry. No telling what else I've forgot."

Ada wondered how she could be missing in Esther's memory when Coley Starber, someone incidental to their lives, had been remembered. It didn't seem fair.

"Mom said you were going to make some fudge," Billie said, holding the magazine under the long ash of her cigarette. "Mom's got a sweet tooth."

"Use that candleholder," Esther told Billie, and Billie flicked the ash into the frosted candleholder.

Ada glared at Billie. Esther was looking at Ada with a bemused, interested air. "I told Billie how we used to make fudge every chance we got," Ada said.

"And what did we do with all this fudge?" Esther asked.

"We ate it," Ada said.

"We ate it!" Esther said and clapped her hands together. "We *ate* all the fudge." Esther repeated the words to Billie as if she were letting her in on a secret. But Billie was staring at Esther's ankles. Ada looked down and saw that Esther was in her stocking feet, and that the legs themselves were swollen and painful looking where the pant legs had worked up.

"What's making your legs swell up like that?" Billie said. Ada knew Billie was capable of saying anything, but she never thought she'd hear her say a thing like this. Such behavior was the result of business, she felt sure.

"I had an operation," Esther said, as if Billie hadn't said anything at all out of line. Esther glanced toward a doorway that led to the back of the house. Then she raised her sweater and pulled down the waistband of her slacks to show a long violet-looking scar that ran vertically up her abdomen. "I healed good though, didn't I?" Esther lowered her sweater, then clasped her hands in her lap.

Before Ada had time to take this in, she heard a thumping sound from the hallway. A man appeared in the doorway of the living room. His legs bowed at an odd angle and he used a cane. The longer Ada looked at him, the more things she found wrong. One of his eyes seemed fixed on something not in this room, or in any other for that matter. He took a few more steps and extended his hand. Ada reached out to him. The man's hand didn't have much squeeze to it. Billie stood up and inclined her head. She was holding her cigarette in front of her with one hand and had picked up her purse with the other so as not to have to shake hands. Ada didn't blame her. The man was a fright.

"I'm Jason," the man said. "I've had two operations on my legs, so I'm not able to get around very easy. Sit down," he said to Billie. Jason leaned forward against his cane and braced himself. She saw that Jason's interest had settled on Billie. Good, Ada thought. Billie considered herself a woman of the world. Surely she could handle this.

Ada turned to Esther and began to inquire after each of her other children, while she searched for a way to bring things back to that time in Springfield. Esther asked Ada to hand down a photograph album from a shelf behind the couch, and they began to go over the pictures.

"This arthritis hit me when I was forty," Jason said to Billie.

"I guess you take drugs for the pain," Billie said. "I hear they've got some good drugs now."

Ada looked down at the album in her lap. She saw children and babies and couples. Some of the couples had children next to them. Many of the faces were young, then you turned a few pages and the same faces were old. Esther seemed to remember everyone in the album. But she still didn't remember Ada. She was talking to Ada as to a friend, but Ada felt as if the ghost of her old self hovered in her mind waiting for a sign from Esther so she could step forward again and be recognized.

"But that wouldn't interest you," Esther was saying as she flipped a page. Suddenly she shut the book and gazed intently at Ada.

"I don't know who you are," Esther said. "But I like you. Why don't you stay the night?" Ada looked over at Billie, who'd heard the invitation.

"Go ahead, Mother," Billie said, a little too eagerly. "I can come for you tomorrow around two o'clock, after the luncheon."

Ada looked at Jason, who was staring out the picture window toward the Mercedes. Maybe she should just give up on getting Esther to remember her and go back to the hotel and watch TV. But the moment she thought this, something unyielding rose up in her. She was determined to discover some moment when her image would suddenly appear before Esther from that lost time. Only then could they be together again as the friends they had once been, and that was what she had come for.

"You'll have to bring my things in from the car," Ada said at last.

"I wish I could help," Jason said to Billie, "but I can't. Fact is, I got to go and lay down again," he said to the room at large, then turned and moved slowly down the hallway. Billie opened the door and went out to the car. In a minute she came back with Ada's overnight bag.

"Have a nice time, Mom," she said. "I mean that." She set the bag inside the door. "I'll see you tomorrow." Ada knew she was glad to be heading back to the world of buying and selling, of tax shelters and the multiple uses of llamas. In a minute she heard Billie start up the Mercedes and leave the drive.

The room seemed sparsely furnished now that she and Esther were alone. She could see a table leg just inside the door of a room that was probably the dining room. On the far wall was a large picture of an autumn landscape in gold and brown.

"Look around, why don't you," Esther said, and raised herself from the couch. "It's a miracle, but I own this house."

They walked into the kitchen. The counter space was taken up with canned goods, stacks of dishes of every kind, and things Ada wouldn't expect to find in a kitchen—things like gallon cans of paint. It was as if someone were afraid they wouldn't be able to get to a store and had laid in extra supplies of everything.

"I do the cooking," Esther said. "Everything's frozen but some wieners. Are wieners okay?"

"Oh, yes," Ada said. "But I'm not hungry just yet."

"I'm not either," Esther said. "I was just thinking ahead because I've got to put these feet up. Come back to the bedroom with me."

Ada thought this an odd suggestion, but she followed Esther down the hallway to a room with a rumpled bed and a chrome kitchen chair near the foot of the bed. There was a dresser with some medicine containers on it. Ada helped Esther get settled on the bed. She took one of the pillows and placed it under Esther's legs at the ankles. She was glad she could do this for her. But then she didn't know what to do next, or what to say. She wanted the past and not this person for whom she was just an interesting stranger. Ada sat down in the chair and looked at Esther.

"What ever became of Georgie Ganz and Florita White?" she asked Esther, because she had to say something.

"Ada—that's your name, isn't it? Ada, I don't know who you're talking about," Esther said. "I wish I did, but I don't."

"That's all right," Ada said. She brightened a little. It made her feel better that Georgie and Florita had also been forgotten. A shadow cast by the house next door had fallen into the room. Ada thought the sun must be going down. She felt she ought to be doing something, changing the course of events for her friend in some small but important way.

"Let me rub your feet," Ada said suddenly and raised herself from the chair. "Okay?" She moved over to the bed and began to massage Esther's feet.

"That feels good, honey," Esther said. "I haven't had anybody do that for me in years."

"Reminds me of that almond cream we used to rub on each other's feet after we'd served at a party all night," Ada said. The feet seemed feverish to her fingers. She saw that the veins were enlarged and angry looking as she eased her hands over an ankle and up onto the leg.

After a little while, Esther said, "Honey, why don't you lie down with me on the bed. That way we can really talk."

At first Ada couldn't comprehend what Esther had said to her. She said she didn't mind rubbing Esther's feet. She said she wasn't tired enough to lie down. But Esther insisted.

"We can talk better that way," Esther said. "Come lay down beside me."

Ada realized she still had on her coat. She took it off and put it over the back of the chair. Then she took off her shoes and went to lie down next to Esther.

"Now this is better, isn't it?" Esther said, when Ada was settled. She patted Ada's hand. "I can close my eyes now and rest." In a minute, she closed her eyes. And then they began to talk.

"Do you know about that preacher who was sweet on me back in Mansfield?" Esther asked. Ada thought for a minute and then remembered and said she did. "I didn't tell that to too many, I feel sure," Esther said. This admission caused Ada to feel for a moment that her friend knew she was someone special. There was that, at least. Ada relaxed a little and felt a current of satisfaction, something just short of recognition, pass between them.

"I must have told you all my secrets," Esther said quietly, her eyes still closed.

"You did!" Ada said, rising up a little. "We used to tell each other everything."

"Everything," Esther said, as if she were sinking into a place of agreement where remembering and forgetting didn't matter. Then there was a loud noise from the hall, and the sound of male voices at the door. Finally the front door closed, and Esther put her arm across Ada's arm and sighed.

"Good. He's gone," Esther said. "I wait all day for them to come and take him away. His friends, so called. He'll come home drunk, and he won't have a dime. They've all got nothing better to do."

"That must be an awful worry," Ada said. "A heartache."

"Heartache?" Esther said, and then she made a weary sound. "You don't know the start of it, honey. 'You need me, Mom,' he says to me, 'and I need you.' I told him if he stopped drinking I'd will him my house so he'd always have a place to live. But he won't stop. I know he won't. He can't.

"You know what he did?" Esther asked and raised up a little on her pillow. "He just looked at me when I said that about willing him the house. I don't think he'd realized until then that I wasn't always going to be here," Esther said. "Poor fellow, he can't help himself. But girl, he'd drink it up if I left it to him."

Ada felt that the past had drifted away, and she couldn't think how to get back to that carefree time in Springfield. "It's a shame," she murmured. And then she thought of something to tell Esther that she hadn't admitted to anyone. "My husband nearly drank us out of house and home, too. He would have if I hadn't fought him tooth and nail. It's been five years since he died. Five peaceful years." She was relieved to hear herself admit this, but somehow ashamed too.

"Well, I haven't made it to the peaceful part yet," Esther said. "Jason has always lived with me. He'll never leave me. Where could he go?"

"He doesn't abuse you, does he?" Ada said. *Abuse* was a word she'd heard on the television a lot these days, and it seemed all-purpose enough not to offend Esther.

"If you mean does he hit me, no he doesn't," Esther said. "But I sorrow over him. I do."

Ada had done her share of sorrowing too. She closed her eyes and let her hand rest on Esther's arm. Neither of them said anything for a while. The house was still. She caught the faint medicinal smell of ointment and rubbing alcohol. She wished she could say something to ease what Esther had to bear, but she couldn't think of anything that didn't sound like what Billie might call "sappy."

"What's going to become of Jason?" Ada said finally. But when she asked this she was really thinking of herself and of her friend.

"I'm not going to know," Esther said. "Memory's going to fall entirely away from me when I die, and I'm going to be spared that." She seemed, Ada thought, to be actually looking forward to death and the shutting down of all memory. Esther got up from the bed. "Don't mind me, honey. You stay comfortable. I have to go to the bathroom. It's these water pills."

After Esther left the room Ada raised up on the bed as if she had awakened from the labyrinth of a strange dream. What was she doing here, she wondered, on this woman's bed in a city far from her own home? What business of hers was this woman's troubles? In Springfield, Esther had always told Ada how pretty she was and what beautiful hair she had, how nicely it took a wave. They had tried on each other's clothes and shared letters from home. But this was something else. This was the future and she had come here alone. There was no one to whom she could turn and say without the least vanity, "I was pretty, wasn't I?"

She sat on the side of the bed and waited for the moment to pass. But it was like an echo that wouldn't stop calling her. Then she heard from outside the house the merry, untroubled laughter of girls. It must be dark out by now, she thought. It must be night. She got up from the bed, went to the window, and pulled back the sheet that served as a curtain. A car was pulling away from the house next door. The lights brushed the room as it moved past. In a moment, she went back to the bed and lay down again.

For supper Esther gave her wieners, and green beans fixed the way they'd had them back home, with bacon drippings. Then she took her to the spare room, which was next to Jason's room. They had to move some boxes off the bed. Esther fluffed up the pillows and put down an extra blanket.

"If you need anything, if you have any bad dreams, you just call me, honey," she said. "Sometimes I dream I'm wearing a dress but it's on backward and I'm coming downstairs, and there's a room full of people looking up at me," she said. "I'm glad you're here. I am. Good night. Good night, Ada."

"Good night, Esther," Ada said. But Esther went on standing there in the doorway.

Ada looked at her and wished she could dream them both back to a calm summer night in Springfield. She would open her window and call across the alley to her friend, "You awake?" and Esther would hear her and come to the screen and they would say wild and hopeless things like, *Why don't we go to California and try out for the movies?* Crazy things like that. But Ada didn't remind Esther of this. She lay there alone in their past and looked at Esther, at her old face and her old hands coming out of the sleeves of her robe, and she wanted to yell at her to get out, shut the door, don't come back! She hadn't come here to strike up a friendship with this old scarecrow of a woman. But then Esther did something. She came over to the bed and pulled the covers over Ada's shoulders and patted her cheek.

"There now, dear," she said. "I'm just down the hall if you need me." And then she turned and went out of the room.

Sometime before daylight Ada heard a scraping sound in the hall. Then something fell loudly to the floor. But in a while the scraping sound started again and someone entered the room next to hers and shut the door. It was Jason, she supposed. Jason had come home, and he was drunk and only a few feet away. She had seen her own husband like this plenty of times, had felt herself forgotten, obliterated, time after time. She lay there rigid and felt the weight of the covers against her throat. Suddenly, it was as if she were suffocating. She felt her mouth open and a name came out of it. "Esther! Esther!" she cried. And in a few moments her door opened and her friend came in and leaned over her.

"What is it, honey?" Esther said, and turned the lamp on next to the bed.

She put out her hand and took hold of Esther's sleeve. "I'm afraid," she said. Esther waited a minute. Then she turned off the light and got into bed beside Ada. Ada turned on her side, facing the wall, and Esther's arm went around her shoulder.

The next day Billie came to the house a little early. Ada had just finished helping Esther wash her hair.

"I want you to take some pictures of us," Ada said to Billie. "Esther and me." She dug into her purse and took out the camera she'd carried for just this purpose. Billie seemed in a hurry to get on the road now that the conference was over.

"I was a real hit last night," Billie said to Ada as if she'd missed seeing her daughter at her best. Little tufts of llama wool clung to Billie's suit jacket. She took the camera from Ada and tried to figure out where the lens was and how to snap the picture. Ada felt sure she hadn't missed anything, but she understood Billie's wanting her to know she'd done well at something. That made sense to her now.

"Let's go out in the yard," Billie said.

"My hair's still wet," Esther said. She was standing in front of a mirror near the kitchen rubbing her hair with a towel, but the hair sprang out in tight spirals all over her head.

"You look all right," Ada said. "You look fine, honey."

"You'd say anything to make a girl feel good," Esther said.

"No, I wouldn't," Ada said. She stood behind Esther and, looking in the mirror, dabbed her own nose with powder. They could be two young women readying themselves to go out, Ada thought. They might meet some young men while they were out, and they might not. In any case, they'd take each other's arm and stroll until dusk. Someone—Ada didn't know who—might pass and admire them.

Outside Billie had them stand below the picture window. They put their arms around each other. Esther was shorter and leaned her head onto Ada's shoulder. She even smiled. Ada had the sensation that the picture had already been taken somewhere in her past. She was sure it had.

"Did you get it?" Ada said as Billie moved closer for another shot.

"I'm just covering myself," Billie said, squatting down on the lawn and aiming the camera like a professional. She snapped a few more shots from the driveway, then handed the camera back to her mother.

Ada followed her friend into the house to collect her belongings and say good-bye. Esther wrapped a towel around her head while Ada gathered her coat, purse, and overnight bag.

"Honey, I'm so sorry I never remembered you," Esther said.

Ada believed Esther when she said this. "Sorry" was the word a person had to use when there was no way to change a situation. Still, she wished they could have changed it.

"I remembered *you,* that's the main thing," Ada said. But a miserable feeling came over her, and it was all she could do to speak. Somehow the kindness and intimacy they'd shared as girls had lived on in them. But Esther, no matter how much she might want to, couldn't remember Ada, and give it back to her, except as a stranger.

"God, kid, I hate to see you go," Esther said. Her eyes filled. It seemed to Ada that they might both be wiped from the face of the earth by this parting. They embraced and clung to each other a moment. Ada patted Esther's thin back, then moved hurriedly toward the door.

"Tell me all about your night," Billie said, as Ada slid into the passenger's seat. But Ada knew this was really the last thing on Billie's mind.

And anyhow, it all seemed so far from anything Ada had ever experienced that she didn't know where to begin.

"Honey, I just want to be still a while," Ada said. She didn't care whether Billie smoked or how fast she drove. She knew that eventually she would tell Billie how she had tried to make Esther remember her, and how she had failed. But the important things—the way Esther had come to her when she'd called out, and how, earlier, they'd lain side by side—this would be hers. She wouldn't say anything to Billie about these things. She couldn't. She doubted she ever would.

She looked out at the countryside that flew past the window in a green blur. It went on and on, a wall of forest that crowded the edge of the roadway. Then there was a gap in the color and she found herself looking at downed trees and stumps where an entire hillside of forest had been cut away. Her hand went to her face as if she'd been slapped. But then she saw it was green again, and she let her hand drop to her lap.

from
At the Owl Woman Saloon

I Got a Guy Once

Danny Gunnerson's mailbox had a serious look, like it could handle any kind of news. Someone had even painted it black, for good measure. I glanced inside to make sure the mail hadn't come, then sat down on the bumper of a blue jeep parked just off the main road. The sun was pushing through for the usual early-afternoon break in the overcast, and I'd started to sweat in my flannel shirt.

Danny owed me what was, in those days, a lot of money—about three thousand dollars. He probably owed others, which accounted for his telling everyone he was going bankrupt long before it happened. At first Danny had told me he wasn't getting checks, period. They just weren't hitting his mailbox. "The mill has quit paying," he kept telling us. "They're just stacking logs in the yard. If Japan doesn't fork over, nobody gets paid." I couldn't figure it. The same company was paying boys in other outfits every two weeks.

He'd been stringing us along like a clothesline to China, and the poor prospects of timber cutting meant he could get away with it. Meanwhile, when I'd missed child-support payments, my ex-wife had turned collection over to the state. I'd moved a renter into my house as a stopgap for some kind of steady income. The state had threatened to confiscate my pickup, plus my land and everything on it, if I didn't pay up. The pickup they could have. I'd even put a sign on it to warn people of its value: NOT A PIECE OF JUNK. GENUINE ARTIFACT OF SPOTTED OWL ERA. I thought tourists would appreciate the local color, since tourists were what we had of light industry these days.

But there had to be an end to Danny's stringing us along. So I worked out which day the check should be delivered to his place, then drove there to sit, big as a jaybird, near his mailbox.

Gunnerson had one of those stump ranches halfway up Lost Mountain. A wooden boat had dead-ended practically on his doorstep. Marooned near a trailer house was a lime green sofa, minus its cushions. Half a dozen fat white geese were pulling tufts of sick-looking yellow grass between rusted vehicles and appliances.

It was peaceful to lean against the jeep with the sun hazing through, and I got to thinking about the mail carrier who'd be coming along anytime now. I knew Joe Cooper had this route, because my aunt Trina lived up the road, and she was always telling me things Joe told her. He was an awful gossip and lady's man. I'd known Joe when he'd been a logger, back when, as they say, the getting was good—long before work in the woods got scarce, with government lands slammed shut to logging. Private timber had been coming down so fast lately that deer were sleeping on our front porches, and a cougar had snapped up a Pomeranian from a backyard near Morse Creek.

Joe hadn't quit logging because of any special eye to the future. Short and simple, he'd developed an honest bad back, like a lot of middle-aged loggers. Then he'd started having some near misses—snags crashing down at his elbow, saws jamming in the butts of trees—things that happen one time or another to anyone who stays long enough with the timber. But Joe read the writing on the wall, while the rest of us just kept getting up with the dawn, hoping for the next stand of timber to cut, even if it turned out to be smack against a playground full of kids.

"How you doing, Billy?" Joe called to me as he pulled up to Danny's mailbox. He leaned out the window of his snub-nosed jeep, opened the black mailbox, and, like he was sliding some awful dish into an oven, pushed Gunnerson's mail inside.

"I'm fit as a fiddle in a hailstorm," I said, and went over to Joe.

We shot the breeze and Joe allowed as how he could get me on with the postal service anytime I wanted to pack it in with logging. "Too dangerous," I said. "You think I don't read about those wacko postal workers who blitz their co-workers and innocent PO box owners to bejesus with AK-47s? And what about mail bombs or poisonous substances? Hazardous duty, I'd say."

"That's what a regular paycheck will do for you," Joe said. "Fearless, I'm simply fearless." But he grinned in a way that said he missed the old sawdust edge a little. He knew I'd been a gyppo logger for over thirty years and regular paychecks are just a dirty rumor to a gyppo.

"There's nothing I like better than to be in timber," I said. "I'm going to last it out until my tailbone drags the ground like a praying mantis." We had a good laugh on that one. The way he enjoyed my stubbornness let me know he envied me for staying with what I loved. He understood how, with hardly a heartbeat between, a logger can love trees and love to cut them, too.

Once Joe was out of sight, I stepped to the mailbox and reached in. I knew Gunnerson or someone must be home, because wood smoke was sifting from the chimney, one of those slow greenwood fires people in these parts light in the spring to shove back the damp. His yellow pickup, a real beater, was parked in the turnaround. It occurred to me Danny might even be watching through the window, so I tried to be quick. I shuffled the mail like a stacked deck, hunting the fifth ace. It was there, too. I brought the envelope with the return address from "Jansik, Inc." to the top.

This company had been buying logs as fast as we could lay down trees, then selling them to Japan. One of the longshoremen I knew told me the trees were being used in Japan to make forms for pouring concrete in high-rises. Then, he said, the wood was tossed. I hated to think of such good wood scummed with concrete and lost to a scrap heap. It hurt me, hearing about waste I couldn't stop.

I let the Jansik envelope ride the pile—mainly bills, along with a tools catalogue and some coupon packets. Then I knocked the mud off my caulks on the bumper of the jeep and headed for Gunnerson's house. I braved it right through the middle of the geese, hissing when they hissed at me. I must have been convincing because they reared their heads back on their slick cobra-sized necks, then waddled to the side of the house. On the porch there was a kid's trike beside a refrigerator with the door ajar. Pulpy apples and limp celery stalks were sinking through the racks. I felt for Gunnerson. The dead food in his recently disabled refrigerator reminded me he had a family to support, same as me. But he was getting his checks. It was an important difference, and why I was standing on his porch with his mail in my hands.

I gave the front door a good hard-knuckle rap and tried to look in through the frosted glass. Suddenly I was nose to nose with Danny. Before he could say a thing, I handed him the mail, check envelope on top.

"What do you know about that!" I said. "Jansik paid today."

Danny looked like he wished he was anywhere but there holding his mail. I'd worked for him many a time before this. He was a person-able enough guy. Could talk you into anything in the way of timber cutting, slash clearing, or snagging a unit, once a cut was finished. I had climbed ridges a mountain goat would have balked at, in order to cut timber for Danny Gunnerson. When the pressure was on to get logs out before closures of one sort and another, I had even cut in wind-storms, one of the dumbest things an experienced faller can do. So I'm saying I had put myself out for this guy, and I wasn't ashamed to be standing there on his porch, asking for pay I deserved.

"Probably more excuses," Danny said, glancing at the envelope he'd been expecting all along. "Come in, Billy, come in," he said, and stepped back so I could see into the rooms. The place was a shambles and his wife was still in her robe, so I stayed on the porch. Danny left the door ajar while he went over to a little piled-up table in one corner that served as a desk and brought back what I hoped was a checkbook. He took the Jansik envelope and tore it open. He examined the check and groaned. "I can't believe these jackasses, shorting me like this," he said. "I can let you have three hundred," he told me when he looked up. "That's the best I can do." He made it seem a stretch. "Surely they'll pay the lot in a couple of weeks."

"Surely," I said. He found a pen on the TV and made out a check, leaning over a bronzed clock with its exhausted Indian rider. Then he folded the check and handed it to me like it was some kind of secret. It hit me that this was exactly what he intended. I wasn't to let on to the others at the job that I'd gotten paid even a fraction of what I was owed.

"Jake and Paul will be glad to hear the payload came in," I said, and unfolded the check to make sure I wouldn't get down the road to find he hadn't signed it. I looked up as his expression fell, then stuck the check in my shirt pocket and stepped off the porch toward my pickup.

Before the day was out, I made sure my partners got around to Danny's for their shares. In no time, I was able to have my phone turned on and to buy lumber for the outhouse I was hammering together back of what I called my hovel. Fifteen years earlier, I'd built an A-frame on my acreage, complete with a beautiful stone fireplace that a logger-turned-stonemason had run twenty-six feet to the pitch of my roof. It was a monument, that fireplace. I'd packed the stones off a mountaintop myself, a few at a time in my saddlebags. "Heather stone" it's called, because it's found on ridges above the timberline in patches of heather.

Now another guy, a renter, a man who'd never set eyes on heather stone atop a ridge, was warming his toes at my fireplace. His kids, from various marriages and byways of desire, were scraping crayons down my walls, and his current girlfriend was burning Spam in my skillet. But what could I say? Hey, he paid his rent.

A month back I'd made this retreat to the hovel, which I'd used as a bunkhouse during elk-hunting season. It had come in handy of late as a fallback position when I'd had to rent my house. Having been run out of house and home, needless to say, it did not sit well when, two weeks after my mailbox visit, Danny came to us hangdog and confessed he was now truly and irreversibly bankrupt. He threw himself on our mercy. Said if we would just cut this one last section, he could maybe sell the logs for lumber to a guy he knew, then put his machinery up for sale. He promised to split the take between us and his other creditors. We knew it was one more promise he was unlikely to keep.

That very day we gathered our gear, took one last look at our spar tree, which was as good as they come—straight and well rooted—and which we hated to leave, maybe for its resemblance to our own stripped-down lives. It was next to abandoning a brother, to walk off from it. But we took our saws, wedges, and falling axes and we walked out of there.

Imagine our surprise three days later when Joe Cooper stopped in at the coffee shop to tell us Danny was still in business, floating home free on a gang of greenhorns. Naturally the new gang had been promised big pay. The truth would only hit them a couple of weeks later.

I didn't say anything to Joe when he told us this. But I had an image at the back of my mind of that great fir spar bouncing up as it fell, then rebounding several times before it settled in its lay. If the spar goes, that's it. There'd be a shutdown and a good while before another could be rigged and put into use. The thought did not let me rest. It occurred to me I would even be doing this virgin crew a favor, saving them from putting in so much as another day's work for which they would certainly never see pay.

In over thirty years of falling I had cut trees in all conditions and weather, including snow up to my nostrils, but I had never cut a tree at night. Luckily there was a bloated moon above the ridge. I was amazingly calm and not the least bit at odds with Danny as I hefted my chain saw from the pickup. I felt that all the worn-out, misused loggers, past and present, were somehow with me. Not that this would truly put right the situation between piecemeal thieves like Danny and honest, hardworking folk like Jake, Paul, and myself. The damage was too extensive and ongoing to kid myself about that. But at least this was some show of spirit.

In my twenties I'd logged with a Swede who had said, "Better to be a tiger for one day than a sheep for a thousand." It seemed, at the time, a fairly dangerous idea. Some twenty-five years had passed. I had been a sheep a long time, had gotten comfortable in my woolly ways. But the Swede's words came back to me, there on that mountainside.

In the moonlight the spar looked silver. The block, which is used like a pulley to run steel cable out to each log, was dangling at the tree's stripped crown. Guy wires were stretched to stumps. Before I could bring the block down, I would have to drop these cables. They were fastened to the stumps with railroad spikes, and I used a crowbar to pry the spikes loose. Then I cranked my saw into the tree itself.

That sound of a chain saw in moonlight—I hadn't been ready for that. It made such a raw snarl that I drew the saw blade out of the cut and throttled back. Then silence dropped over me—the velvety, deep quiet of clear-cut, and above that, of trees still growing, untouched high on the ridge. It was a fresh, unwearied silence that probably belongs to the instant before the world was born. The moon seemed to look down at me and to make a great show of itself in all the blue-blackness of sky around it. I felt watched as I cranked the saw again and stepped to the spar.

I set a cut into the base, two feet from the ground. When a pull of air hit the saw, I yanked it out, just as the tree began to hinge from the stump and break into its fall. The spar gave way in slow motion. Its falling seemed so outside time that I was glad to see it finally reach the ground. On impact there was a brittle sound of machinery and I could make out the yarder crushed as easily as a beer can under the trunk.

Just as the spar rebounded I glimpsed something live making a run from the clearing. It was the size of a large dog. A cougar, I guessed, probably displaced by the recent havoc we'd wreaked on that hillside. "It's all over, here," I shouted, my voice coming back to me with too much importance. "Don't you worry," I called into the night. I was speaking to the cougar, but also to the trees, and to the stare-down moon that was shining over what I had just done.

After the spar settled, I went over and ran my hand the length of it, right up to the block, past the bashed-in yarder, its snapped wires gone slack. The tree still had plenty of quiver, and I felt sorry all over again to put to waste such a perfectly good spar. At the same time a giddy light-ness came over me. I felt like a man with cougar in his veins. I could have clawed my way up a hemlock or skimmed five miles at a bound. It was energy I couldn't account for. Sheep energy, built up for years, working on and off for Danny Gunnerson and the like.

Standing there in moonlight, next to kinked iron and that downed spar, I felt that, at least for those moments, there was something peaceful in having called a line on what you were willing to put up with. Pride is an awful engine, mind you. I had been raised to keep a clear heart, not to do wrong to anyone, and if anyone asked me today, I would stand by that view of life. I would not bother to argue for rightness in what I'd just done, and done out of the usual misbegotten notions that add ruin to ruin in the world. No, this night's work was somewhere out there with cougars and bobcats, with instincts we pledge to mostly over-come. But I figured, right or wrong, that for all the daylight I'd given up to Danny Gunnerson in good faith, I had one such night coming. My mind seemed eerily far-reaching, like that moon-washed night. If an army of Danny Gunnersons were to line up in my future, I hoped maybe I'd walk away with a little more backbone for having taken that spar down, wrongheaded as it was.

The moon was sinking fast by the time I'd finished dropping the block and dragged it a hundred yards into the brush. I piled limbs and salal over it, then went back to the clearing for my saw. The spar was white as a tusk, right where I'd left it, resting on the yarder. I looked toward the edge of the clearing and thought I caught a glimmer of the cranked-up, mad-to-the-core night eyes of a cougar.

I let a day pass, but I couldn't keep away from that clearing. At day-break on the second day I found myself near the work site with my hounds. Danny's new men had already sawed the spar for stove wood. There were fresh jets of sawdust in the dirt where they'd cut it to length. Danny was rummaging the carcass of the yarder when he saw me. "Hey, Billy," he shouted, "some sonofabitch took out my spar and my yarder." He had the brow of an angel when he said it, and it was a wonder to me that a man like Danny could carry himself so pure and wronged. But that quick, I saw myself—not so different from him as I had been.

My hounds were crooning, a sign the trail had suddenly gone live, and I knew they'd be high notes over the ridge in a matter of minutes, so I waved at Danny like the man of leisure I'd suddenly become, thanks to him. I put my eyes to the ground for track. I admit it did my heart good to see I'd given him pause, made him take stock of a shift in his stature in the universe. Maybe what I'd done was the start of a true downward spiral for Danny's life. All I know is, he really did go bankrupt after that.

One day five years later I was driving to Discovery Bay to shoe a horse for Joe Cooper, when I saw a man walking at the side of the road. It was pouring rain and he was thumbing without looking as he walked.

I pulled over, thinking it could be me anytime now, since I was odd-jobbing it to hold things together, one step ahead of the Devil. The guy opened the truck door, tossed his lunch bucket onto the seat, and climbed in. When he turned his head, I saw it was Danny. He'd aged considerably, to the point it made me wonder if I looked as bad. There'd been a twinkle in his eyes in our logging days, and he'd had charm that could cause a man to put aside his better judgment.

"Billy!" he said, like I was someone he'd been missing, and he put out his hand. We caught hold of each other's palms and gave a squeeze. Rain was pelting the windshield. I could smell his clothes, wet and acrid in a mix of wood smoke and denim.

I was driving the same amazing piece of junk as when I'd worked for him, and we remarked on the sturdy nature of junk, that it should be given more credit on the world's balance sheet. "I'm not much better than a piece of junk myself," Danny said, and smiled. I was glad to hear something in his voice that meant this wasn't such a calamity for him to admit. At the same time, I saw that whatever he'd been traveling on earlier had left him. He could no longer strike deals, borrow money at banks, or convince a crew their paychecks were just around the corner.

"I'm splitting shakes in Chimacum," he told me. I looked down at one of his hands, resting palm up near the lunch bucket, and saw it was torn all to hell. We didn't talk for a stretch while I chanced passing a string of trailer houses leaving the west-end campgrounds in the downpour.

"I got me an indoor toilet again," I volunteered, as if to let him know I'd improved on where I'd been in our final days, when he'd joked that he'd advance me one crescent moon for my outhouse door.

What does one piece of junk say to another piece of junk anyway, going down the road? We talked a little more damage. One of his kids had turned wild as rhubarb in August, he said, and his wife's ex-husband had recently flipped his lid, rushed into their house one morning, yanked the phone off the wall, then lunged out again, using it as a walkie-talkie to God.

"I wish I had connections like that," Danny said, and laughed in something akin to his old self. I told him how my drunken renter had run over and killed my favorite hound. I even exaggerated the state of my finances, telling him I was nearly down to washing cars at the Jack-Pot, trying to steal customers from the cheerleaders on Sundays.

It was still raining when I came to my turnoff. I pulled over to let him out. He stepped onto the roadside, then reached back into the cab and offered me his beaten-up hand again. I leaned across the seat and took it, then let it go. I looked down and waited as he slammed the truck door. For a few moments I idled in the truck and watched him start off down the road without looking back.

The amazing thing was that there was still a lot left to Danny, even with his life savvy and charm out of the way. It occurred to me that if revenge is sweet, it's because it is also more than a little sad, sad and a weight to carry. And more often than not, we mistake sadness for sweetness.

When I glanced in my side view, Danny was swinging his black lunch bucket and holding out his thumb. Cars were passing him up, one after the other. I considered turning around and driving him to

Chimacum myself, just to save having to think of him that way, a man without so much as a piece of junk to drive down the road.

But the past is a sure bullet with no mission but forward. I could feel it zinging straight through the stray, half-smart thoughts I wanted to have about my life or the fate of Danny Gunnerson. So I just kept herding my piece of junk down the road, to shoe a horse for Joe Cooper, a horse not unlike Joe, with more than a few bad rumors attached to it. Joe's ten-year-old granddaughter had named the horse Renegade, a name that gave me pause, thinking how even a kid knows, without being told, that wildness ought to be honored, ought to be called to. Like a horse named Renegade, that I was about to humiliate by pounding nails into its hooves to hold on rims of steel.

To Dream of Bears

If you could get Tivari to talk about his fear of water, he'd say it had to do with his Romanian mother's vivid descriptions of a drowning she'd witnessed on the last day of a summer holiday at the Black Sea. Mostly, though, he wouldn't talk about his phobia, as if some dangerous, yet-to-be-crossed body of water might overhear and take note of him.

"I flew over an ocean to get here. Now I'm sleeping on water and taking a boat to work," Tivari said to me one day in disbelief. We were housed on a float camp snugged offshore in a small bay near our logging site on Prince of Wales Island.

My friendship with Tivari had begun in Washington State in 1965, during a logging job near Sappho. We'd both been in our early twenties, cutting the '21 Blow on a six-month job, so there'd been plenty of time to get to know each other. The "Big Blow," as the windstorm was called, had leveled an entire forest in 1921 at the ocean end of the Olympic Peninsula. Cutting in those return stands was an eerie undertaking and if the wind came up, we respected it and called it a day.

Tivari had long, sinewy arms like a wrestler. He wore his black beard well trimmed and this made his milk white teeth seem false. While the rest of us were calling our tatters fashionable, Tivari's overalls would be mended, because he was good with a needle—something taught him by his Romanian mother. If anyone had a splinter in his palm or needed a wound lanced, he would call for Tivari as if he were a doctor.

We always knew he was at hand because he carried a transistor radio and tape deck everywhere. He loved opera or any serious classical station. When reception was poor, as it mostly was, he would punch in a tape. He often turned up the volume until we had to shout to be heard, and there were times even I missed the silence of the trees. No question, we were the only gyppos in the world cutting timber to *Aida*. The men joked freely about Tivari's music, and I once heard him called the Volga Boatman, though not to his face.

"You think trees don't have souls? What are you, some dumb stumps?" he shouted, until the word "stumps" echoed in the clear island air. He contended that the forest was in the presence of its tragedy and its beauty when he played this music. "If I had to fall," he announced, "let me hear *Twilight of the Gods* while I'm crashing down." Tivari also applied music as a preventative against drowning and would sing along to the best of his ability as we motored across the bay between our float camp and work site.

By the time I hit Alaska, I had a healthy respect for what it took to keep any logger's fears in harness. We were at the prime of our lives, our pleasures on hold back in the towns we'd left. Tivari's music came to represent more than what we were missing. It stood for gentility and ease we'd probably never get. I found myself enjoying the rigorous emotional keening of those operatic voices—and I'm sure there were one or two others who more than submitted to its mournful intoxication. I even took to carrying a spare set of batteries in case Tivari's should run down, as they often did. Tivari cutting a tree in silence—now that was an experience to be avoided, the way others avoided Saturday night whores.

Tivari did not avoid the ladies. It was as if, having escaped a week of water crossings, he had an impulse to reward himself, to drown in the calculated attentions of women. He paid over his earnings and this brought all he could drink, plus a sodden sort of company into Sunday.

When all was said, Tivari transcended his breakout time. I'd seen him so wasted he couldn't get his chain around his saw blade, but by the next workday he was still the best bushler and blowdown bucker there was. He knew that a blowdown can look dead, but have vicious turns of life left in it that could whip around and run a man through with his own saw. He also knew the cardinal rule of such cutting—when to quit.

Tivari, in short, was, by nature and necessity, an artist of the moment. To work, eat, and move daily in his company was to feel that any instant might break open to hilarity or sorrow or some joyful clamor that lifted, for an instant, the weight of the day, and could be traded out as story during the relentless daylight evenings of Alaskan summers.

"Tivari," someone would say, "tell us about the time you wrestled the bear." And it was true, or should have been if it wasn't, that Tivari had once wrestled a bear in a logging camp near Homer. He took his shirt off on occasion to display a scar that ran diagonally across his back to his right hip. The bear, he said, had been raised in captivity by a young boy, then sold for spectacle.

The match he'd fought was not the first for the bear. Word reached camp that it had badly mauled the last man it had encountered, so expectations were tilted heavily in the bear's favor. Tivari realized from the start that the animal intended to do damage. It entered the makeshift ring with its head low, its ears back. A raking moan unwound from it. This woeful sound was punctuated with chuffing noises. Tivari's mates were there to cheer him on, though several, he later learned, had placed money on the bear.

"I held his jaws like this," he said, grabbing the head of the logger sitting next to him and forcing his mouth wide, "and I gave that bear mouth-to-mouth resuscitation." He did not demonstrate this. "I might as well have poured gasoline down that bear and dropped in a lit match," Tivari said, playing to his audience. He claimed that prior to the fight he'd eaten a powerful amount of garlic, and that while breathing the bear into submission, it had raked its claw down his back.

On one occasion I saw a logger who kept hounds attempt to get Tivari to discuss bear hunting. It ended with the logger slapping down a hunting magazine and telling Tivari to "read up" if he wanted to pretend he knew anything about bears. Then the man pulled the ultimate dismissive and called him "a goddamned environmentalist." But Tivari was beyond the assumed slur of "environmental." He had set his own course for understanding and valuing bears. He held no false pieties about the animal he clearly loved and, before anything, he was a storyteller.

Each time Tivari removed his shirt, the scar ran before us like an angry river in which he'd narrowly missed drowning. We were believers then, carried beyond faith, into the place where story outleaps what happened and still, in some cow-over-the-moon fashion, stays true. A creature or someone had raked a knife, a scythe, or a claw deeply down Tivari's back, and it became the hieroglyphic of his survivals.

In 1972, when he was thirty, Tivari had, against his mother's pleas, gone back to Romania in search of his father. His father had become a political prisoner in 1969, under Ceauşescu's regime, and had not been heard from since. Not surprisingly Tivari managed, in short order, to get himself thrown into prison. We'd heard his descriptions of cold beyond cold, how the men would lend each other warmth in the clammy, rat-infested recesses of the Bucharest prison. But whatever Tivari had experienced made him fog over with silence when anyone came too near the site of those experiences.

"No, friend, don't ask," he'd say. "I lost some brothers there, and that's not the worst."

Whatever the worst was, we would only catch glimpses in his desperate drinking bouts. I assumed it had something to do with whatever he'd discovered about the fate of his father. But someone started a rumor that Tivari had been castrated in prison and that this was why he was forever begging the whores to "take pity" on him—an unfortunate phrase he would utter during pangs of drunken abandonment on the floating tug *The Gallant Lady,* where few of the ladies were exactly gallant, though, by report, they had other favorable attributes.

"Take pity!" Tivari would implore from inside the cramped below-decks compartments of the tug. His voice drifted to those of us at float-camp who had girlfriends or wives to whom we were safely sworn. The word "pity" never had such resonance as when I heard it, from my bunk, in Tivari's unmistakable voice, torn across the short Alaska night, like the plea of a man with his head on a chopping block. I did have occasion, in the casual life of men thrown together in close quarters, to be able to report at large that Tivari had his equipment intact. Still, I suspected something completely unmanned him when it came to women.

Nonetheless, the more fickle the woman, the more ardently Tivari would pursue. We all felt he'd topped his mark when he fastened on a woman we called the Blond Bomber. Her true name was Rena and she was married to our hook-tender, Al Worthington. Al had situated Rena on shore in a cabin an hour from camp. We were under pressure to get the timber down, and had light enough to cut until 3 AM, if we wanted to use it. Because the pace was just short of killing, Al visited Rena at weekly intervals and spent most nights at float-camp.

The Bomber, on occasion, and much to Al's dismay, made appearances at camp. She was a showy woman with Marilyn Monroe–style bleached-blond hair. Her breasts were a prominent feature and she dressed to their advantage, her waist cinched so tightly that her voice seemed to come from her nostrils. On one of her sudden visits to camp, Rena caught Tivari's eye. Not long after, I noticed he would be away nights when Al stayed at camp.

Rena had a passion for clothes that bordered on mania. She kept Al working seven days a week to buy her the latest styles, which she ordered from catalogues and had delivered by float-plane to the cove near her cabin.

Once Tivari made up his mind to have Rena, his campaign was swift and determined. He took her to Anchorage, behind Al's back, and fitted her out like a runway model. Then he paraded her through the bars, snatching the envy of men and the jaundiced scrutiny of the barflies. It was a heady concoction that fueled them into their elopement out of Alaska.

When I next heard of Tivari, he'd moved Rena to Aberdeen, where once again he found himself living at the edge of water. I had recently come down from Alaska when he phoned to ask me to partner up with him. It would save time and money, he said, if I stayed with him and Rena.

In Aberdeen I had a close look at how Tivari was managing life. I was glad Rena hadn't shut down his love of opera. The tide lapped not a hundred yards from the door and he kept the windows open so the music swirled out to fishing and pleasure boats offshore. A revival CD, *Caruso in Song,* was on before we left in the morning, accompanied us to work, and played into the night when we returned. It amounted to total immersion. His favorite cut, "Guardanno 'a Luna," lapped away consciousness that it was even playing.

My friend so indulged Rena in her quest for the flashiest, most outrageous clothes that there didn't seem to be money left for much else. They had one comfortable piece of living room furniture, an antique maroon velvet couch, of which Tivari was inordinately proud.

"Think of it," he would say, when he'd entered his nightly ritual of cauterizing the day with drink. "I've taken thousands of dollars' worth of clothes off that wicked woman right where you're sitting."

Rena would be propped in bed with one of her fashion catalogues. But Tivari seemed in no hurry to go to bed these nights. He wanted to regale me with stories of bears. How Indian hunters had used every part of the bear when they'd killed it—eaten the meat, made the teeth and claws into charms, given the paws to their medicine men, turned its skin into blankets and clothing, melted down the fat for cooking oil, even twisted its intestines into bowstrings.

"No one will ever use us so well, my friend," Tivari said, licking his beard from his white teeth and bowing his head toward his jelly glass with its potent triple shot of *ţuica*—a rheumy-looking plum brandy he'd learned to make in Romania. Tivari's philosophy was simply that one of the worst things that could happen to a creature, man or beast, was not to be used up, to be in some sense wasted.

Tivari continued to lean over the knees of his perfectly patched overalls, telling me how the Pueblos had, according to accounts, believed their medicine men could actually change themselves into bears.

He'd discovered the library and read deeply on the subject. He'd become curious about a passage in one of the books that described how the Michigan tribes, the Cree and the Ojibwas, were said to have turned against black bears and killed them for government bounties after smallpox had devastated their tribes. "The Bear Wars," Tivari called them. "Some say the Indians believed those bears were in a conspiracy against them. That the bears could have healed them, but refused, and let them die of smallpox. Remember, these are white historians. Nobody, except maybe the ghosts of those Indians, really knows why they started to kill bears for bounty."

I learned much later that Tivari's mother's maiden name was Ursu, which means "bear," and may have partly accounted for his fascination and respect for the animal. He could snap out figures about the early decimation of bears in America like sparks from a campfire: West Virginia hunters who took eight thousand black bears for skins early in the 1800s; trappers in the Dakotas who racked up 746 skins in five years through 1805.

"Sportsmen will tell you today this country is overrun with bears, and in some places maybe it's true, so they're never entirely wrong. But somebody sure took care of those black bears in the Dakotas. No bear problem there now," Tivari said and fell silent. We could hear the waves rushing against the logs below the house. They tossed and hissed, then sighed into the huge dark that was the Pacific. Finally Tivari began to tell about the execution of eight bears in Yosemite National Park in 1979—"problem bears" who'd had a history of bad interactions with humans and paid the ultimate price.

"They kept files on them, and when they had enough evidence, they shot those bears," Tivari said, as if the bears were the brothers he'd lost in the prisons of Bucharest. At some point I asked him how the Indians had been able to kill bears at all, if, as he said, they'd considered them healers.

"Those bears, even when they were dead, just somehow went back to live in the forests. You couldn't really kill them. That's what the Indians believed. I'm not going to die either," he said with a grin. "I'm just going back to the forest." Then he roused himself and found a pillow for me so I could make my bed on the velvet couch. I watched him careen toward the bedroom, where I imagined Rena lay asleep, wrapped in the sexiest negligee money could buy.

That night I fell into dreams of bears. I was hopelessly attempting to frighten off one with a water pistol. I pulled the trigger to no avail, then managed to shoot a pitiful stream of water toward its toothy snout as it advanced, upright like a man. The steady sound of collapsing and retreating waves against logs on the beach came through the open window to mix with menace in the dream, and I was glad for daylight and the smell of coffee.

"That's good, to dream of bears," Tivari said, the next morning as we filled our coffee bottles. "It means they've noticed you. They're looking out for you. But I'd drop the water pistol if I were you."

Someone besides bears had noticed me. Rena's sleepy morning glances seemed to have fastened inordinately on my needs. She rustled between us in a red silk kimono embroidered with dragons, marshaling us in the dawn light before the "crummy" would take us to work. I had a sinking feeling that Tivari might soon have his hands full. The prospect was cheerless as sunrise over a clear-cut. Even though I'd done nothing to invite Rena's attentions, and even though they'd passed seemingly without my friend's noticing, they left me with a guilty residue, her assumptions about the fragile nature of friendship having caused me to call myself into question. It was luck and providence that our work suddenly ran out and I moved to another part of the state.

An interval of months passed with no logging to be found. Then I took work as a "casualty," longshoring. It was good pay with overtime. The next thing I knew I was traveling to unload a ship in Aberdeen. I was glad to have an excuse to visit Tivari. I'd gotten married by this time and rented a small house in Port Orchard. My wife worked as a nurse in a retirement home. She wore a uniform and was as far from the Blond Bomber as they come. Word along the gossip line was that Tivari and Rena were openly at odds. She'd taken a job as a cocktail waitress at a local resort and had subsequently overstimulated the imaginations of some of her customers.

"There are bears who get to be panhandlers," Tivari said to me on my first night back, with Rena out of earshot. "People feed them—panhandlers are mostly females—and it's like signing their death warrants." We were talking about bears and we weren't. Tivari had bought a freezerful of beef, which sat on the back porch, and all week we ate steaks and prime rib, cooked to a bloodless turn by Rena.

When I arrived back at Tivari's after a three-day weekend with my wife, havoc had struck. A window had been shattered on the back porch. I looked in at the freezer, and saw the kitchen door standing open onto the porch. I walked around and glanced through the front window. The space once occupied by the velvet couch was bare.

It was scorching, hitting the mid-nineties. My mind fastened on locating a dark bar and a cold beer. As I drew up in front of the Red Ranch Tavern, I spotted Tivari's pickup. White packages of partly frozen beef were heaped on the velvet couch in the truck bed. Blood was soaking into the couch in the noonday heat.

Inside the tavern I found Tivari. He recognized me through the beery dark as I approached, raised his right hand, extended his index finger, and drew it swiftly across his throat in a cutting motion. He made a gurgling noise like the sound of waves withdrawing over small stones, then turned back to his drink. I took the stool beside him. The music was country western and I knew he must be punishing himself. Or maybe the stock dilemmas of opera and country music had run together for him of late. My life, by comparison, seemed far from the turnstile future he was meeting with Rena.

"A guy actually came up to me today and asked did I know where he could get himself a bear's gallbladder," Tivari said in disgust, offering me a door into his general despair. It seems the Chinese had been paying big money for bear gallbladders. They believed them to be aphrodisiacs. Tivari allowed that any number of bears all over the country had been killed recently for their gallbladders alone.

"Bastard," Tivari said. "Sonofabitch," he added for good measure. "And no part of *him* worth killing for."

I rested my arm across my friend's back. I knew that just under my forearm ran the long angry scar that Tivari claimed a bear had given him. Whether or not it had actually been a bear, he'd earned its connection by now, through respect and his earnest attempt to discover something of their nature and history. Male black bears, he'd been quick to tell me, lived and died mostly alone.

But today he had another story in mind. Soon the Black Sea stretched before us in the early dawn. The lifeguards had not yet come on duty. His Romanian mother was still a young woman, collecting seashells on the last day of her summer holiday. Since my own mother had died when I was a baby, I had no such stories or memories of her. Consequently, Tivari's recounting of this incident concerning his mother held a fascination for me.

"Suddenly a man's voice crying for help causes my mother to look up," Tivari said. "She sees a man on shore leap into the waves and swim to a man who is surely drowning. She watches the swimmer catch the man by his hair and begin to pull him toward land. She was taking this in with her eyes, but also her soul, she told me. Somehow, after a long time in the water, the swimmer lost his grip on the man. When he reached shore, he stepped out of the water alone.

"A woman ran up to my mother," Tivari said. "She asked, 'Did he drown? Did a man drown?' 'Yes,' my mother told her, 'I'm sorry, he's lost. He couldn't be saved.' Then the woman said, 'That was *my* man,' and began to wail. She rushed toward the sea and into the waves. She stood up to her knees in the water and cried, 'Give him back! Have mercy! Give him back!' But the sea just kept being the sea.

"My mother cast her eyes back and forth," Tivari said, "but she saw only waves, rising and falling. Then a young girl came toward the woman in the waves. She was weeping and she held out a man's shirt. That must be the drowned man's daughter, my mother thought. She watched the woman and daughter holding each other with the shirt between them. Then my mother took the shells she'd gathered, drew her arm back, and flung them hard into the sea.

"After that," Tivari said, "my mother was angry about bodies of water. When I was little she wouldn't let me swim with my friends. She'd tell me this story and warn me, until the only safe water for me was in a tap or on a postcard."

Unlike Tivari, I'd had no such warnings. No mother's fears to temper what I dared to do. My father had raised me to feel able for anything. "He can swim like a seal," my father had bragged. Tivari could not swim, but he admired those who could, as if they were specially gifted, like the opera singers he loved.

He told me once about three troublesome Newfoundland bears whose swimming had brought them notoriety. They'd been removed from the mainland by park officials to an island in Bonavista Bay. But the next day the bears swam off the island through stormy waters, then they walked eleven miles back to their home territory. Tivari believed so much was coded into us, we'd probably never know why we did what we did.

"Mother Nature leaves a survival map in each of us," he said. "We just have to know how to read it. My mother read it, and it said: 'Keep your kid terrified of water.' But, my friend, you can drown anywhere."

Suddenly I remembered the blood-sodden couch and decided to try to move my friend.

"Tivari," I said. "I know a butcher with a big heart and an enormous freezer." He followed me unsteadily into the searing daylight. I opened the passenger side of the pickup and he obediently handed me the keys, then climbed in.

We drove to my friend's shop and stacked the beef in the corner of his walk-in freezer. Tivari took delight in the cold as we moved back and forth, dodging the hanging sides of beef and pork.

"Shut the door and take me out in the spring," he joked with typical bravado. Then he stepped from the freezer, grabbed the palm of my hand, and pressed it to his chest. "Imagine, if I was a bear in hibernation, this heart would be down to eight beats a minute. We're nothing but halfway primitive meat compared to bears," he said and let my hand drop from his icy grasp.

Later that night I drove Tivari to another of my friends' to sober up and to sleep. This friend was a retired high school coach who'd recently gone through a divorce. We slept on mattresses on the floor of his workout room, among weights and fitness machines. The next morning we each showered and sampled my friend's wide spectrum of toiletries, then, smelling like pimps, drove to Tivari's house. As we parked at the back, I was somehow not surprised to see the sheriff coming off the porch to meet us. He had the clouded look of a man who's learned to expect the worst and is not often disappointed.

"Your wife says you stole her clothes. That right, Tivari?" the sheriff asked, retreating a few steps when he caught wind of us. Tivari didn't answer. "Your wife's down signing a restraining order on you," the sheriff said, and folded his arms in a gesture of contained official pleasure. "You want to tell me about the clothes?"

The sheriff and I followed my friend onto the porch. Tivari lifted the lid of the twenty-one-foot chest freezer and stepped back. Inside, frozen in a solid four-foot-deep block of ice, were the fur coats, sequined gowns, and sheer negligees of Rena's long career. We stared at the frozen garments, as if the Black Sea of his mother's story had suddenly risen up and deposited the congealed debris of a life. Tivari quietly bent over and pulled the electric plug.

We left the sheriff to inventory the damage and walked back toward the truck. Dried maps of blood splotched the cushions and arms of Tivari's velvet couch on the pickup bed. It looked like the site of a massacre. But I knew that Tivari, as he took note of it, was probably recalling his misbegotten hopes with Rena, their late-night erotic rituals— reduced to this sad, unseemly display.

Tivari climbed behind the wheel and we drove to my truck at the tavern. I could stay with Tivari, but couldn't attempt to keep up with his drinking. I knew he was about to head over the top and out to sea. Soon images of his mother in a summer dress would surface like a strange obliterating sun.

These glimpses of her belonged so much to me by now, they were nearly my own. I thought she had somehow made sure, across time and death, that I was there, next to her son. Her defiant gesture, as she'd thrown the shells back into the sea, seemed the long arc of her connection to me—a man drawn taut as a bowstring by things he did not understand and could not control. I was sure Tivari had no notion why he'd been held in lockstep with a woman like Rena, whose surface was glassy as a waveless sea. Likewise, I couldn't figure why I wasn't in my car driving hell-bent-for-leather for Port Orchard and my wife.

The jukebox had begun to play something so melancholy and awash with heartbreak that Tivari's voice from our Alaskan days rang out again across water and darkness—"Take pity!" And I did. I clung to his slumping form in the downward spiral of that music, swimming against fate and memory, with Tivari's thin hair wrapped around my fingers.

Creatures

Elna had once said that beautifying was nothing more than grabbing Mother Nature by the throat and showing her who was boss. When Shelly arrived for her appointment, her friend was vigorously at work on an alabaster-complexioned teenager. Testimonies of terse, coiled ringlets spiraled past the girl's ears and down the back of her neck.

"Hey there!" Elna called as Shelly settled into a chair across from what they laughingly called the hot seat.

"Where's your cat population?" Shelly asked. She unbuttoned her coat and slipped it onto the back of the chair. Elna's cats were a quick barometer for the household's travail now that Elna's marriage was in trouble. Shelly always felt strangely cheered by the prospect of Elna's troubles—maybe because they were harder to solve than her own.

When Elna and Eugene had tried to split up the previous year, the clients had commiserated with Elna, said she was "doing the right thing," that Eugene was "only along for the ride," et cetera. But in the end, Elna had let him stay and her clients now kept their opinions to themselves.

This time around, Eugene was calling the shots. The day after New Year's he'd announced he was moving out, but not until spring, when an apartment he wanted would come available. Elna had complained so bitterly about the marriage that her friends were astonished she'd agreed to this. But theory had it Eugene might settle more congenially if she did things his way. Shelly knew it was harder for Elna to let the marriage go, now that Eugene was the one heading for the door. Still, things had been building up.

In the months prior to their current situation Eugene had been giving all the signs of a man having an affair—late nights, strange excuses. Once he'd even called Elna to say the gold cap on his front tooth
had fallen into a load of gravel. It would be awhile. Another time he'd
phoned from a training session in a nearby town. He'd been learning
to install a new kind of insulation. The afternoon meeting was supposed to allow him to come home that night, but he'd called Elna with
a change of plans. His hemorrhoids were bothering him. They were so
bad, he said he couldn't make the two-hour drive home. He'd have
to spend the night there alone, in pain. He was sorry. He was having to
stand up while making this very call, he said, an odd catch in his voice.
Elna's friends said it didn't sound like your regular excuse. He'd also
started bringing home single rosebuds wrapped in cellophane from the
supermarket. Out of the blue, he'd call Elna from a pay phone to say,
"Hi, honey, just wanted you to know I love you."

It had been hard for Elna to believe Eugene had somebody on the
side—even harder to admit, once she believed it. Shelly had been all
too willing to confirm the diagnosis. She'd had her own experiences
with cheating men. She'd been glad to share with Elna an article in
a women's magazine that told all the signs. "Constant irritability and
fault-finding"—those were two they'd agreed especially fit Eugene.

As she settled herself in her chair, Shelly continued to scan the shop
for the cats. When she didn't see them, she called to them by name.
Elna, who'd been methodically swiveling the curling rod to the teenager's head, withdrew it and stepped over to Shelly. She bent and, in
a confidential tone, said, "Honey—Lucky and Lightning are no longer
with us. They've gone where all good, but sadly flawed creatures go."
Then she retreated to her client, having seemingly dispensed with a
very unpleasant matter.

Clearly things had taken a desperate turn. Shelly consoled herself,
noticing that the remaining young black cat, Veronica, was basking in
the last rays of afternoon sunlight. She nudged the cat with the toe of

her shoe, and its eyes blinked open and shut several times, as if completing some coded message from a dream-filled interior.

"I wish I could have gone with them, straight to kitty heaven," Elna was saying. "Do not pass Safeway or Twelve-Star Video. One minute the needle, then poof! Heaven."

The idea of Heaven had always eluded Shelly, and, linked to "kitty," the word only revived images of the two missing cats, stranded in some lonely outpost of the mind. They had been fixtures the ten years she'd been coming to the shop, always curled in one chair or another. Each time a client uprooted them they would tolerantly resituate themselves.

Lightning, a huge white cat with a streak of black down one side, was forever inviting himself into a client's lap and having to be scolded down. The other, Lucky, a tea-colored part Siamese, was like the sleep of the world. She had once crawled into the clothes dryer for a nap and managed to endure several minutes on Knits/Gentle/Low with a load of bikini panties. "If she'd been on Cottons she'd be looking *up* to mice," Elna had quipped. She'd been affectionate about even the failures of her cats. It was hard to believe she'd had them put to sleep.

Recently Shelly had heard on a talk show that willful deaths or injuries to innocent pets often signaled a worsening of relationships between their owners. Elna leaned against the mirror that ran the length of the room and appraised the rather glum-looking teenager undergoing transformation. She used a comb to tease a fringe of bangs onto the girl's forehead as she continued. "Lucky, with her own little motorized tongue, licked down an entire cube of butter, then did her job in my yarn basket. *One* of the clinchers," Elna said. "They just got too old." Shelly didn't contradict her friend, though she suspected age had nothing to do with it.

"Veronica, you lucky devil," Shelly said conspiratorially to the remaining cat, "to be young and in control of your functions—housetrained like the rest of us."

Shelly had been feeling the closest thing to joy in a long time when she'd entered the shop. She hadn't been prepared to hear about the disposal of Elna's cats, and was dismayed at how suddenly any relief in life could be so quickly burdened again with sadness. Her eighty-year-old mother had completed a diagnostic test that afternoon, which had taken longer than expected. During the test, Shelly had sat with a magazine on her lap, imagining the long thin probe being worked into her mother's stomach and upper intestines while the doctor's eye searched for the reason she had been bleeding. Shelly had mentally entered that darkness as a small wink of light, grazing and scraping the deep interior. The trouble with the imagination, she thought, was that the mind could go anywhere, so you could never tell from one moment to the next where you might end up.

The doctor had prepared Shelly and her mother to deal with stomach cancer or ulcers, but miraculously nothing had been found. She had come to her hair appointment prepared to celebrate her mother's good fortune. But the deaths of the cats had changed that.

"Oh, honey, we were just bawling our eyes out after I took them to the vet's. My clients sat in their chairs and cried, and I blubbered right along with them," Elna said, bending to the teenager. "Cousin Flo came over on her lunch break to say good-bye to them. Then I closed those poor babies into the same cardboard carrier and drove them to the clinic."

To be shut into a small dark space against your will was one of the most frightening things Shelly could imagine. Her mind veered out of the box with its doomed cats and back toward her friend. Shelly could see Elna didn't know at all how to represent what she'd done. She was alternately hot and cold over it—pitying the cats while trying to justify her part in their fate.

The bells on the shop door jangled and Gretchen, Elna's daughter, entered with her two children. Her face looked puffy to Shelly, like a person who'd been either hit in the face or crying, or both. "I need some of your magic hair spray, Mom," Gretchen announced. She picked peppermint candies for her children from the fishbowl Elna converted to a candy dish after the fish were found floating belly-up one morning. "Hey, it's like a funeral in here."

"If you only knew, dear," Elna said.

"She *offed* Lucky and Lightning," said the teenager, like the surviving member of a Greek chorus.

Gretchen made a sound deep in her throat—an eruption that sprang from the unpredictableness of human utterance itself.

"I can't believe you did that, Mom," Gretchen said, holding her children by their jacket collars to keep them from taking another step toward their grandmother.

"I suppose I could have just let them scramble for it outside," Elna said, ignoring her. "But I would have been worrying all the time. Besides, it's cold out there, and if something chased them—"

"My cat sleeps with me," said the teenager, a beacon of ruthless insinuation.

"Lightning slept with me, too," Elna said quietly, making clear that intimacy could not have staved off the inevitable. "The last straw was him spraying down the floor vent. We breathed cat piss for a week. I dumped cologne, Purex, baby powder, a bottle of cedar scent down it—even got back into my hippie days and burned incense."

With the cats gone, the shop felt larger, less cozy. Shelly noticed Veronica had moved to the back of a chair at the window, one paw V-ing the venetian blind where she gazed into the yard. "She's looking for them," Elna said. "She can't imagine what's keeping them, thank God. Lucky and Lightning," she mused, "forever expected in Veronica's cat mind."

"We didn't even have a funeral," Gretchen said plaintively.

"Flo and I thought about burying them in the backyard with two little stone markers from one of those catalogues, but I chickened out," Elna said. "No—they just went into the incinerator. 'Cremate them,' I told the vet, 'and do whatever you do—I mean, when no one takes whatever's left.'"

At the mention of the backyard, Gretchen's children wriggled from her and eased out the shop entrance. Shelly wished, for a moment, she could go with them. She knew Elna made light of things when she felt them most, that she would be cryptic with bursts of admission until she had eroded some kind of invisible barrier between her actions and her feelings.

"Honestly," Elna said, "Lucky would sashay in from the great outdoors, stand right up against the door she'd just walked through, lift her leg, and spray, right in front of me!"

"I didn't know female cats lifted their legs," Shelly said.

"This one did. Lifted it just like a tom, smart as you please, and shot her tank, then pranced off like she'd accomplished something."

"Little did she know," Gretchen said.

"You bet," Elna said, with muscle in her voice. "The Kevorkian of cats had called her number." It was five o'clock. Elna walked over and closed the venetian blinds. "Open them, shut them. Who cares?" Elna said. She returned to the girl in the swivel chair and rotated her toward the mirror. With the blinds closed, the eyes of the shop seemed closed, and Shelly felt the particular intimacy of women alone in a room, talking, trading confidences, speaking their minds.

"Kimberly's wearing forest green to the prom," Elna said, her voice rubbing the consonants in "forest green." The ebony of trees at dusk entered Shelly's mind—a pungent, under-boughs' darkness that overpowered the smell of hair spray mingled with cat urine. She imagined night falling in the forests on the mountains behind the town, creatures alive there, able to survive nights and days in snow and rain, searching for food, for shelter.

A strong draft ran through the shop as Gretchen's children burst into the room again. "Stay inside, please, children, or stay out," Elna said. Shelly realized eerily that Elna was using the same tone with the children she'd used with the missing cats. The children had just dropped to their knees in the middle of the floor with the black cat when the shop door opened suddenly and Eugene entered. He veered around the children and, without a glance, shot past everyone into the kitchen.

"Brace yourself," Elna said with a knowing look.

"Mom, okay if I make a long-distance call?" Gretchen asked, seizing the moment. "It's about a job. They shut off my phone." Shelly saw Elna go into her stoic helpful-against-the-odds mode.

"Use the kitchen phone," Elna said, "but make it snappy."

Shelly could feel how stretched beyond limits Elna was because of Gretchen, yet she knew Elna would likely do a lifetime of setting aside her own boundaries for her daughter. Shelly hated her friend's helplessness, but she also took pity and even admired her, because at least helplessness meant you were out there in the deep water, risking things. Her friend lived somehow beyond the prudent, fix-it mentality of others she knew. For Elna things were patently wrong, and they were going farther in that direction, no matter what Shelly or anyone wished for her. She tried to imagine a life where Elna wouldn't be burdened and ensnared, but no matter what she considered, no likely solution occurred.

Soon Gretchen's laughter drifted through the open door to the kitchen. She was always "looking for a job" or "about to get a job." In this, it struck Shelly, she wasn't so different from Eugene. After a few minutes the register of her voice changed. Now she was talking to Eugene. Her tone was placating, the way someone used to calamity tries to soothe away consequences.

"All that room out there!" Eugene blurted. "All that ocean and forest, and she has to ram a goddamn California lawyer with two kids in a goddamn camper." On the way into the house, Eugene had spotted a dent Gretchen had left in his pickup. Elna stopped what she was doing to listen.

"Why not ram the ocean? Something with a little give-and-take," Eugene cried at the top of his voice. "Aim for an oil tanker, be ambitious—a raft of logs, a fishing trawler. Give chaos a chance!" he ranted.

"Eugene's off his spool again," Elna said, a high ripple in her voice meant to counter his tirade by seeming to indicate the malfunction of an ordinary household appliance. Eugene had always claimed that

Gretchen's problems, her sudden incursions on his and Elna's lives, her bad choices in men, two children by an absent father—these ongoing pressures had made it impossible for him and Elna. To a certain extent, Shelly thought he was right. Whatever faults Eugene had, no one could dispute that he'd been a veritable blue-ribbon champion at living with things in a mess. He reentered the beauty shop now, drawn backward by some invisible force centered in Elna.

"You never asked *me*," he said to the company at large, his back to Elna. "The queen of demolition derbies, and you loan her my truck like loaning a can opener."

"My God, Gene, it's only a dent," Elna said, hardly grazing his attention.

"I can't get over it," he said. "Snuff the cats. Ram the truck. I'm lucky to have a door to walk through." He hitched his jeans and ducked to look at himself in the mirror. His black hair roiled in a glistening wave he pushed back from his forehead.

Shelly noticed Eugene had dark circles under his eyes and he'd lost weight. So had Elna, for that matter. She'd always been wasp waisted, but now her skin seemed oddly transparent, as if everything inside, the entire circuitry of her body, were visible to whoever came within her parameters. Eugene disappeared into the kitchen.

Elna spun the prom girl toward her and gave her a hand mirror so she could see the back of her head. "Mister Righteous," Elna said. "'Honey, honey,' he'd say—'there's a mess in here. You might want to check it out.' Well, I checked it out all right!"

The prom girl stared into the mirror, adrift on the small bright raft of her face in a shark-infested sea. She bobbed her head, and the drooling curls danced briefly.

Meanwhile Gretchen's children had forced the surviving cat under the nail-polishing table. Shelly had the all-encompassing sensation that places of refuge were thinning out across the face of the planet. Soon enough, if a human impulse fixed its mark on a creature, it would be found and destroyed. There could be delay, but no lasting retreat. Maybe it had always been this way and she was just now realizing it.

"You're going to look amazing in that forest green," Elna chimed to the teenager. "If that boy was shy before, he's going to be speechless now." The girl frowned and pulled at the neck of her T-shirt. It was clear the shirt wouldn't lift easily over her hairdo.

"Is that expendable?" Elna asked.

"I guess so," the girl said vaguely.

"Darlin, you'd be surprised what's expendable by the time you get my age." Elna reached into a drawer and took out a pair of scissors.

"I still don't see how you did what you did, Mom," Gretchen said, reentering from the kitchen. She was speaking to her mother in the mirror. "Just because you and Gene aren't making it. We had those cats fifteen years," she said. "You're mean. Just plain mean!" Shelly could tell her friend was carefully not letting herself be provoked.

Elna took the scissors and began a vertical cut from the girl's neckline between the hints of her breasts. The scissors snipped viciously in the silence. When she finished, she dropped them into the drawer, then slid it shut with a decisive thud.

From the kitchen a loud cascading of pans sounded. Eugene swore and Shelly looked up to see him pace past the doorway. He returned to stare briefly at the women in the shop, then broke away into the kitchen again, having evidently collected fresh energy from just glancing at them.

Child voices murmured from under the table. Shelly felt an undercurrent in the room, as when messages and secrets are being exchanged. She remembered what it was to be a child, crawling into the musky darkness under beds and tables, able to hear everything that went on; being there, yet not there. Once a pan of grease on the stove had caught fire while she'd been exploring the space under her parents' bed. Her mother had run through the rooms carrying the flaming pan, yelling "Fire!" and calling for her in a tone of ultimate panic, which changed to fury when she eventually discovered her under the bed. To this day, Shelly instinctively connected certain states of anxiety and threat with fire.

"Things are going to change around here," Elna said. "I see to everything else, and I'm seeing to that. There you go, dear," she said to Kimberly. Elna helped her lift the T-shirt over her head through the rough slit. The girl sat uneasily a moment in her bra until Gretchen reached into the little side room where her mother mixed hair colors and handed her a flannel shirt.

"Kimberly's going to dress in my bedroom," Elna said. "I told her I'd do her hair for free just to see her in her dress." Kimberly slipped on the shirt and moved toward the kitchen on her way to the bedroom.

A mournful howl came from the cat, then giggling from the children. Their legs spidered from under the frilly table. "Jo-Jo, come out!" Gretchen called to her son. When he didn't appear she pulled him forth like a wheelbarrow by his legs.

"After what she did, I'm scared to leave my kids with her," Gretchen said. She took up a comb from the counter and raked it across her son's scalp. Gretchen's daughter approached Elna's work area clutching the glaring cat by its middle.

Shelly was used to the charade of Gretchen and her mother fighting over the children. She'd been in the shop once when Elna had called the Children's Protective Services, threatening to take them away. But since Gretchen left her children with Elna most of the time anyway, the threat was empty.

"When I was pregnant with her," Elna once told Shelly, "if I'd known the trouble I was in for, I'd have climbed onto the roof and dashed myself to the pavement like a watermelon."

Kimberly slowly eased into the doorway from the kitchen. Everyone had turned to look. Eugene was visible over one bare shoulder in the fluorescent light. Gretchen pulled at one of the small gold rings in her nose and, with her eyes on the girl, sat down under a dryer that was cocked open near Shelly.

The girl rustled forward, leaving a cool tracing of air in her wake.

The taffeta sheen of the dress dimpled with dark whispering pools as she glided toward them, her arms lightly at her sides. Like a calm fir tree in their clearing, she stood a moment, then began again to turn, slowly, like someone in the vortex of a dream.

Suddenly the black cat let out a long, involuntary moan. It struggled free of the child's grasp and leaped precariously onto the swivel chair. Before they realized what was happening, the cat was midair in a short unwieldy arc toward the girl's bare shoulders. Its claws sank into the pure fleshy center of the room. The girl gave a raw cry of pain. If an eagle had dropped onto her shoulder to lift her from earth, she might have given such a cry. Poised, electric, the cat stared violently at them from its human perch.

Elna rushed forward with her face turned away, like a woman about to handle fire. She caught the cat by its fur and flung it from the girl's shoulders against the mirror. For a moment the animal appeared to be leaping out of itself, multiplied, quenched and resurrected at once as it rippled along the counter, then became airborne again, clearing the fishbowl before it dropped to the floor and streaked past their ankles. The girl began to shudder, then to sob, holding on to herself.

Shelly moved to catch Elna firmly by the shoulders. "There," Shelly said as she held her. "There." She took Elna's helpless blows against her back until they subsided. The cat had made its escape through the kitchen. Shelly imagined it tunneling into the farthest recesses of the house.

When Elna broke free and turned to the others, it was clear she'd crossed some boundary from which she looked back at them like one who holds a territory beyond challenge. Everyone in the room balanced unsteadily on the rim of the moment. A switch had somehow been thrown in all their heads at once. Night had fallen suddenly in their clearing. Each of them gazed warily out of the darkness at the others with the lime green eyes of the young black cat, a creature forced to its limits and past.

There was unearthly calm and stillness in the space they now inhabited. They seemed suspended in the close chemical smell of the room,

but elsewhere in the house they heard things falling, shattering—the rac-
ing, desperate plunge of an animal seeking its full measure of darkness.

Shelly stared at her friend and realized she didn't know what Elna
might do next—that everything, and everyone, had somehow been reduced to their simplest, most destructible element. She was aware that
her childhood dread of fire was unreasonably alive in her. Whatever
was flammable in the room rose to make itself known—the nylon
flounce along the mirror, cans of hair spray, raw clumps of hair at the
base of the swivel chair, cellophane glinting from a wastebasket, hair
again, the very hair on her head. The hair on all their heads. A woman
with a pan of fire seemed to be running through her mind, fanning
oxygen into flames, igniting whatever she passed. Shelly knew she and
the others had arrived at some precarious boundary—where, despite
their strongest instincts, they seemed to have agreed that no one would
run from this room.

A Box of Rocks

Arlen gazed out the bedroom window facing onto the pasture and saw Elida as she passed in silhouette over the ridge. He went to the bed, sat down and pulled on his socks, then slipped into his trousers and shirt. He returned to the window in time to see his wife reemerge, as if she had climbed out of the earth itself. The only acknowledgment she'd made toward the cold was a light jacket and head scarf.

In the half light he could see she was carrying something, but he couldn't make out what. Her shoulders were drawn forward, and she looked old to him, though she wasn't yet thirty.

Arlen had been in love with Elida since she was fifteen, had chosen her over her sister Dory, whom he had fancied briefly. There had been something too sudden and elusive about Dory. "A girl made for tragedy," his mother had warned, and after that he could not look at Dory without feeling that her life did not belong to her.

Only once before had Arlen seen his wife locked obsessively to an action, and that had been two years after their marriage. They'd learned Elida would be unable either to conceive or to carry a child. The situation couldn't be reversed, they were told. They had considered adopting a child and had even begun the process. Then Arlen had lost his job delivering oil for a company that had fallen on hard times. The agency advised them that their case would be reexamined at a later date, since the lack of a steady income made the couple ineligible.

It was then Elida had begun to raise ducks. Arlen had persevered with her, even though the ducks were messy and the noise they made got on his nerves. One day Arlen found his wife holding a sickly duckling at

the kitchen table, forcing water down its throat with a medicine drop-
per. Its eyes were hooded, its head drooping. Elida had asked him to
hold it while she continued to drop water into its throat. When they'd
succeeded in reviving the bird, he'd felt joy with her at having been a
part of another creature's survival.

After the ducks had attained some size, he would see her followed
by a line of them across the field. They joined her whenever she left
the house. She had delighted at each stage of their development, especially the day she'd watched them begin to swim in the pond near the
house.

One morning she and Arlen had discovered a clump of feathers on
the porch. More feathers were caught in the chicken wire around the
pen, as if forced there by a fierce wind. Inside the pen were the grisly
remains of the ducks. The scene looked to Arlen like the afterbirth of
some creature he could not fully imagine. Elida sat around the house
for several days, turning away food, talking little.

A letter from Dory in Kansas City arrived during this time with an
unexpected request. Dory had written that since her husband had left
she'd had to get a job. She could no longer manage her child alone, a
little girl named Elmi whom Arlen and Elida had never seen.

Dory's husband traveled for a company that sold fencing. The relatives had taken one look at her salesman husband and said that Dory
ought to use one of the fences on him. Dory might have had some of
these feelings herself. Whatever the reason, she'd taken their child
and gone on the road with her husband. Though the relatives said
Dory had smartened up, her vigilance hadn't saved the marriage. Her
husband had left their hotel one night in Saint Louis, saying he was
going to gas up the car for the next morning's drive, but he had not
returned.

Dory's letter asked Arlen and Elida to take on the raising of Elmi.
It had been no surprise that Dory's marriage had ended, but they'd
never expected to become involved in this important way. Dory said
she would send checks to help with the girl's care so it wouldn't be a

financial burden. She thought the child would be better off with Arlen and Elida, there in the country, and even though she was two hundred miles away, she said she would try to come on the bus to see her as often as she could.

Until two weeks ago the child, Elmi, had been living with them. They'd kept her for three years. They had even celebrated her fifth birthday by planting five plum trees in the orchard. Dory had seldom visited, although she'd kept her word about sending money from her paychecks. She had acted as if her daughter would always stay with Arlen and Elida. It had been easy for them to believe Elmi would never leave them.

Shortly after the child's fifth birthday, Dory remarried. This time she'd found a man of some means. Her circumstances were so much better she'd decided she wanted her daughter with her again. She announced in a letter that she would, in fact, be coming to get Elmi. Would they please write to let her know when would be convenient.

"We won't answer," Elida had said, as she'd lifted the lid of the woodstove and dropped the letter into the fire. After that they would catch themselves looking at the red-haired child as if she were a photograph of a child running, or laughing, or sleeping. At these times Arlen would feel her preciousness so fiercely it would sweep over him like an invisible wave that forced him downward into its undertow. The bleakness of the feeling seemed a preparation for what was coming, as though the pain of separation were being pulsed into him in minutely bearable doses.

On his way outside to see what his wife was doing on the ridge, Arlen automatically glanced into the child's room. Elida had arranged the stuffed toys on the bed as Elmi had liked to find them before bedtime. The child's clothes hung neatly in the open closet. The room itself seemed to accuse him, to ask what kind of protector he was if he had allowed its inhabitant to be taken from it.

"Elida," he called, when he saw his wife moving downhill. Only when she'd dropped what she'd been carrying did he see it was stones. She was piling them near the swing set he'd built for Elmi. The rocks were heaped onto a scuffed patch of ground where the child's feet had touched down each time she'd given herself a boost into the air.

"I want you to build me something," Elida said when he reached her. He glanced to where she was looking. Some of the rocks were the size of a fist. Others could be carried in a pocket, and still others were as big as a cantaloupe or a person's head.

"What's this going to do? What good's this going to do?" He bent down and picked up one of the rocks. There was frost on it and it was damp on the side that had touched the ground. He brought it close to his face. The smell of dirt still clung to it. The cold coming from the stone was like a small intimate engine whose workings were hidden.

The sun had come up and the frost on the other stones was starting to melt. They glistened and their colors deepened. He could see which were moss green or slate colored. Others had bright flecks of fool's gold or were speckled like a bird's egg.

"She can't have it all her way," Elida said. She took several coin-sized stones from her jacket pocket and let them clatter onto the others. Arlen could see there was no reasoning with her. He went to the shed and got the hammer, handsaw, some nails, and a few rough boards, then set to work.

At the end of the morning she came to see what he'd done. The box was nearly finished. He'd fashioned a lid that could be nailed on, once the box was filled. The hammer blows made a bright definitive sound as he tapped in the last nail. Elida ran her hands inside the space as if to take its dimensions fully into herself.

On the day Dory had come to take Elmi, the sheriff was inside the house when Arlen returned from town. For a moment Arlen stood outside, taking in the scene. Then he moved to pass Dory where she leaned with a deputy against the sheriff's car just outside the gate.

"You got my letter, Arlen G.," Dory said to him. "Don't pretend you didn't."

"You just come on back," the deputy said, as Arlen moved past them. "You go in there and we'll never get this done." He tried to take hold of Arlen's arm but Arlen stepped aside and quickened his pace until he reached the house and climbed the steps.

When Arlen came into the living room, Elmi was kicking and screaming in the hold of the sheriff. He had thrown her across his shoulder, meaning to carry her out of the house. Elmi looked straight at Arlen, then pushed her face inside the man's collar and clamped her teeth into the sheriff's neck. The sheriff let out a string of curses and lost his hold on the child. Once she was free, Elmi seemed to realize that neither Arlen nor Elida could stop what was happening. She ran to Arlen long enough to grasp his pant leg before she made for her room and disappeared under the bed.

"Damn!" the sheriff swore, as he took his hand away from his neck. He left a thin streak of blood on khaki where he wiped his trousers. He scowled at Arlen and walked past him out the front door and onto the porch.

Arlen saw Elida braced against the living room wall. A deadness had come into her eyes that made him want to throw something, anything; to pick up his easy chair or the entire dish cabinet and hurl it. He had that kind of energy. Crazy energy. But he didn't want these to be Elmi's last memories. So he stood still as the wildness rippled through his shoulders and upper thighs. With the front door open, he could see the sheriff go over to Dory and the deputy. Then Dory headed for the house, with the sheriff behind her.

"She's my little girl and I aim to have her," Dory shouted loud enough for them to hear inside the house. Then Dory was in the room, striding past them and into Elmi's bedroom. The sheriff was close behind her.

"I'm not yours! I'm not a bit yours!" Elmi cried between bursts of wailing from under the bed. Dory got onto her knees and peered into the darkness under the child's bed.

"She has a right," the sheriff warned when Arlen moved as if to enter the child's room.

Arlen watched as Dory reached her entire upper body under the bed and took Elmi by the arm. Elmi gave a shrill cry, as if she had been caught in a snare. As Dory pulled the child into the light, Arlen felt Elida come to his side and put her hand on his arm. His forearm was tensed and flexing, as if he were lifting something. The sheriff stood between them and Dory and the child.

"Now see what you've done," Dory said to Elida. She stopped a moment in the bedroom doorway with the child pressed to her hip. Elida seemed unable to move or even to speak. Her eyes were searching the child for some way of holding to her beyond all this. Dory managed to lift Elmi, but was barely able to contain the struggling, wailing child. She and the sheriff moved toward the front door.

"You can do this, but that don't make it right," Arlen said to Dory as she swept past with Elmi. But his words were drowned out by Elmi's inconsolable cries as she was carried down the steps. His whole body felt as if it were being funneled upward, against all nature, as in movies he'd seen of waterfalls run backward. He heard the sheriff tell his deputy to open the car doors.

"Settle down, honey," the sheriff said. From inside the car Elmi's cries seemed those of a small insistent bird as it is closed into the dark. The car doors slammed and they heard no more. Soon the car spun away down the gravel road.

Elmi had been gone a week when Dory wrote to tell Elida to pack the girl's clothing and toys and send them to her in Kansas City. She didn't ask; she told her. There had been "such a commotion," as Dory put it, that she'd come off without Elmi's things. "I paid for those things and Elmi needs them," she wrote. Dory said she would be glad to pay the postage once the package arrived.

Arlen carried the box and lid he had built over to the pile of stones at the swing set and placed them on the ground. He put the hammer and a packet of nails beside it. Elida lifted the stones, one and two at a time, and began to drop them into the box. They made a blunted sound that fell back into itself as they struck the boards.

Arlen's body seemed to thicken with resolve as he watched the box fill. They had been unable to say much to each other, either to comfort or ease the fact that the child was no longer with them. He began to bend, take up stones and drop them into the box. The child was gone. Alive, but gone from them, probably forever. Elida held the lid as he hammered it shut. Their muscles strained as they lifted the box and carried it to the truck.

As if they had planned it, they climbed up and sat for a while on the truck bed with the box between them. A stillness rose from it that calmed and fortified them, as if something of the child's joyful presence lagged behind, something that had nothing to do with belonging. Finally Elida took a black marker, and wrote Dory's name and address onto the box. Then she eased herself down from the truck and walked back into the house.

When, after a week or two, no reply or reaction came from Dory, they were not surprised. It didn't matter whether they heard from her since there was no release for them from Elmi's absence.

After a few weeks Dory sent photos of Elmi, and later, notes about her progress, as if nothing had occurred between them. For a time this continued. Then even these communications dwindled and finally stopped altogether. Elida had made no reply to her sister, and Arlen hadn't interfered. Other relatives would pass along glimpses of the child from time to time, but it was like news of a ghost, the images faded as though not meant to last.

When anyone tried to soften the incident between the sisters or to move them back toward each other, Elida would withdraw. Arlen had watched her get up and leave the room more than once. After a while his own longing for the child seemed inexplicably to fall away. He hadn't asked anything for himself after the ordeal, even though he would have liked somehow for the photos to have continued to arrive, each one moving the girl a step farther away from him, yet closer in his imagining of her. They never spoke again of bringing another child into their lives.

Those who knew the situation had said that when Elmi got a mind of her own, she'd come back to them. These friends meant to comfort, but Arlen and Elida knew it was only what people said when things couldn't be changed or resolved. They knew that a child lives the life it is given, and that Elmi had been too young for their love to have left more than a trace of memories, in which they too were fading.

In the standoff between the sisters, Arlen was aware that Elida held the balance of power. It was Elida who had to be moved. But she had no intention of relenting and, as time passed, Arlen assumed more of her attitude than he sometimes realized.

In the twenty-five years that then passed, Elida's slow, wordless sorrow had become embedded in Arlen's own grief. He would have liked, in time, to have seen the break between the sisters mended. But time had all but run out. Elida was going down fast now. From the day they'd discovered the cancer, the doctor had given her six months and all but a month of that time was gone. So when a knock came at their door and Arlen opened it to find Dory standing there, his first impulse had strangely been relief.

Then his gaze fell on the bouquet of mums and carnations Dory cradled in her arms. He stared at the flowers, trying to catch their meaning, the pungent smell of carnations working on him like an irritant.

He had been feeling both used up and rooted by the daily necessities of tending his wife. The memory of Elmi still ran like a river between them. Even after all this time, it was cool and mysteriously sustaining, could prick the heart unexpectedly and seep into the farthest reaches of his being, especially now that he was losing Elida. He felt the child had somehow been gathered back, the way he had seen horses foraging in spring, finding hidden tender shoots and pulling them deeply in.

"No, you can't see her," Arlen said. Then before Dory could hand him the flowers he closed the door. Dory's look of pained astonishment stayed in his mind long after he returned to Elida's bedside. He knew it would rise up in him when this time of watching after Elida had passed, and that he would wonder if he had done the right thing, even when there was no going back. His heart hadn't been hard when he'd turned her away, only sad, as if it were the only way he could handle the situation at the moment.

When he opened the door later he feared Dory might have left the flowers, but she had taken them with her. He'd worried about explaining them. He could shut a door, but throwing out flowers—that would somehow have been harder, away from what he'd meant. He had thought of telling Elida that her sister had come. That, at least, would have included her in his decision. But there was always the chance Elida might have objected to how he'd handled Dory. The more he played this out in his mind, the more he felt he should simply let it stand, and not trouble these last hours. Whatever happened, he would be the one who had to remember, and that would be punishment enough if, later, he felt he'd been wrong. One thing was clear. He had kept his wife from painful affairs that might have consumed and unsettled her when her life ought to be calm and in order. This was no time for Elida to have either a reunion or an argument with Dory.

He propped a photo, of Elmi taken in the swing, near the headboard where Elida could see it when she reached for her water glass. Elmi was a woman now. They'd heard she had children of her own, children they might have seen and known had the sisters relented. But over the years everything had become irrevocable, closed. And Arlen had, at last, taken his own part in this. But how strange it was, Arlen thought, that his heart could be completely without malice, yet allow him to do a thing others could see as cruel. If he stood away from himself, he saw that under different circumstances he would have embraced Dory and shown her to the bedside. But in the moment, his choice had somehow involved his loyalty to Elida and that pent-up time when Elmi had depended on him and he had done nothing. Closing the door to Dory had carried him far outside the reasonable wish to resolve one's differences whenever possible. It had been possible, but something had jammed in him and he'd had to trust it.

Arlen had managed the immediate details of Elida's death with more ease than he did the days he now spent alone. He seemed awash in time. Still, he'd become used to supplying Elida's view to the questions he'd had to answer. He was amazed at how naturally this occurred.

He'd known, for instance, immediately after Elida's passing, exactly what to write on the obituary form the newspaper had sent. Under "survived by" he had printed his name, and after it "husband." Then he'd added: "one daughter, Elmi, of Kansas City." He'd paused over the word "daughter" to consider "foster daughter," but finally had written "daughter." He hoped one of the relatives would send Elmi a copy. He was certain someone would.

This morning he had gone to the bedroom window again, as if he might find his wife walking to the crest of the hill as she had on that morning not long after Elmi had been taken. It was nearing the end of winter now, as it had been then, only during the night snow had fallen.

He dressed and walked out into the orchard. The cupped branches of the fruit trees seemed unnaturally bright, as if the whiteness of the snow caused them to vibrate in the sunlight.

One low branch of a plum tree under which he stood seemed laden with white blossoms. But when he reached for it, snow sloughed onto his jacket sleeve along the crook of his arm. He didn't shake it off, but began to walk with it, as if an invisible bird had landed on his arm and he wanted to carry it a few steps before it flew. When he finally let his arm drop, he felt a lightness ripple through his body, then lift away.

Coming and Going

The man at her door was bald and wore a blue windbreaker. She had asked him twice what he wanted, but he only said, "Are you Emily Fletcher?" as if he knew she was, but needed confirmation.

It struck her from the man's salutary tone that she might have won something—an envelope was about to be handed over with a check inside for a million dollars. She was sixty-five years old. It was about time.

"Yes," she said, her tone cascading downward, as if she were stepping onto an unsteady footbridge over a high mountain pass. The man looked harmless enough, there in the doorway. On closer observation he seemed less sure of himself, as if he couldn't quite fathom why he was there. So many things had seemed unfathomable to Emily since her husband's recent death that she'd begun to accept "unfathomable" as an ongoing state.

Emily suddenly remembered she'd left Hanson, her lawyer, waiting on the telephone. It had taken her three phone calls to get a return call from him and now the dollars were ticking away while she stood there with this awkward stranger. She looked him over again and felt the moment seize her in which women hurriedly judge a man safe with the scantest evidence—that split second in which they lunge past fears into an unreliable security.

"Please step inside," Emily said. "I won't be a minute." She moved back to allow the man into the entry, then shut the door behind him and automatically turned the deadbolt. She knew it was crazy, to lock people in after she'd locked them out, but at least no one else would come in. She'd been interrupted by the telephone as she'd been taking a quilt from its shipping package. The gift from her sister fell from the back of a hall chair. She left the man standing as if he'd come to a halt before the flag of some unknown nation.

Speaking again to Hanson, she experienced the odd sensation of being two places at once. She heard her voice going out over the telephone lines, but she was also uneasily aware that her side of the conversation was entering the acutely attentive but uncommunicative head of the stranger in her entryway.

"Nyal spent a month in Italy while the house was under construction, but it wasn't a vacation!" she said to Hanson. "Martin tells me this woman called him before his father died." She revealed this almost involuntarily. Martin was their son and she had confided unnecessarily to the lawyer during their last discussion that she feared Martin was a womanizer. She hated how she found herself blurting the most personal things to the business people she dealt with now. "It was while Nyal was very ill, and the woman must have intended to put pressure on him by calling Martin." She paused here to calculate the echo factor of the stranger's overhearing this last piece of information. Though what did it really matter? The man had no context in which to place these fragments of her life. Hanson's incisive voice, heading for the crux of the matter, began impatiently sweeping aside what he seemed to consider mere female baggage.

"The legal issue is: did your husband modify, use, or appropriate another man's house design? And if so, is that man's widow entitled to recompense? The statute of limitations unfortunately has not run out on this. You're further involved because Nyal completed this job under the business partnership you both formed to reduce his tax liability. You signed off on this work and took payment with him in the partnership."

"I recall something about it," Emily said. "But Nyal took care of all that." She'd signed whatever Nyal had asked her to sign. At the time they'd formed the partnership, paper had flown by with blizzard force. But, as representative of her husband's estate and also in her tutelary capacity as his surviving business partner, she would now, Hanson reminded her, be the defendant in any action. The other woman, also a widow, and representing her own deceased husband's estate in Rome, would be the plaintiff. On his behalf, she claimed part ownership in a house design. Nyal had only been asked to modify the design. The plans had resulted in a construction in Italy that Emily had never seen, but which her husband had supervised. Both men who'd contributed to its design were now dead—her husband from cancer and the architect named Riccardo from a stroke in Rome some ten months previously.

During the final months of her own husband's illness, Emily had been aware of murmurings from the widow in Rome, who believed Nyal owed her payment for Riccardo's original design. Ultimately a letter had arrived full of allegations. And Nyal, on his sickbed, had reasserted it was nonsense. Riccardo himself had invited him to modify the plan. Riccardo's widow knew this all very well. It was unfortunate Riccardo wasn't alive to corroborate it. But the whole matter would subside on its own. No, they needn't hire a lawyer in Rome.

For a time, Nyal seemed to have been right. They'd had their hands full, with people coming to visit and pay their respects, once it became known that Nyal's cancer was no longer in remission. Also, there was the finishing work on plans for the ecological center. Nyal had been the lead architect, and this project had been his final passion. All else had been swept aside so he could concentrate his remaining energies. The strange Italian murmuring had become inaudible, all but forgotten. Now Hanson informed her that yet another letter had arrived, one that framed the complaint so aggressively he suspected it was preliminary to a suit.

"We may need to get representation in Rome for the estate and for you as well, if she decides to press the matter," Hanson said. Emily tried to gauge the emphasis he was putting on the "if." Why was her lawyer so lackluster, such a practitioner of the uninflected? She could never tell where the meaning lay in his sentences. Since her husband's death she craved emotion in all her communications. This lawyer was an ongoing disappointment in this regard.

"Rome?" she heard herself saying, like a word spoken aloud in a dream. It was as well to say Djakarta or Bandar Seri Begawan. The only personal connection she'd had with Rome, other than her late husband's sojourn there, was having avoided the city while she'd traveled alone as a young woman in Europe. She had pointedly not gone to Italy when she'd heard that Italian men randomly and impulsively pinched women.

"Do you think I'll have to go to Rome?"

"It's possible," Hanson said. "But worse things have happened than a trip to Rome." Emily took note of a sound in the entryway and remembered the unknown man who, by now, must certainly have become restive. He might be deciding to go without having handed over the important, long-awaited envelope. She still behaved as if Nyal were in the house. Had he been there during the time prior to his illness, he would have heard the man at the door and come down. A mere two weeks had passed since his death and the house seemed swollen and randomly eruptive. At times it pulsed with an absence that was a kind of presence, a hum of consciousness that ran parallel to her own.

"I'm glad Nyal didn't have to bear this," she found herself saying to Hanson, as if Nyal could still somehow overhear. But what she really meant was that she was sorry she was having to bear it alone. "I have to go. There's someone here," she said, allowing a provocative edge to slip into her voice. They agreed to speak later. She paused a moment before hanging up, hoping Hanson would give a small reassurance that this trouble was likely to subside, but he gave none.

She hung up feeling betrayed by things beyond her control, as if some still trembling fiber of her dead husband's actions had brought them into an unfamiliar alliance. Why had he taken on the project of a house in a foreign country? This Riccardo—someone he'd known from his college days who'd married and settled in Italy—he'd involved Nyal, brought him in to solve an impasse on the project he'd begun. She only vaguely recalled. Nyal's expertise in the particular building materials had been important. But also something to do with an inflexible situation. Now some inflexible element had acquired another impetus. It was hardly conceivable that this had gotten so out of hand.

When she returned to the entry she found the casually dressed, rather timorous man examining the quilt. Black arrowhead-like sets of Vs dovetailed down the white fabric. There was something almost cruel about the pattern, but she identified with its pain-in-flight quality.

"It's the Widow's Quilt, a nineteenth-century pattern," she said to the man. "But the quilt books call it the Darts of Death."

"A lot of work there," the man said quietly, raising his eyes to her with a sepulchral gaze. He let the quilt edge slip from his fingers.

"I don't know quite where to use it. It's single-bed size." She felt at once she'd volunteered too much in speaking of a bed to a man she didn't know. She noticed him pull nervously on his jacket zipper, running it a short way down, then up toward his Adam's apple. There was a wedding ring on the hand. She felt herself drop her guard another notch.

"I have something to give you," the man said. The insupportable idea of the prize envelope fluttered tantalizingly again through Emily's mind. If it were to happen, it was a pity Nyal would miss it, she thought, characteristically undercutting anticipation with disappointment. The man definitely unzipped the jacket and reached inside to his shirt breast pocket. Next he extended a black leather holder the size of a checkbook and flipped it open to reveal a gold star on a dark velvet backing. It was a badge. It seemed the man was some sort of official.

"I'm a United States deputy marshal," he said, expertly returning the badge to his breast pocket. "And since you are Emily Fletcher, I have papers to leave with you. You'll need to sign, just to acknowledge you received them." He reached farther inside his jacket and brought forth a sheaf of official documents and handed them to her. She could see that everything, except the receipt form, was in another language.

"If you'd just sign here, please, Mrs. Fletcher," the man said without the slightest doubt in his manner that she would comply. He now had the air of someone for whom these matters were beneath notice. He produced a black pen and handed it to her. She followed his index finger to a signature line, under which she saw her name typed. She was still quaking from having glimpsed the gold star. What exactly was a deputy marshal? She felt unable to speak the question aloud. To ask could invite a revelation as to the seriousness of the matter. Was she about to be arrested?

She folded back the signature page and quickly scanned the document for clues. It was in Italian, she confirmed from the legal address in Rome. Here, then, were the very documents her lawyer had feared were on the way. The word "press" came back from Hanson's characterization of what the aggrieved woman might do. She might *press on with things.* A sexual verb, Emily thought. So here the woman was, indeed. Pressing on. It struck her oddly that the coincidence of her lawyer's warning had merged into the arrival of the process server. It carried an eerie resonance, as if something awful were masquerading as normal, a thought she had experienced most poignantly at the moment of Nyal's death, the way his breath, in its final rush, had been so like a sigh.

Their son had said that when the woman telephoned three weeks ago, she'd claimed Nyal had once given her his number "in case I ever needed to reach your father." She'd informed Martin she would soon be taking the "necessary steps." Evidently it had not deterred the woman to learn from Martin that Nyal was terminally ill. Only after Nyal's death had Martin told Emily about having received this puzzling call. Maybe the woman, even now, believed and intended that her letters, followed by the serving of papers, would catch Nyal on the brink of his death. What sort of woman would do such a thing? She never wanted to become such a woman.

Emily held the papers and stared at her own name—again, the feeling of forces conjoining against her. She wanted to be rid of this man as quickly as possible. She moved her hand through the deft strokes with which she traversed her signature. During the days since her husband's death, she and their son had only once again referred to the woman in Italy.

"She can claim anything she likes, now that your father's dead," Emily had said. "She could claim they'd had an affair and that he promised her the moon!" The remark had flown out of her and she'd reveled briefly in the absurdity of its fictional self-inflicted wound, or perhaps the wound had been meant indirectly for Martin. "To call you—she seems desperate," Emily said. Her son dismissed the woman as the sort of person who's delusional, who has nothing fruitful to do with her life, so she runs around trying to extort money and to get attention by threatening to sue. He'd met this type, he said, in his job as an insurance adjuster. Martin was forty-three, had a darling third wife and five children from his two previous marriages. He loved to evaluate propositions, buildings, objects, and the erotic parameters of any female with whom he came into contact. Emily knew all this without surrendering affection for him. The more untrue he'd been to his wives, the more attentive and solicitous he had tended to be toward her. It consoled her now that he seemed to give no credence to this woman's claims.

"I'm sorry," the bald man said, lifting the stapled pages to yet another signature page. "Just here on the duplicate, if you'd be so good." He pointed to a red X near a blank. Emily wasn't at all sure she should be signing for these papers, but doing so was strangely as simple as the fact that the pen was in her hand. She signed again, then, without replacing the cap, handed the pen back to the man. His hands, like her own, were trembling. He was also finding the encounter stressful.

"Now," he said, and glanced pointedly toward the living room. "Could you tell me, please, is Mr. Fletcher here?" He paused and looked in the opposite direction, toward the kitchen. "Or has he relocated?" This second question startled her in the possibilities it opened up. She thought of the woman's audacity in having telephoned her son, the invasiveness of her having insinuated a dispute into such a time, when her husband's life had been reaching its final days and hours. And now this woman, who should have known what it was to suffer such a loss with her own husband not dead a year, had propelled a process server into her entry. There had obviously been some delay in the arrival of the papers, which must have been in the works prior to Nyal's death. The U.S. deputy marshal probably did not read Italian and had no idea what this was about. He was restless and only half satisfied in his accomplishment. He tucked the signed receipts inside his jacket, allowing Emily to retain the sheaf of paper in Italian. Then he regarded her as if she were withholding something. He seemed precariously on the verge of becoming less courteous. A set of undelivered papers still remained in his hands.

Emily's mind was speeding through the town. She could picture exactly where her husband lay—the freshly disturbed plot that overlooked the town at its eastern edge. There was a large evergreen wreath at the head of his grave, with NYAL and BELOVED HUSBAND AND FATHER in gold lettering on wide strands of velvet ribbon. It would be months before she arranged for the stone and decided what to inscribe on it, but there was a poem she had in mind. It was a tanka by the Japanese poet Bashō—whose poem was modeled on yet another poem sent by a woman to a man after their first love-meeting. She might use only the first three lines:

> *Was it you who came*
> *Or was it I who went—*
> *I do not remember.*

She approved of the casualness of these lines, how they held a definitive absence in suspension, as some mere coming or going. The words would have yet another dimension, she realized, when her own remains eventually entered the plot beside her husband. It would be as if a conversation were still ongoing between them. Even while the poem subtracted their "remembering," it would insist on memory all the more for anyone who paused before the stone. But most of all, she agreed with how the words cast away life and death at one fell swoop. There was something at once simple and expansive in that motion.

"Yes, my husband *has* relocated," she said, bringing her attention back to the man. It occurred to her that although she had no control over the serving of these papers, she did hold sway over this exact moment.

"Would you be so kind as to tell me where I might find Mr. Fletcher," the bald man said.

"Certainly." Emily spoke clearly and decisively. "I'd be glad to help you find my husband." The man was clearly taken aback by her cooperativeness. He shifted the remaining papers to his right hand and ran the hand with the wedding ring over the top of his pale head, then let it drop. The motion brought him into contact with the Widow's Quilt. His demeanor, she saw, had visibly softened when she said she would help. It was likely he'd experienced harsh treatment many times. He did not smile, but dropped his shoulders, which had been held high and rather formally.

"There's a very nice view of the town where my husband has landed," Emily said. She disliked the casual implication of "landed," since she and Martin had carefully chosen the site. Nonetheless, she was determined to continue in this fashion, to reveal exactly where her husband was.

"Oh, very good," the man said. He resituated the sheaf of documents meant for her husband inside his jacket, then plunged a hand into his trouser pocket, jingling some loose change, no doubt an unconscious expression of delight at the surrender he assumed on her part.

"Go east on First, past the bowling alley, and down Race until you come to Caroline," she directed. The man took a small notebook from a side jacket pocket and began to scribble. "Then turn right and continue past the hospital. You'll approach some grassy fields, then go up a steep hill. At the top you'll find the development you're looking for." To call a graveyard a "development" would never have occurred to her, but she supposed death was a development. Still, her husband's death was beyond the word in such a physically challenging way that she felt an involuntary shiver.

"I imagine there's a house number," the man said.

"If you need assistance to find exactly where Mr. Fletcher's situated,"

Emily said, "ask at the little white house just inside the gate. There's someone on duty until 5 PM."

Emily thought she'd deflected the reference concerning the house number nicely. The man glanced at his watch and Emily automatically checked her own. She saw that only half an hour remained for the man to get further help in finding her husband. He slipped the notebook with the instructions back into his side pocket.

"You've been most cooperative," he said, and glanced uncompre-hendingly at the ferocious black darts of the Widow's Quilt, which, as he brushed against it, seemed to be jutting directly into him. For a moment she thought crazily that, in his mute exuberance, he intended to embrace her. The idea made her quake, as when he'd flashed his deputy marshal's badge. She was relieved when he reached for the door handle and attempted to let himself out. She moved near his shoulder, turned the deadbolt, and moved back so he could pass. On the steps he paused, turned, uttered some final sentence of courtesy, then crossed the driveway to his white Volvo. She was taking pleasure in the very fact of his going and that he would now be following her directions, this minion of the widow in Rome. He climbed into his car, and lifted his hand in a mild wave. She did not return the gesture.

She was thinking of her husband now, that he could not know these unpleasant things that had befallen her since his death, stran-gers who wanted to use his silence to beleaguer and ensnare her. Nyal would have enjoyed how she'd just acquitted herself. She imagined the two of them laughing about the U.S. deputy marshal's driving into the cemetery, hoping to be directed out of a wrong turn, asking the caretaker where Nyal Fletcher "lived." Well, the widow in Rome had misused Emily's husband, and now Emily would make use of her mes-senger. The man could stand before her husband's wreath as long as he wanted. Maybe Emily's circumstances would prick his heart. He might fully experience the weight of his actions that day. After all, they had each been reduced to functionaries.

She continued to follow the man in her mind as she gathered the quilt so the darts folded against her breasts and grazed her neck. She carried it upstairs to the queen-size bed she now occupied alone. She spread the quilt out on her side. With the pattern unfurled, the bed seemed to be sliced in two, but the quilt gave her side fresh vitality.

Even though it was hours before bedtime, she unbuttoned her dress, stepped out, then lifted the covers and crawled between the sheets in her slip. The added weight was an unexpected comfort. She closed her eyes, then eased her hand onto her husband's side of the bed. It was cooler and she realized that her cheeks, against the white pillowcase, were flushed.

She thought of the woman in Rome. *What if?* she thought, and Emily smiled to recall the moment with Martin in which she had cast her dead husband into the woman's arms in a sentence uttered more as a challenge to the unlikely than a true possibility. But what would it change if her husband had sought the company of another woman? How casually the thought came to her. They had been married the same forty-five years. She believed they had loved each other beyond all others. She even recalled the exact site of her faith, her steadfast belief. One night, before they were to go out in company, he'd put his arms around her at the door and said, "If I should ever say anything to annoy you while we're out, dear, ignore it, because I adore the ground you walk on." It was gallant and wide, and no one had said anything so beautiful to her before or since.

Death had added another dimension to that long-ago gift. Perhaps it was death, that ultimate release from belonging, which made even the idea of infidelity ludicrous. She suddenly caught a glimpse of a possibility she'd kept quietly in reserve. She wondered if all wives held aside a reserve of forgiveness for unrevealed betrayals, believing their husbands could, in some pull of opportunity, go astray in fact, if not in heart? She had put aside such a reserve, she saw, without really having had to know it, until now. Yet: *so what?*

Prior to the Italian woman's intrusion forcing her to tremble in her own doorway, she'd had no idea of the degree to which she could still volunteer acceptance of all Nyal might have been. It was really in behalf of them both that she could manage this leap. At his death she had thought mistakenly that an end had come to the growth of their earthly loving, but instead she had stepped onto unexpected terrain where what she held precious had become even more so. In these thoughts she was able to reach herself newly, and this both surprised and enlarged her sense of Nyal and of their life together. In her reception of all her husband might have experienced, in and out of her knowledge, she saw with an ungaugeable onrushing force, how deeply she'd loved him and loved him still. Would always love him.

"You're so very kind," the U.S. deputy marshal had said to her as he'd gone down the porch steps. Her throat tightened now as she recalled his words. She had not been at all kind toward this man, and by now he would be realizing this. What was there in being kind when life itself and the actions of others were often monstrous? Yet she continued to believe kindness was, when one could manage it, the ultimate checkmate, and beyond that, the one enviable gift. But could there be a hidden sleeve of malice inside too much kindness? Whatever else, she'd been true to her feeling.

Nyal's silence seemed more vast than ever, and she felt included there—allowing all things to be absorbed, to coexist—fidelity and infidelity, residence and grave, coming and going.

By now the man had likely reached his destination. He would have come to stand before the wreath. For a moment he might have studied the name on the fluttering ribbon. Then, deciding to go, he would have turned and begun to walk back to his car. Perhaps he was ruefully thinking of her this very moment, of how artfully she'd misled him. But maybe, if he hadn't passed too far into disgruntlement, he might pause and look back toward the grave, realizing that, on either side of the town, they could both be faintly smiling.

My Gun

I am thirty-eight, have straight teeth and good hygiene. When anyone from the thin-is-godly camp looks me over like I should lose a pound or two, I tell them, "Sorry. I protect my roundness." Although I haven't yet tried to write a personal ad to attract somebody new, I think once I figured out the codes, I could come up with something punchy and tantalizing. Now that a year has passed since my husband's death, I start to think about such things.

Lately, however, whether or not I should buy my own gun seems to preoccupy me more than whether I should look for a new mate. I ask you, what kind of country is it where a woman finds herself considering a gun for a companion? When my husband was alive, the idea of owning and using a gun never occurred to me. I'm not even sure at this point why I feel myself inching toward actually forking over cash for a little snub-nosed silver something, dropping it into my purse, and walking out of this one particular gun shop I've had my eye on, just east of town.

This shop attracts me because it sprang up overnight like a bad mushroom. It looks as if it could be staffed by the same men—why am I certain they are men?—selling arms elsewhere in the world—to Bosnian Serbs, or helping the Macedonians get ready in case their towns are next, or beefing up Croatian arsenals. Just the thought of those Serbs, raping several thousand women for three years as an actual so-called "weapon of war"—now this makes me want to rush right out and buy my gun.

It scares me when I think like this. But then, many things come to

my mind, now that I'm alone. I have too much time to think, according to my friends. Most of the time I wouldn't even say I am "thinking."
I muse. I especially like to muse in my flower garden, which borders
the property my husband and I kept as a summer home, but to which
I have now retreated full-time. When I'm musing I dislike being interrupted. My neighbor, who's about fifty and who practically lives in her
yard, is always trying to carry on conversations with me.

"We have twenty-one cats in our neighborhood," she says. "I didn't
count yours since he never comes outside. These are outdoor cats I'm
talking about."

My neighbor is fuming on the cat question because *someone* has
dropped a flyer into her mailbox. It suggests that those who have outdoor cats keep them indoors during the entire spring and early summer months, because birds are nesting and raising their young.

"Cats have to do their cat things," she says. "Why should I confine
mine when twenty other cats are on the prowl?"

At precisely 8 AM every morning my neighbor scatters a stingy
handful of seed on a hip-high platform in her backyard. I have never
pointed out to her that these feeders are patently death traps for birds.
In neighborly tolerance I allow her to bait, entrap, and tantalize to her
heart's content.

Aside from cats and birds, my neighbor can be nosy in other ways.
Like asking if the investigation is still going on as to why my husband,
a well-known progressive senator from a southern state, committed
suicide. I correct her right away.

"Not suicide. Nobody knows. But not suicide."

"I'm sorry," she says, and I believe she is, in her own way, sorry. "I
only know what I read in the papers," she says, deftly hinting.

"I can't really talk about it," I say, though I'd like to. But I don't want
to ruin the nest of my musing. How would it be if, every time I stepped
into the yard to water my sweet peas, my neighbor and I had to talk
about my husband's death?

One thing I know: my husband was a man who loved every instant of life, and no way did he shoot himself in the back of the head at that impossible angle. For one thing, he had a muscle problem in his right shoulder. He had dislocated it a number of times during the three years we were married. I used to rub liniment on that shoulder every night.

Of course, it's true, I didn't know he kept a handgun that was registered to him with his own apparent signature. If he could keep a handgun secret from me, he could also conceivably intend suicide and not give hints. No matter what anyone says, I think suicide is totally out of character for him.

From her remarks in the press, his ex-wife seemed to accept the idea of his suicide a bit eagerly, I thought. At the funeral I wanted to ask her a few things, but never got a chance. She made an awful racket at the graveside and had to be kept from leaping onto my husband's coffin. It was probably a mistake even to think we could have spoken peaceably to each other, since now she considers herself the "authentic widow," essentially because she put in more time with my husband.

My husband was an obsessive preparer. This may have caused me not to notice things I should have. I don't know if he had this habit of preparing for the worst during what he referred to as his "interminable marriage" to his first wife. Right from the time we were married he frequently used the phrase "If anything happens to me . . ." He was twenty years older and he knew it was likely I would survive him.

"Here's my safe-deposit key," my husband had said. "Notice the shape and color. Your other keys look silver, but this one's tarnished, clouded like pewter." He slipped it onto my key ring, right next to my rabbit's foot. "If anything happens to me, look in the safe-deposit box."

My husband believed in safety nets and he told me from the start he had insurance to cover payments on both our houses, the one on the East Coast and the one where I now live, the location about which I can't be specific. Naturally the suicide question put a kink in his preparations, and I am on the verge of losing both houses. Soon I may have no garden in which to muse, no well-meaning neighbor to avoid.

"You should get yourself a gun and let me teach you how to use it," my neighbor is saying, as I douse my sweet peas with Miracle-Gro. "Bruce and I worry about you," she says, "over there by yourself in that big house." She doesn't say *alone*. And *woman* is the other word we take for granted.

"I'm a crack shot," my neighbor says. "I could snap off the nose of a reindeer at two hundred yards." It's when she says things like this that I realize I wouldn't trade this neighbor for anyone on the planet. She is better than a security system or a pack of pit bull terriers. Plus, she makes me laugh, which is curative.

I'm aware that she practices her marksmanship because on Sundays I see her blue Ford station wagon parked just off the highway in front of the shooting range. She goes to church, then comes home, grabs her gun, and drives over to the range to shatter clay pigeons for an hour or two. Sometimes Bruce goes with her. Maybe she and my husband shattered clay pigeons elbow to elbow, but I don't ask.

When I'm unresponsive she says, "If you need me, I'm just a phone call away." She is a good and thoughtful neighbor, it's easy to see, and I believe she would bring her loaded gun over here in the early morning hours and shoot to kill if she found me in any possible danger. And Bruce, he would be right behind her with his gun. I would have a small but capable army of two at my disposal. These are people whose consciences would not wince, or be hampered in the least, by slamming a bullet through somebody's heart or brain if they found such a person climbing through one of my windows or breaking down a door. "Hesitate and ye are lost" is their motto, and "Let the police ask questions of their relations later." When I muse about getting a gun I often think I should instead put a sign at the entrance to my property that says: BEWARE: NEIGHBORS ARMED & DANGEROUS. Then I wouldn't have to continue this dialogue with myself about the advisability of owning a gun.

It's funny how just beginning to consider getting a gun feeds all sorts of personal encounters into the question. Last week a girlfriend in an upscale area of San Francisco calls me, shaken to the core. She has zapped open her garage door and gone inside, only to find a man behind her. Two seconds later he puts a knife to her throat. She is dressed in a pretty summer smock with a dropped neckline and carrying a purse, just for looks, with no more than twenty dollars cash in it. My mother would say my friend has brought this on herself by dressing this way. Whatever. My friend is under attack and coming up short. Her credit cards—she can see them now—are zippered into her regular purse in the downstairs closet. Listening to her is like watching a reenactment on a TV cop show.

"The guy is pissed because I'm an empty cash register," my friend says. "Then he spots my wedding ring. He orders me to take it off. It's my great-grandmother's ring and just to think of this worse-than-scum taking it is like throwing generations down a sewer. But I can't get it off my finger.

"'Let up on my neck,' I breathe to the creep through my teeth. 'Maybe I can suck it loose.'

"'Get it off, bitch, or you're blood on cement,' the guy says.

"I can't see the man's face because he's behind me, but I'm ashamed to be glad the arm around my neck is white. Honey, why, as a white woman in America, have I been caused, against my will, to think, *Hey, shouldn't this guy mugging me be black?* Where did this designer thought come from, and why do I suspect I'm not alone in having it?" my friend asks.

I'm used to her rants and can generally cut through the haze to touch down on the other side. I admit I'm more concerned about her throat getting sliced than her political and sociological quandaries. But then, just having a throat to be cut, like having a gun to fire—these are new concerns for me. And white arm, black arm—if the throat is cut, it bleeds.

"So I'm sucking away on my ring," she says, "and the white arm has let up enough that I could get my whole hand into my mouth if my mouth was big enough. Finally the ring clinks against my teeth, and rolls to the back of my tongue so I nearly swallow it. I have to bend into the knife to keep the ring out of my throat. I manage to spit it onto the garage floor, and he shoves me to the cement where I get a mechanic's view of my car. This is life in America.

"I am still afraid he's going to bend over and slit me open like a melon," she says. "But the white arm reaches behind one of the car tires and grabs my ring. Next, I see these big feet in high-powered Nikes loping off into the daylight. I reach up and touch my throat. There is blood on my fingers when I bring them away. I pull myself up and tremble back inside the house to a mirror. There's a hairline slice where I had to bend into the knife. I call the police, then I phone Bobby, who's so furious I won't even repeat what he said, and who assumes I've been raped. And hey, there is that black guy again. The one who wasn't there. 'Was the guy black?' That's the first thing Bobby wants to know. Not: 'How are you, babe? You all right?'"

Bobby is my friend's husband and it turns out he owns a gun. He's been trying to convince my friend she should get one too. By the time of this conversation, she has been to her first gun-handling session. She has her mind around a trigger and is saying, "I never thought I'd be so totally *into* anything like this. Our instructor put it to us like this: 'Would you rather be carried by six or judged by twelve?'"

"And do you feel safer?" I ask, dreading the answer.

"You bet holes in your panty hose," she said. "I'm not to be messed with." She went on to say that just having the gun in her possession made her more aware of danger. "I will never go into my garage again without my hand in my bag on my loaded gun." She had bought a special purse, she said, with a Velcro side pocket made just for her gun. She won't even have to take it out of the compartment to fire it. Just pull the Velcro tab, and BLAM!

It all sounded eerily reasonable, given what she'd been through. The hairline slice on her throat lingered in my mind when I walked into my own garage after that, and I thought of my gun out there somewhere, waiting for me to buy it and carry it everywhere like a mother kangaroo. I felt a glint of unattached affection for it spike off me into the cosmos.

I have begun to think a revolver would be my weapon of choice. I just like the word "revolver," though the word "automatic" also has its charm. If I were buying a new microwave I would go into the store and look at them. Run my hands over them. Open and shut them. See what buttons there were to push and how big the cook space is. Muffins versus turkey—that sort of thing. But going into a gun shop—the idea strikes me the same way going into a porn shop might. I feel all scummy and wrong just thinking about it. Like something I don't agree with is going to happen.

But then, I'm a widow and this is also something to which I didn't agree. I think of him all the time, my husband, out there under the dirt where I know he doesn't want to be.

Not long after his funeral I'm back to doing just what he told me. I take the deposit-box key down to the bank and have the girl let me into a room that is positively chilly with money. We each insert keys. I turn mine, then she slides out a long metal box. I carry it to a little alcove and sit down. For a moment I think of my husband, that he intended for me to do this. It's a bustling place, this bank, but my alcove is a still pool of silence. The sort of silence I imagine around my husband when he was shot. Or, if I'm wrong, the silence he broke when he shot himself.

I lift the lid. Inside are my husband's will and the papers on our houses. But in a long brown envelope I discover several thick bundles of traveler's checks. One-thousand-dollar checks, unsigned. Packets and packets of checks. Why did my husband put so much money in here, money that was never invested and also has not been collecting one cent of interest? Where has this money come from? Did we pay taxes on it? Should I report it to someone? I mean, this is more money than I have ever seen before in my life. I am not even going to mention the total amount.

My mother's descriptions of hot flashes come back to me because I'm sweating right through my favorite apple-print top. The traveler's checks seem tainted, cut off from the whole idea of spending. It's true

I could use them, even bail myself out of my current financial problem caused by my husband's assumed suicide. I could pay off the mortgage on one of the houses, probably the one next door to my armed-and-dangerous neighbors. "If anything ever happens to me," I recall my husband saying. But what did he intend with this stash of ready-to-travel money? Am I supposed to go someplace, and if so, where?

I hate the paralysis of this decision period I'm in. I phone a woman I met at a fund-raiser for my husband's last campaign. She's a performance artist living in LA. When she started telling ex-wife stories at the party, we hit it off right away. We even joked about doing a book together called *The Men We Love and the Bitches They Left.* Our plan would be to write this under aliases, so as not to get sued by our respective ex-wife antagonists.

"What about guns?" I ask her. "Do you own one?"

"No," she says. "But I've handled one. I went over to this guy's, Stan Mosman—Mossy, we call him. He has guns all over his apartment, the way some people collect masks or ships in bottles. I tell him, 'I want to do a performance piece in which I load a real gun with real bullets, then point it at my audience while I do my monologue—some ramble about having gone off my meds because I was losing my edge.' This appeals to him. 'How can I help you?' he asks. I tell him I need to learn to handle a gun so it's second nature. He takes a handgun out of a locked cabinet and slides it onto the coffee table in front of me with a shivery metal-on-wood *thunk*. When I pick it up, it's heavier than I expected, but more than that—the power, the diabolical feel of the thing. No doubt about it, I've got my hand around pure evil, something made to kill people. My whole body is horrified. After a few moments I just ease it back onto the table and say, 'Mossy—thanks a lot, but I'm going to have to borrow a gun from props. A real gun is just a little *too* real.'"

Listening to my actress friend's experience is like being an astronaut of my gun question. I begin to see all sides of it. The way she'd felt about the gun is close to how I'd felt about the checks in the lockbox.

Something unsavory. Too many unknowns. Then my friend begins to describe her neighborhood and I realize she has more reason than me to start down this should-I-get-a-gun path.

"So I walk back from Mossy's to my apartment," my friend continues. "Remember, I live in the Echo Park area of LA. Still, it's weird to see black spray-painted messages that say RIP SPOOKY on the sides of buildings." She assumes I know what this means. When I ask, she translates: "Rest In Peace, Spooky."

"Spooky," she says, "was a kid not six blocks from me who was shot to death in a gang showdown." It gives me a jolt of confidence to know that my friend, in such an environment, has chosen *against* owning a gun. But then she's an actress and could probably fake her way out of anything. She would just bite the white arm, and if the guy caught up to her, she'd offer first aid so convincingly he'd forget whatever he meant to do to her.

Recently I've tried to shift the focus of my musings from guns to a certain man who attracted my attention at a party after a production of *My Fair Lady*. He is physically impressive, looks able to lift and move things—more and more this is how I judge the desirability of a man. I noticed immediately that he would be fit enough to help reorganize the boxes I've stored in my garage—my husband's things, which I've kept for a museum. This man talked about how he loved to hike in the backcountry and, before I left, gave me his phone number on a scrap of paper he tore from a newspaper. He said he had a van that he often used as a camper. This added information seemed a little forward and suggestive, but I ignored it.

Even though my husband is gone, I still have friends in helpful places. One of them has access to records at the county courthouse. She offered to check out this gentleman. A day later she calls in a state of alarm. She has not only checked the courthouse files, but has asked around at her hairdresser's and the tanning salon.

"This guy's a real zero," she says. "Less than zero, if you want to know. Besides that, he has a permit to carry a gun. Trouble," she says. "If I were you, I'd just crumple that phone number and toss it into the nearest public toilet."

But I don't do anything of the sort. I put the number into my coat pocket and head for the supermarket. It's a ten-minute drive through the usual heavy afternoon traffic. I go inside and locate the magazine racks. At least ten different gun magazines are available. I decide on one with a photograph of a woman, arms extended, both hands grasping her handgun with the tension of a slingshot, before the target of a shadow man. There are already lethal holes in this "man."

It occurs to me that if this target were in the shape of a woman, with bullet holes arranged like erogenous zones, I wouldn't be buying this magazine. I notice I am willing, at least in my imagination, to shoot holes into the shape of a man. I wonder, could this be one of those designer thoughts my San Francisco friend was talking about?

The female cashier acts like I'm not doing anything special buying this magazine, but I've camouflaged it with necessities—milk and raisin bread. Maybe she's a gun owner herself. It's not something I'd know how to ask. As I walk to my car I think I see the attractive man getting into his van. I situate my groceries in the backseat, then reach into my coat pocket and touch the slip of newsprint on which our link is scribbled.

Back home, I carry in the groceries. I take my gun magazine into the bedroom and place it on the nightstand, saving it for bedtime. It's late afternoon, so I go outside and unspool the hose to do my watering. A fat white cat dodges into the shrubbery when he sees me. I assume he's had experiences.

I muse about the attractive man as I water my sweet peas and glads, the hanging baskets and rosemary. Then I muse on the word "inevitable," whether my husband felt his death was, in any sense, inevitable when he loaded up the lockbox with traveler's checks for me to find. My neighbor fills her birdbath and we wave reassuringly to each other from the parameters of our yards.

Later I make a trip to town because I need to drop something at my lawyer's, the one still trying to unravel my husband's financial affairs. I drive past the gun shop, which is covered with fishnet and painted camouflage green and gray. The phone number of the attractive man with a gun permit is in my pocket. I wonder what make of gun he packs. Having his number is like having a gun, without having it. Just to know he's there, if I need him. Loaded and ready. I am certain he would teach me all I need to know about guns. I might even invent some trigger-happy love-name for him, like Spooky or Mossy, and we'd go off to shoot clay pigeons together on Sundays. Or maybe he lives in the country, where we could shatter the windshields of junked cars. The scrap of paper curls around my finger and causes a ripple to run up my spine, just to know he's there. Naturally, I don't plan to use his number. I hope that's clear.

Mr. Woodriff's Neckties

Every now and then one of my neighbor's visitors carries an item of clothing out to their car and hangs it with their own. Sometimes they're clutching a paper bag and I can't see what she's given away. Shirts, books, and even his toiletries, though I'm just guessing here. I'm probably mistaken about the toiletries. But things have been trickling out of the house ever since she began to get a grip on herself.

About a year ago she told me over the fence that she might not be able to keep her house. Legal matters, including Mr. Woodriff's royalties given over to pay off a publisher for books he'd never write. It's been a hard time for each of us in our own way.

Mr. Woodriff only managed to live ten months in the house next door as my neighbor. I'm a good neighbor and I would have enjoyed living next to him into old age. Maybe even seeing myself depicted as a minor character, walking a dog or passing by just as his main character needed to clarify something by speaking with a stranger.

Even though our time as neighbors was short, I had some good influence on things next door. Mr. Woodriff used to ask me about my roses. I guess he noticed me working in them all the time. He told me a fan had sent him and his wife three rose plants—Love, Hope, and Cherish. The next thing I knew he and his wife were making a small rose garden over there with about ten bushes. She would dig a hole with a mattock. Then she would haul a gallon bucket of water over next to the planting bed and he would tip the water into the hole, then wait for it to seep into the soil. Finally, he would get down on his knees and set each plant into place.

On Sundays I see her gathering these same roses to take to the cemetery. It makes me wonder if they both knew, while they were planting them, that this was in their future. Or maybe they were so involved with earth and root-balls and whether the holes were deep enough that they didn't trouble to think ahead, except that eventually there would be roses. Maybe their minds were mercifully clear of the future. That's what I hope, anyway.

I own signed copies of all of Mr. Woodriff's books, except this last one he was writing next door to me and which didn't get published until after his death. I called out to him one day while he was sitting on the teak bench in his yard. Even before I saw it, I could smell he was smoking one of those small, stinky cigars. I stood at the fence and asked if I could please get his signature on a few books.

I was afraid he might be working, puzzling over a character in his head. I hated to disturb him. I've tried my hand at writing and I know how it goes—courting the imagination, putting words down until a new world builds up, mixing a little of the real with some of the made-up until it starts things you couldn't expect. I also know I'm never so happy as when I am reading, and I had never imagined that a real and famous writer—in fact, a pair of them, since the missus is also a writer—would move in next door to me.

When I asked Mr. Woodriff to sign the books, he appeared almost boyish. He seemed eager to do it for me, so I climbed through the rail fence and went over to him. I think he was not supposed to be smoking, because he acted like I'd caught him at something. He puffed a rancid swirl of smoke onto some red peonies at one end of the bench and ground the cigar into the grass with the heel of his bedroom slipper. I noticed his heel stayed on the cigar.

"Sit down, sit down," he said to me, because he could see it was going to be a while, as I had brought six books over that first time. I sat down at the far end of the bench and put the stack of books between us, then handed him my pen.

My wife was still living at this time and Mr. Woodriff very kindly inquired after her. I said she was now in remission and we were hoping, God willing, she would stay that way. I felt a little emboldened by actually being in his yard. I told him I lit a candle for him at Mass every time I lit one for my wife. He didn't seem embarrassed at all about this. In fact, he just very quietly said, "Thank you." Maybe I should have let it go at that, but I added that I hoped his treatments were going okay. There was no use pretending I didn't know he was traveling back and forth every week for radiation.

"I'm doing just fine," he said. "Nothing to it. It's over in sixty seconds and I don't feel a thing."

Before they left for Seattle one day I'd asked if I could do anything to help out, and his wife allowed me to water her sweet peas, which are on a trellis against my fence. That's when she'd told me about the brain radiation.

The brain—well, it gave me pause, I can tell you, to think what might be going through Mr. Woodriff's mind, and his wife's, too—knowing there was a tumor where he worked and imagined. Still, I learned later he was going to his desk every day, writing those last things, and she was helping him.

After my wife's death, when I finally came to myself again, I noticed my neighbor's yard needed mowing, and I asked her would she mind if I ran my mower over it. She said her brother had been mowing it while he'd been out of work, but he'd recently found a real job. She would have to hire somebody all right, she said.

I told the widow it was no trouble and it would give me pleasure to mow her lawn, as by now I had read her stories and poems, too, along with Mr. Woodriff's. I'd also read about their life together—the final portions of which I'd witnessed without quite knowing what I was seeing.

There was the day a stocky Mexican with a pretty blond woman and

a dark-haired beauty of a girl, his wife and daughter, I assume, pulled
up with an unwieldy flat object strapped to the top of their avocado
green station wagon. At the time I thought it was a piece of construction
material and that maybe this fellow was doing Sheetrock over there.

Later, when I'd been invited into the house, I saw that what I'd
thought was Sheetrock was actually an oil painting this Mexican had
painted. The canvas had been wrapped for transport in a bedsheet. If
it hadn't been for this, I would have seen salmon leaping up a waterfall and the faint images of spirit-fish headed the opposite direction in
the painted sky—all of this bobbing down the driveway between the
Mexican and the blond and onto the porch next door.

I discovered about the painting on the day Mr. Woodriff motioned
to me and asked would I come into the house to help him with something. "Sure. You bet," I said, and followed him into the entryway under
a chandelier tall as one of those thirty-gallon galvanized garbage cans.

I thought he was going to ask me to help him move something and
I was already deciding not to say anything about my sciatic nerve—
just to take a chance I'd be okay. But instead he opened the hall-closet
door and took out a necktie. He left the door open and I couldn't help
noticing there were a lot of ties looped over wire clothes hangers. These
neckties were already tied, as if around an invisible neck, and the neck
holes had been left wide to let the guy breathe or at least relax.

Mr. Woodriff ushered me into the TV room, which was very comfortable. I saw he must be spending a lot of time reading. At one end
of a leather couch that faced into the room was a stack of books on the
floor. I appreciated that the natural light over the back of the couch was
good for reading.

When I turned back to Mr. Woodriff, he was holding this slightly
metallic-looking, pale, salmon-colored necktie. There was an expression of utter helplessness on his face, and the tie was limp across his
outspread palms like a priest bearing the Eucharist. If we had been
in church my chin would have been up, eyes closed, and my tongue
slightly extended.

"Do you know how to tie one of these?" Mr. Woodriff asks.

At first I'm taken aback—a grown man who doesn't know how to tie a necktie? Then I recall reading somewhere that his father carried a lunch bucket. So did mine, and he didn't own a tie for some years himself. Still, I had to wonder how Mr. Woodriff made it in the halls of academe back East when he occasionally held a lectureship or a chair at this or that Ivy League university, times he must have had to meet a dean or two, or to look snappy in his tweed jacket at a banquet. Who was tying his necktie then? Somebody, or several somebodies, had certainly stocked his closet with a good supply of ready-to-slip-on neckties.

I am a man who is always learning things, so I assumed that finally Mr. Woodriff had decided to transcend his working-class preference for an open collar. He was ready to tie his own necktie and I was to be his teacher. I felt flattered by this. I almost wished his wife were there to witness the patience I was about to expend in showing her husband how to do something that, for unknown reasons, he'd been avoiding all his life. But I'd seen her leave half an hour earlier in the car with some book-sized packages I'd assumed she was mailing.

"It's a tie one of my friends gave me," Mr. Woodriff said, "and I want to wear it at the book fair in Anaheim."

"Fine," I said. "We'll fix you up." He stood looking at me with a kind of friendly curiosity while I draped the tie around my neck. It did not coordinate with the mostly red plaid flannel shirt I was wearing. I asked Mr. Woodriff to move parallel to me while I went through the steps. I flipped the tie this way and that, as slowly as possible.

Finally, when I'd asked several times, "You got that?" and repeated the procedure, I handed him the tie and told him to give it a shot. He looked baffled. Like I'd just asked him to nail his eyeball to the wall while holding the hammer between his teeth. He laughed nervously. His fingers seemed ribbed together like wings. Then he made his move. He fanned one end of the tie over the other with a nice emphatic gesture that allowed me to think briefly this would come out okay after all.

But then he just stood there, elbows out, and looked down at the tie, which was shooting off a cruel iridescent sheen in the mid-morning sunlight. I wanted to give him a hint, but I also didn't want to insult his intelligence, which was considerable, despite what I'm portraying here.

When Mr. Woodriff made the first wrong move I reached up and gently got him headed right again. Finally, though, he'd made enough wrong moves that I realized something. I'd done it. I'd tied the tie for him!

He seemed very pleased. Extraordinarily pleased. He shook my hand enthusiastically, I remember, just like I'd done something for him nobody else had ever done. But it was dawning on me that this must have happened many times before, and that Mr. Woodriff had no earthly intention, before death and God, of ever learning to tie a necktie. I mean, it was right over there on the side of his ledger with bungee jumping and ice fishing, with camel rides across the Australian desert, maybe even the Pogo Stick Olympics.

"This is great! This will keep me going just fine!" he said, and walked a few steps away into the bathroom to check my work in the mirror. The collar on his sports shirt wasn't right for a tie, but I guess he was picturing himself in his dress shirt and suit jacket. He liked what he saw.

Then he did something I realized I'd seen in my mind's eye a moment before it happened. He reached up, and like a sheriff who has interrupted a small-town lynching, he loosened the tie from his throat and lifted it over his head.

My neighbor seemed suddenly more free, like any man who's nearly lost his life. How could I help but be glad for him? I knew what he was up against, in more ways than one. I forgot all about being his failed teacher-of-the-necktie. Instead I looked around the room at the warm spruce paneling, the braided rug, the way the sun, shining through the skylight, illuminated the very place he was standing. I just appreciated the comfortable circumstances Mr. Woodriff had managed to find for himself. I knew from things his wife had said over the fence that it was a difficult time for him.

"Look at this painting our friend Alfredo gave us," Mr. Woodriff said, as he pushed me eagerly along by my elbow toward the living room. But I stopped in the dining room doorway, staring into the living room at this huge painting. Salmon were leaping across it. I took in how they were balancing there on the edges of their deaths. Some were in the river while others were leaping above a waterfall. I had to fight the impulse to touch the painting, to feel the ridges in the river current and the waterfall. Mr. Woodriff must have noticed my hands rising, hovering before the painting, because he said, "Go ahead. It's okay."

I looked to see if my hands were clean, then I moved them very lightly with the current, across the canvas. It felt like minnows flicking against my fingertips. Still, I knew nothing was really moving except the blood in my veins. I let my fingers follow the lines of color and shape the Mexican painter had spent a month or more pressing into this canvas with oil paint on a brush. It occurred to me that all the time he must have been painting he had to know his friend was dying. He would have had to guess that. Yet he'd also probably been glad Mr. and Mrs. Woodriff had each other—that had to strike him. And the fish too. He must have been glad, as he painted each one, that nothing was going to get in the way of their leaping along like that.

It was all there in that painting—joy and sadness and destiny and friendship and farewell. I admit I was weak in the knees when I turned back into the room. I saw Mr. Woodriff, my neighbor, still holding the necktie he was going to slip back over his head in a few days in California, cinching it up to his Adam's apple, like he'd tied it himself.

I was his accomplice, and we smiled at each other that day in his living room, like we'd just cleaned out a bank and each of us had a pretty woman waiting for us to spend the money on. And we did, too—both our wives still with us then, and that miracle of life itself, too, ours—for however long it lasted. We had it all.

That was the most memorable encounter I had with Mr. Woodriff. When his son comes to stay a few days each summer with his stepmother, my widowed neighbor, I feel strangely like I'm back in Mr. Woodriff's young vigorous days, shaking hands with him at full strength, his hand pressing so hard on mine that the wedding ring I've moved onto my right hand smarts to the bone.

"So, you knew my dad," the son says to me in a kind of simple wonderment, smiling. He's the spitting image of his father, only young and alive.

"I did," I say. "I sure did." And I'm sorry I don't have more to add, since my meetings with his father were really so incidental. I suppose I could tell him about the neckties, but somehow I think that's just between Mr. Woodriff and me.

Sometimes I look over and see the son sitting alone where his father sat on the teak bench. I've noticed him helping my neighbor pick the apples when he occasionally visits her in September, and once in February, they pruned and mulched the roses together. Each time he leaves he is carrying a few things of his father's. He had a briefcase and raincoat this last time. He was beaming and he came over to the fence to show me and to thank me for helping "my mom." That's what he calls his stepmother. I think to myself this is decent, kind of him, really, to refer to her as his mom, since she has told me he is the closest to a son she will probably ever have. I tell him it's no trouble. I just do her lawn when I do mine.

But mowing my neighbor's lawn has gotten to be something I actually look forward to. I like to make a swirling green current the way I cut the grass, so the lawn has a river, an invisible river of pattern with ridges of energy cut right where I've moved my body along behind the mower. I work up a good rhythm. There's a kind of hum running inside me so pleasurably I forget what time it is, or whether the darkness is falling, as it often does. I'm moving with the current under the boughs of the cedar trees. When I'm finished and have shut off the mower, my neighbor comes out of the house to stand next to me.

I've never told her about the dream I have repeatedly, in which she crosses to me on the freshly cut lawn and holds out one of Mr. Woodriff's already-tied neckties, loosened to slip over my head. I bend my head down, but even so, she still has to reach up. It's like I'm receiving a medal after performing in some amazing exhibition of human will and daring, only I can't think what I've done to deserve this tie coming over my head. I feel ordinary and humbled as the tie slips down to my shoulders, but my neighbor seems so sure about what she's doing that I just give over. I go ahead and cinch the necktie, sliding the knot under my Adam's apple. It's then I feel an unexpected moment of satisfaction. Like the already-tied necktie, this peacefulness also seems somehow to have been ready for me.

In the dream I have the sense that Mr. Woodriff is advising me, telling me it's okay to leave some things to others, the way he managed his closetful of neckties. I wake up feeling greatly calmed and included, remembering how he let me help him that day. Then I realize this is the same feeling I have after I've cut my neighbor's lawn.

We admire the lawn together awhile, taking silent note of its rushing, a low murmur in the leaves of the big maple near the garage. After a minute or two she thanks me, but neither of us goes anywhere. We survey the sweep and eddies of the lawn together, and for a moment a stupendous calm falls over that small corner of the world. It's then I take leave of her and go back to my own house to fix the evening meal. The same way she must be doing over there.

Rain Flooding Your Campfire

Mr. G.'s story, the patched-up version I'm about to set straight, starts with a blind man arriving at my house. But the real story begins with my working ten-hour days with Norman Roth, a blind man who hired me because he liked my voice.

My job included typing, running errands, filing, and accompanying the blind man to court. But most of the time I was reading out loud to him from police reports. We were working research and development for the Seattle Police Department.

Those days, before qualified people like Norman got real consideration, a blind man working for the police was rare, not to say bizarre. But they left us alone, those other researchers and developers. They gave us a cubicle with no windows and shut the door. That was okay by Norman. He liked it fine and I guess I did too. It was my job, after all.

Norman was a chain-smoker. He had a little chain he pulled from his vest pocket and rattled the first time he broke the news. Then he laughed and lit up. Sometimes I could barely make out the silo on the state fair calendar behind him. But we did okay. We listened to each other's stories, tried to make work interesting, even brought treats to share. Frequent breaks made sense, once we realized nobody was keeping tabs on us. What I'm saying is, we edged into friendship during those ten-hour days.

After our work at the SPD wrapped up, Norman and I corresponded by tape, and once in a blue moon we'd telephone. A while later he got married and passed through a series of low-grade jobs for the feds.

Then, with the help of his wife, Caroline, who was sighted, he quit the government and started his own business.

I'd made a few wild swerves and ended up moving back East, working at a gas company and living with Ernest, who, for the most part, understood a woman's life hadn't started the minute he walked through the door. He also knew about my ten-year friendship with the blind man. So, when Norman came out East and called from New York City to arrange a visit, Ernest didn't make a big deal. He griped a little, sure. But that's in the nature of things. It probably made things easier that Norman was in mourning after his wife's death, and that his visit to me was part of his journey to see her relatives. Ernest could hardly object under these circumstances.

Norman and I had a saying in our Seattle days when things bummed us out. "Rain flooding your campfire," we'd say to each other, and whatever it was didn't seem so bad. But there was no one to say that to after I read Mr. G.'s version of Norman's visit. All I could think of was the tender, painful things about my friend Mr. G. hadn't known to tell.

Gallivan is Mr. G.'s real name. He and I work graveyard at the gas company. I have a repertoire of sixties songs I hum, two of which will send him flaming from the room—"Maggie May" and "It's All Over Now." I'm also an intermittent whistler. If Mr. G. were doing the work he's paid to, my habits wouldn't be a problem. But most of the time he's stealing time at his novels and stories. Nothing he writes gets published. Does that stop him? He claims he needs a breakthrough with the editors. My opinion is, he'll type till kingdom come, inflicting this stuff endlessly on his unfortunate fellow workers.

If Mr. G. were an out-and-out liar I would have more respect for his storytelling. As it is, he can't imagine anything unless he gouges himself with the truth, and that makes it hard for those who know what really happened. The result is the "marble-cake" effect. Aside from this, he's not an altogether bad guy. He did, by default, invite Norman to dinner when he appeared a day earlier than expected.

Ernest and I were just locking the front door, heading to Mr. G.'s, when the phone rang. It was Norman. He was at the train station, wondering where I was.

"I'm here in my house," I said.

"Oh dear," he said. I could picture him touching his watch with the days of the week nubbed into it—a watch he no longer owned, as it turned out.

"It's Friday," I said. "You're a day ahead of me, Norman. No problem," I lied. "I'll be right down to get you." I managed to sound cheerful, practically eager. I phoned Mr. G., who said it would be fine to bring Norman to dinner. Ernest had beefed up a drink, switched on the TV, and stretched out on the couch, so I decided to drive to the station alone.

"Ernest," I said. "Please clear those keepsakes and stack the throw rugs on the porch." I was still worrying about electric cords and a faulty railing as I pulled out of the drive.

When Norman married, I'd been grateful for his having Caroline, but I also liked her on her own ground, not just because she was devoted to my friend. I'd been sorry, for both their sakes, that I was so far away when she fell ill. Norman told me in one of his calls before her death more than I could absorb about the cancerous brain tumor that was taking her from him. There'd been months of deterioration. Near the end, we'd recalled better times, once early in their courtship when I'd taken them camping at Mount Angeles. Before she lost her voice, his wife had been looking at the pictures with him, describing them to Norman. The photos of that long-ago trip gave them solace, he said. He used that word, "solace."

"Strange, her losing her voice like that," Norman told me. "Oh, she knew everything. Just couldn't make a peep." He said she would give him little pressure signals on his hand—yeses and noes to questions he formulated. "I had to talk for both of us. 'Want to try some physical therapy?' I'd ask. 'Okay, sure,' I'd say. 'Need that pillow under your shoulders? All right. The window up? Some fresh air?'"

When I arrived at the station, Norman was standing next to a small black valise.

"Norman!" I said, locating myself in front of him. We embraced, then he stepped back, leaned forward, and fumbled for my face.

"I'm so humiliated," he said, then planted a kiss hard on my jaw. "A day early! I could evaporate!"

"Now, now," I said. I took his arm and he picked up the valise. "You're here. That's what matters. I just wish I'd had the whole day to look forward to you."

We made our way as far as the taxi stand when he stopped, let go of my arm, set the valise down, and took an object the size of a deck of cards from his shirt pocket. "Look at this. My new computerized watch. I guess it was misprogrammed on the day." He pushed a switch activating a voice: "Sat-ur-day: Fi-ive for-ty-ni-en and fif-ty sec-onds." A melodious bell tone sounded.

"That's something," I said. He returned the voice-clock to his pocket, took up his bag, and we made our way to the car. I situated him, stowed the valise, then got behind the wheel. "Good to see you, Norm!" I said, and patted him on the arm.

I genuinely liked this man and was very moved by the fact he'd taken the trouble to visit me at this difficult time in his life. "Don't you worry about a thing," I assured him. "Mr. Gallivan says you're welcome to join us for dinner. He's a writer," I told Norman. "He's written six novels and three books of nonfiction. Right now he's suffering writer's block, so he's taking up slack by entertaining people from work."

Norman was fresh from having visited his dead wife's relatives in Vermont. (Mr. G. places them in Connecticut.) Visiting me was his last stop before returning to Seattle. He confessed he didn't miss Caroline as much now as he'd thought he would. "It's a terrible thing," he said. "But true." He was fingering my dashboard, trying to tell the make.

"This isn't the same car you had," he said.

"That one bit the dust long ago," I said. "I call this one 'Old Blue.'"

Mr. G.'s story begins as we get out of the car at my house and I help Norman up the steps. The narrator sees his wife (that's me!) gripping the arm of the blind man, guiding him toward the house. Here he is, catching a view of the wife in a moment of intimacy with a blind man.

Norman leaned on my arm as we took the steps. "That one nearly got me," he said. On the porch I held back the screen and asked Norman to step inside.

Ernest wasn't around. I set the valise at the end of the couch, moved some newspapers, and Norman sat down. In no time I'd stepped into the kitchen and mixed a couple of Bloody Marys.

Soon we began to reminisce. We sipped our drinks and called up names at the police department—Barbara Dukes, a female officer we'd liked—still and forever, we imagined, in juvenile. Then I mentioned Sergeant Smiley, in the bad checks department.

"Oh, you mean *Chuckles*," Norman said, arching his chest and leaning back to laugh. "Gee, it's so dark in here I can't *feel* where I'm going," Norman used to say, then purposely bang into a file cabinet. He used to do that a lot, change things from sighted terms to hearing, smelling, or touching. Then he'd laugh his big, booming laugh.

Norman was trying to locate an ashtray on my coffee table. I placed one under his hand. I'd nearly forgotten Ernest when he came down the stairs. Before he could sit down, I motioned him toward us.

"Norman," I said to my friend, "this is Ernest, the man I live with. Ernest, Norman Roth." Norman got to his feet. His hand came up like a pistol, thumb cocked. Ernest looked at the hand, then took it. He was not thrilled to have a blind man in his house. (Mr. G. at least has that much right.)

"Pleased to meet you," Norman said brightly, furrowing his brow as if straining to see. He pumped Ernest's hand like the Tin Man in *The Wizard of Oz,* then reached to relocate his place on the couch before stiffly sitting down again.

"Heard a lot about you," Ernest said.

"Nothing too bad, I hope," Norman said. "I wonder, could I get a light off you, Ernest, if you're still up?"

Ernest fished for his lighter and handed it to me. I flicked it, then touched the flame to the cigarette Norman held between his lips. He inhaled deeply. Smoke issued from his mouth and nose. Once he was satisfied he couldn't be seen, Ernest took a chair near the couch.

"How was the train ride?" he asked. He lifted his bourbon and took a swig.

"Swell, just swell," Norman said. "After I got the porter trained to bring me drinks, it was very pleasant." He put a hand awkwardly inside his jacket lapel and kept it there. He smiled, nodded silently. Suddenly he remembered his cigarette ash. He withdrew the hand and started pinching the air above the coffee table. When he'd located the rim of the ashtray, he knocked his ash expertly and smiled toward the unknown room, obviously enjoying the fact he was on top of things. He lifted his drink and took a long draw.

I should say he's not blond, as Mr. G. describes him. He's bald, except for close-shaven sideburns and a band of hair at the back of his neck. Because his eyes are clouded he's always seemed balder to me than he is. From the start I felt invisible when Norman looked at me. A person could stare back as long as they wanted and not meet the smallest glimmer in those eyes.

"Ever see one of these?" Norman said, offering his voice-clock in Ernest's direction. "Little bugger got me here a day early."

Ernest reached across the coffee table. "Six-twen-ty-four and ni-en sec-onds," the watch said, then the cherubic bell sounded.

"Great little gadget," Ernest said. "How much did it set you back?"

"Got a deal from the Bureau for the Handicapped," Norman said. He waited for the watch to touch his hand, then slipped it into his pocket.

"Good to see the taxpayers' dollars helping a few needful sorts," Ernest said. I shot him a shut-up-or-I'll-kill-you look, but he just grinned.

"We'd better head to Gallivan's," I announced. Anything to get Ernest's mouth full of food before he started wishing out loud a little federal aid would come his way. We hadn't finished our drinks, so Ernest dropped our glasses into the slots of a carry-out and headed for the car while I helped Norman.

Mr. G. lives in a brick duplex. Shrubs crowd the walkway, but Mr. G. has clipped a little passageway to his door. The whole neighborhood's a mess—cans, bottles, old newspapers, yards knee-high in grass. Naturally Mr. G. does not mention this in his account.

When Mr. G. opens the door he has on what I call his uniform—a yellow shirt, green tie, khaki trousers. He's worn these at the gasworks the three years I've known him. He probably likes not having to interrupt his thoughts with decisions while he dresses every morning.

"Welcome," Mr. G. says to Norman. "Nice you could join us." I stepped to the side so Norman could give Mr. G. one of his pile-driver handshakes.

Ernest squeezed Mr. G.'s arm conspiratorially as he walked past into the living room. Mr. G. positioned my two fellow workers in front of Norman. They each met his grip and stepped back: Sal Fischer—the soft-spoken foreman on swing shift, there with his old Lab, Ripper, and Margaret, a secretary who was dating Sal, pretty in a blue cotton print dress with red tulips along the hem. Ripper nosed Norman's crotch, then grudgingly allowed himself to be petted.

"Smell that food, Norm?" Gallivan said. "We're in the homestretch."

Norman rolled his head toward the kitchen. "I'd know pork roast at fifty paces." He fixed a grin on his face like someone waiting for his picture to be snapped.

"Amazing," Mr. G. said. "You're close. It's back ribs, made with my special Texas barbecue sauce."

I situated Norman on a sturdy chair and went into the kitchen. I knew the dinner had been on hold until we got there, so it was decent of Mr. G. to smooth that over. I could hear Norman's voice above the others. Mr. G. had begun to question him about the free availability of "talking records" for lazy but sighted readers.

"My father *can* read," Mr. G. was saying, "but he doesn't. He might listen, though. If he could just plug in a novel while he shaves or tidies up."

Norman was acting very deaf.

"Ernest," I called into the living room. When he came into the kitchen, drink in hand, I gave him the platter of ribs.

"What're you doing?" he asked. "This isn't your kitchen." His eyes had that glassy look of someone warmed up for a party long before it had started.

"I know," I said. "I'm taking charge." I dished up coleslaw and beans. I filled the water pitcher, then went into the living room to announce we were ready. By the time the others wandered into the dining room, Ernest was seated.

"Here, Norman," Mr. G. offered. "Sit next to me. I want to hear about your Independent Management Enterprises."

"Oh, that's finished," Norman said. "Now that my wife's gone, I don't have the heart for it."

"I'm sorry, I didn't catch that," Mr. G. said and cocked his head. "Gone?" He held his eyes on Norman a moment, then unbuttoned his cuffs, rolled up his sleeves, and forked a side of ribs onto his plate. He raked another portion onto Norman's, then reached across him to serve Margaret, who kept trying to catch my attention, as though I should signal her what to do.

Norman lifted a row of ribs from his plate and began to chew vigorously. He leaned over the table so as not to drop anything onto his lap or the floor. We got into some serious eating. Bones clacked onto our plates. I imagined Norman heard that sound. I'd been enjoying how, without the slightest concession to the sighted world of manners, he licked barbecue sauce from his fingers, when suddenly he pushed his chair back and stood up uncertainly.

"Where's the loo, if you'd be so kind?" The British accent he put on made his question sound refined, almost invisible. He asked it roughly in the direction of the light fixture, then took a step into the table, like one of those TV monsters who can see to kill, but that's about it. Margaret looked alarmed, as if he might stoop and carry her off. I got to my feet and led Norman down a hallway.

"The facility's to your right," I said. "I'll wait for you, Norm." I switched on the light for him, realized what I'd done, then flicked it off.

I heard Norman's watch go off, then the water running. It ran a long time. When he didn't come out, I listened harder. I could hear sobbing. I stood there thinking what to do, then knocked softly and the sobbing stopped. I thought he might really break up if I took his arm when he came out, so I went back to the table and asked Ernest to go get him.

"What'd he do, fall in?" Ernest said. He moved the bones on his plate to one side and helped himself to more ribs. Then he looked wearily at me, pushed his chair back, and got up.

In a little while I could hear Ernest and Norman bumping along the hallway. It was then that Ripper broke from under the table. He scrabbled across the hardwood floor and began to tear at Norman's trouser leg. Norman would have been hearing a lot of growling and slavering at his ankles. Sal cursed, rose from his chair, and caught Ripper's collar. He pulled so hard he collided with the table edge. For Norman it was a yowl, then a series of thuds spiced with cursing. He looked strangely disheveled with his trouser cuffs askew.

When things settled down, I mentioned a TV special I didn't want to miss, thinking to head us home. "It's on the continuing threat of nuclear war," I said. Mr. G. threw down his napkin and said, "I'd love to see that. My TV's on the fritz. We need to face up to the horror of what *could* happen, even if we can't do anything." Mr. G. deftly turned the cleanup over to Margaret and Sal, and followed us through the undergrowth to the car.

"I want to hear about your dreams," Gallivan said to Norman as he slid into the backseat beside him. "Is it true that if someone were throwing, say, a lemon meringue pie at you in a dream—you'd experience the taste of 'lemon pie'; then you'd feel sticky meringue all over your face?"

Norman rocked back and forth against the seat. "That's about it, kiddo."

None of the dinner scene just described or the lemon pie remark makes it into Mr. G.'s story. He also removes himself entirely from a scene in which, purportedly, a blind man, plus a husband and wife, watch a TV program and the wife falls asleep. One thing is true: I did fall asleep. But not before I'd taken Norman and his bag upstairs to the spare room. I plumped his pillows and helped him locate an ashtray and towels I'd placed on a nightstand. Then he sat on the bedside, tipped his head back, and his blind eyes ranged off toward a Mexican vaquero on a velvet wall hanging my brother had bought me in Juárez.

"Caroline's mother," he said. "I think I could have gotten through it okay except for her."

"We'll have a good talk tomorrow, like old times," I said. The vaquero in his spangled sombrero, poised to give a bull the slip, begged me to mention him, but I didn't. Norman could get along without him.

"I just want to tell you this one part," Norman said. He let his head roll back, righted himself, and leaned forward. "After the biofeedback petered out, Caroline's mother'd do things like have her refuse drugs for the pain. 'She says she doesn't want those pills,' her mother would say. 'She says she can handle it. Can't you, honey?' I mean, imagine me watching someone *else* put words into Caroline's mouth."

I thought about the word "watching," how some of my friends would have tittered at this. But I knew Norman *had* "watched." He gave keen attention to details. I remembered the last time I'd heard him say the word "watched." "I love to *watch* the flames"—he'd said. Our campfire was blazing on that long-ago mountainside and the heat of the flames danced against our faces. We watched.

I stood up and eased my hand under Norman's elbow. I wanted to hear him out, but knew it wasn't the time.

"We'll sit a little, then say good night," I said, as we entered the living room. I coached Norman past my big paradise palm toward the couch. Mr. G. was fine-tuning the set. Ernest had his shoes up on the coffee table. I seated Norman, then told him I was going upstairs to get ready for bed. I glanced at Ernest, who jiggled his eyebrows when he heard me say "bed."

After I'd changed I came downstairs and took a place on the couch near Norman. He'd begun to nod, but I couldn't tell if he was napping or just agreeing to something he was thinking. Mr. G. was banging ice cubes in the kitchen. Ernest lifted his glass in my direction and gave me the old glitter-eye, so I flipped my robe, hoping it would accelerate getting upstairs. But the TV was on and Norman suddenly asked a question.

"What's he mean, 'limited nuclear war'? How limited is it if they obliterate Europe?"

"Next war you're fried, eyeballs and all," Ernest said.

"Or gassed or shot," Norman said. "For once I'm glad I'm not able-bodied."

Mr. G. returned, a drink in each hand. He'd loosened his tie and I could tell he was on the scent of "material." An aircraft carrier as big as three hotels moved heavily across the screen. My eyes were shutting down and I'd be asleep sitting up in no time, but I couldn't seem to move. Ice cubes were clinking in glasses. *Norman hears those ice cubes,* I thought hazily, and felt close to him in the old ways, those times I'd had to think what he needed for an entire day. I also recalled helping him across a log over a river as we'd headed up Mount Angeles, how scared Caroline had been. But Norman had trusted me on the unsteady log, the river rushing and deep, ten feet below us. That trust still held a place with me, that's why Norman is here, I thought.

The word "capability" occurred repeatedly in the voice from the TV. Then I heard Norman ask Ernest to find a piece of paper and some scissors. I must have dozed because when I woke up, my robe had fallen open. Ernest, Mr. G., and Norman were bent over the coffee table. Mr. G. had Norman by the hand and was moving his fingers over a piece of paper. "That's the nose right there," Mr. G. was saying. "Feel that?"

"What are you doing?" I asked.

"Helping him *see* a missile," Ernest said. "We cut one out of paper."

"Flash," Norman said. "That means a sudden burst of light."

Ernest laughed. He shook Mr. G.'s arm. "Hey, try cutting out a flash."

"But the word 'light.' What does that really mean to you?" Mr. G. asked Norman. "I mean, I could say 'a sudden flash of sagebrush' and it would be all the same, wouldn't it?"

"A nuclear flash would be blinding," Norman said. "In some things, I'm ahead of you."

As Mr. G. tells it, the program was on cancer hot spots in the body, so they weren't examining the cutout of a missile at all, but a drawing of the stomach. Mr. G. ties this in nicely with the death of Norman's wife. The narrator in Mr. G.'s story, an inarticulate sort, experiences blindness through his blind visitor. Mr. G. says he's considering a twist in his rewrite, maybe bringing in Norman's intrusive mother-in-law.

What really happened was that I cinched my robe shut, got up, and switched off the TV. "Enough's enough," I said. "Good-bye, world."

I left the three of them sitting there and went upstairs. It was a hot, muggy night. I took off my robe, then my nightgown, and got into bed. I could hear Ernest on the stairs, but he didn't come into the bedroom. Then I heard voices outside on the lawn. It was summer and the screens were on, so whole good-night love scenes from the neighborhood teenagers, or even lovemaking noises from the nearby houses, would drift through the windows.

"Where have you been?" I asked when Ernest finally came into the bedroom.

"Having a cigarette," he said.

"Where's Norman?"

"Nobody ever told your blind man the constellations, so Gallivan's doing it. Out there telling him the stars." He undressed, put on his pajamas, and got into bed. Soon he reached over and began patting my hair the way he does when he wants to get something started. Then he discovered I was naked and his motions took on another eagerness.

"How's Gallivan getting home?" I asked, paying Ernest no mind.

"It's a great night for walking," he said.

I threw back the covers, got up and went over to the open window, raised the shade, and looked down. There was Mr. G. holding Norman's arm over his head as if he'd won a prizefight. They were illuminated from above by the street lamp.

"This here, see? That's the Big Dipper." Mr. G. moved Norman's arm in an arc. "The Dipper's handle is along there."

I couldn't see the stars. Nobody could, because the sky was overcast. I'd looked at stars since childhood, but never learned much about constellations. Oh, I knew some bore the names of animals, and Greek gods, and I might have found Orion if my life depended on it, but so far it hadn't.

"What stars?" I asked. "Ernest, take a look at this."

Ernest got out of bed. He stood behind me and leaned over my shoulder. Two men stood in our front yard with their arms raised. Mr. G. was calling out the stars like a stationmaster.

Ernest cupped his hands around my breasts and rested his chin behind my ear. We saw Mr. G. lead Norman into the middle of the street. Then a siren went off somewhere. I began to think how strange it is that stars are silent. What if each star made the smallest noise—say the insistent tone of Norman's watch—what an enormous din would pour down on us!

Mr. G. had turned Norman in another direction entirely. Headlights of a car rose like a strange bloated moon over the hill, beamed on them a moment, then swept precariously down another street. Ernest and I got back into bed, but we could still hear them. It would be just like Gallivan, in some jaunty hail-fellow-well-met good-bye, to forget totally Norman was blind, and simply strike out for home. Which is exactly what he did.

I had wanted to stay awake until Norman was safely inside and in his room—but Ernest's hands began to move over me until my shape seemed to rise and drift from the room. I don't even remember when I closed my eyes.

Somewhere in my uneasy sleep, I saw Norman standing in the front yard. His face was turned skyward and he was holding on to a tree as if he were afraid some force might pull him from the earth. The sky inside his mind must have seemed hugely populated after all the instruction he'd taken.

About then I jerked awake. It was so warm in the house I didn't bother to put on my robe, just made my way downstairs in the dark. My dream had uncannily intersected the real—Norman was there under the trees. I unlatched the screen and went down the porch steps toward him. I didn't speak, but I had a feeling he knew I was there. The houses were dark now and the maples, in a light breeze, made a soft rushing above us that could just as well have belonged to the stars, visible now and blinking calmly down.

I should have been cold in the night air, but I wasn't. I heard myself say something consoling as I stood beside Norman. I felt completely unconcerned that I was naked, as if I were somehow still dreaming and protected by the blindness of the world to dreams. It was one of those crossover moments where life overflows, yet somehow keeps its shape. Norman let go of the tree and said, "That you?" "Yes," I said. Then I slipped my hand under his elbow and, as if the entire world were watching and not watching, I guided our beautiful dark heads through a maze of stars, into my sleeping house.

The Mother Thief

With the electric attentiveness of a deer in headlights, Jeanette fixed on the contents of the six-page letter. It had been composed by her cousin Felicia while she and her live-in love, Dave, had been on a camping trip in Canada. The envelope exuded the heady scent of kerosene and cinders from their campfire sifted from the pages. It was the first letter written by lantern light Jeanette had ever received. She assumed that the primitive lighting and general surround of darkness, inhabited by wildlife, had contributed to the toothy nature of the letter's contents.

"Dave is not a drug addict," Felicia insisted in a script that flickered at an uphill slant. "This untruth, spread so thoughtlessly to the family," Felicia believed, "must have started with you." Furthermore, Felicia maintained that any damage to a borrowed chain saw had been purely accidental, and if Jeanette had not been prepared for damage, she shouldn't have lent it.

"Dave," Felicia continued, "takes nothing stronger than aspirin or Tylenol. An occasional Advil." There was a coda about the nature of unconditional love, which Jeanette guessed had been meant to reassure her, but which tasted strangely, given the rest. Finally, Felicia cautioned her once again about "thoughtless and gossipy remarks to others."

Still and all, gossip had become the family's order of the day—ever since Felicia had been contacted by her birth mother. The family had been moving vicariously toward the reunion of birth mother and daughter, as if it were happening to each of them. Jeanette, however, felt the whole affair had thrown the family out of alignment. Prior to this, Felicia, because she was adopted, had belonged to them all, but now she seemed to be moving beyond them. Jeanette's participation in this new dimension of Felicia's life had been complicated by their falling-out over the borrowed chain saw.

Jeanette hadn't minded lending the saw. It had belonged to her father and had been given to her after his death. But when it came back with the chain broken, it unexpectedly acquired fresh stature in relation to the loss of her father. She'd made the mistake of mentioning the incident to one of her mother's three sisters, who then mentioned it to Felicia's adoptive mother, Ricky, who took the matter straight to Felicia. By this time, whatever Jeanette had said was significantly embellished by the family penchant for drama and chaos.

Jeanette had been stung to the core by Felicia's punitive campfire letter. When she told her mother about it, she was shocked to learn her mother had received a copy of the letter. Felicia also mailed a copy to Aunt Hallie, the cousins' mutually favorite aunt—the person Jeanette believed most likely to have speculated about Dave's post-Vietnam drug habits. Aunt Hallie's own son had been sent for drug rehabilitation and it had been such a blow to her that she now saw drugs everywhere. When she visited someone's house she would disappear into the bathroom. The muted snapping of plastic containers, as they spilled from medicine cabinet to sink, would signal her inventory. Aunt Hallie could tell you what everyone in the family was "on."

Jeanette felt betrayed and isolated by the circulation of what she would have considered personal correspondence. Had Felicia really imagined she could turn Jeanette's own mother against her? *And* Aunt Hallie? She smiled to realize her mother must be taking pleasure as she watched her daughter and adopted niece try to outdo each other in their ministrations toward her.

Ultimately Jeanette arrived at the conclusion that Felicia was a woman starved for mothers. Ever since Aunt Ricky and Uncle Jack, Felicia's adoptive parents, had retired to a small town in Oregon near their natural daughter, Phyllis, Felicia had been quietly bereft. Now it seemed her cousin had converted her grief into action and was aggressively shoring up her familial bulwark by attempting to appropriate Jeanette's mother, both in sympathy and fact.

However hurt she'd been by Felicia's recent actions, Jeanette still regarded her as the sister she'd never had. Their misunderstanding had unexpectedly forced Jeanette to experience what it was to be outside the family enclosure, something her cousin probably experienced more often than she'd been aware. To set things right, she'd invited Felicia to Sunday brunch. The meeting, at one of the town's more upscale restaurants, was timed to follow Felicia's return from Miami. By then Jeanette knew her cousin would have encountered her birth mother and there would be plenty to talk about.

They hugged each other in the entry of the restaurant, a faint-hearted motion that lingered awkwardly as they waited for the hostess to seat them. Not a moment too soon she maneuvered them to an empty booth. They slid onto vinyl-cushioned seats that gave sad little puffs of air as they settled. The bustle of the restaurant quickly drew them in, enclosed and protected their meeting. They'd barely glanced at the extensive menu when Felicia's account of her birth mother began to tumble forth with the excited onrush of a waterfall. From sheer force, all else receded.

"I woke up to find this woman rubbing my feet!" Felicia said, as if a python had cinched her ankles. "Imagine! I'd just met her the night before and she takes this liberty."

Because Jeanette was particularly sensitive in her feet, she felt her toes draw inward in her white slip-ons. The pressure of Felicia's story caused the cousins to choose their breakfasts hurriedly while their waitress hovered.

"Totally weird," Felicia said, rushing on. "She asks, 'Do you mind if I give you a massage?' and I say I'm not exactly comfortable with that; no, I'm really *not*. She tells me I don't know what I need, that *she's* the mother and *she* needs to 'bond' with me. She says, 'You were just days old when I last set eyes on you.' She tells me she has to rub my fingers and toes, to get the *feel of me* back into her."

"And you let her?" Jeanette asked. Felicia had always been so take-charge that this scene refused to include the collected person sitting across from her, who didn't break stride in her account, even as their breakfasts arrived.

"The woman," Felicia said, "Bernadine's her name, but now I call her 'the woman.' She says my body came out of her body and she needs to touch me *all over.* 'I want to give you an all-over body massage,' she tells me. For two years she's been reading books on birth mothers getting back with their children. But she came up with this idea herself—a full body massage."

"You let her?" Jeanette asked incredulously.

"I kept saying I wouldn't be comfortable," Felicia said, an edge to her voice. "But she'd say something else. Not persuasion, really, but like it was going to happen, no matter what I said. Then I'd say *again* I wouldn't be comfortable. Don't ask me how—before I knew what was what, she got me to take off my clothes and lie on the floor. There's a blanket under me. I'm in the buff, not a stitch over my hind end, and she's oiling me like she's basting a roast. I mean I was in the oven and cooking." Without taking her eyes from her cousin, Jeanette lifted a small pewter pitcher and absently drizzled hot syrup over her pancakes.

Later Felicia would tell Jeanette's mother, as if to shield herself in aftermath, that she'd never allowed her birth mother to so much as lay a pinky on her. The discrepancy in the stories caused Jeanette and her mother to break into an unexpected round of hilarity. It was contagious. They didn't even know exactly why they were laughing, but they laughed until tears ran down their cheeks. Jeanette thought it was relief, pure and simple, that Felicia had her evasions and moments of unaccountable surrender too. Still, their sympathies remained firmly with her. They saw that whatever she told others, it was important to Felicia that her birth mother had accepted her in the moment, no matter how unsympathetically she might present the woman afterward. They also saw that the presence of the birth mother had been so powerful that she'd managed to drive Felicia into a panic of capitulation, and this reluctant giving over, as much as anything, had managed to alienate Felicia from the birth mother, at least for the time being.

"Why'd you stay at her house in the first place?" Jeanette asked her cousin.

"I didn't want to insult her before I even knew her," Felicia said. "Hospitality was the first thing she wanted to give me. I thought okay, I didn't take anything from you all these years, it's okay to accept this. Wrong," Felicia said. "Dead wrong."

"Why didn't you go to a motel when she started getting weird?" Jeanette was thinking what she might have done.

"The plane ticket took everything I'd saved," Felicia said, as if stating the obvious.

"You're lucky she didn't try to spoon-feed you icky yellow squash from a baby-food jar," Jeanette said.

"Pablum," Felicia said, picking up the tease. "I should have screamed for my pablum!" Now they were giggling like schoolgirls and Jeanette began vigorously to slice her pancakes into bite-sized pieces. Felicia spooned salsa over her omelette, then speckled it with Tabasco for good measure.

"What's scary is how reasonable she sounded. She told me my father is Colombian. (Don't tell Aunt Hallie!) He came to the States to train for his family's hotel business back in Cartagena. He'd wanted to adopt me on his own, take me back to Colombia, but the woman, Bernadine, was too furious. My birth mother discovered he'd not only cheated on his Colombian wife, but on her, too. She told me that his having a wife was one thing, but she couldn't forgive him for making it with this 'two-bit hussy' who slung hash in the cafeteria. So the big news for me is that I got adopted out by default. Bernadine caught my birth dad at sexual Ping-Pong, then dumped him *and* me. Now when I do something nuts I have to wonder if it's the Bernadine in me," Felicia said. She tore off a hunk of bread from the sourdough loaf and glanced furtively around the restaurant at customers dressed in their Sunday best.

"Before, when I didn't know my bloodline," Felicia said, "I could just be once-in-a-while-crazy like I'd invented it. If I blow a fuse now, it goes back in my mind to this woman. Bernadine. I have to wonder now if it's my genes. Maybe I'm stuck with it."

"You must feel lucky she gave you away to Aunt Ricky and Uncle Jack," Jeanette said quietly.

"We're talking big-time luck," Felicia said, her green eyes widening. "Luck so good not even the Irish have it. This woman is rubbing my butt crack with almond oil. Is this supposed to calm me down, or what? It's not to be believed. She says, 'If you were my son and you were a Sicilian bandit who'd been shot at my feet, I'd love you so much I'd lick your blood out of the dirt.' I mean, we're talking *behavior* here."

Jeanette felt more and more refreshed by the chaotic vibrancy of her cousin's ordeal, but she also began to marvel at the simplicity of her own mother and father's coupling, their steady bearing and raising of her.

"After me, she'd had two more girls by her next man," Felicia said. "She never got a son. Maybe she was imagining I was her son. Who knows how a Sicilian bandit got into it! Remember, I don't know this woman."

They seemed to have drifted far downstream from the petty disagreement over the chain saw and Felicia's accusatory letter. Maybe her cousin's "Bernadine side" had penned the campfire letter. Jeanette's mother would, of course, want to hear all the details. She was already thinking how to elude her probings when Felicia launched into the final episode.

"We fought like piranha, all teeth and gullet. God knows how I made it home without smacking her one. 'You can't win,' she kept telling me, 'I've been at this too long.' And she was right. She carried me into meanness further than I've been or ever want to go again. She's obviously tanked her way through life and never taken a direct hit. I wimped home on the plane the next day."

"What did Dave think about it?" Jeanette asked. She didn't know why she'd brought up Dave, except she was sure Dave would have freely volunteered opinons she couldn't chance making herself.

"He's such a sweetie. He felt sorry for Bernadine when she first located me. Even went to a lot of trouble helping me imagine her pain and guilt. But he's done a one-eighty. She really stripped Dave's gears." Jeanette hadn't realized Dave had gears.

"The woman phoned after I got home and said I'd treated her *just like a man.* 'A man,' she says, 'draws you up close, then pushes you away. You have to plead and beg and worm your way back. I'm your mother and you're treating me just like a man would, making me crawl and grovel, like I don't deserve anything from you.' You could wonder what kind of men she's had, right? Then she tore out all the stops. She said, 'I pity your adopted mother.'" Felicia's eyes snapped with righteous anger. She drew herself up against the back of the booth. Jeanette located her napkin and held to it in the close quarters.

"I went totally ballistic," Felicia said with obvious pleasure. "I borrowed a page from Dave. I said, 'You fucking-bitch-motherfucker, don't you *ever* call this house again. Don't you assume you know *anything* about the people who loved and raised me while you were so busy nursing your ego.'" Jeanette felt singed. She took a sip from her water glass.

"Then I got off the phone and just cried and cried 'til my sides ached," Felicia said. "Dave said, 'Don't waste tears.' But I said tears are never wasted. If they don't fall, what's going to soften up the hateful meanness in this world? 'Hush up,' he told me. 'If she were here she'd probably lick those salty tears right off your cheek.' It was such a dumb remark, I started to laugh. Then he called me his little Sicilian bandit and said if it would make me feel better he'd get a job working construction and hook up with the local Mafia. After that, the whole thing seemed like the worst soap opera. But you know," Felicia said, "I hadn't fazed that woman. In ten minutes she phoned me right back, and you know what? I listened. I just shut my mouth and I heard this woman talking, calm and sweet, into my ear like there was nothing I could say to make her hate me or change her mind. What could a person do? She'd decided what she needed, and she was going to have it, come hell or high water. In a certain way she still didn't need me."

Felicia seemed to have voiced the whole of it in this last remark. She'd grown calm and now appeared more fully aware of Jeanette. "I don't do everything perfect," Felicia admitted and looked down at her hands folded on the table.

It seemed for the first time during the meal that they were speaking about their misunderstanding. Jeanette marveled at how much sympathy and genuine feeling for her cousin had replaced the sense of betrayal she'd held earlier. She even felt better about sharing her mother with Felicia. She saw that her cousin might be a long while allowing herself, even in her imagination, to accept her birth mother—if she ever did— that everything was not what she'd hoped for, or expected. Until now, Jeanette had taken her own birth circumstances for granted. But she saw that to be born out of the body of a mother who'd loved and protected her and stayed beside her from the beginning was pure accident and more than that—a gift for which there was no deserving.

Jeanette knew her cousin had shared things with her she wouldn't have, except that they'd been in this family together since childhood. They'd gone swimming in the same rivers, raced ponies at the county fair, and as teenagers played Monopoly over the telephone long into the night. They'd been through deaths in the family and illnesses, weathered the inevitable feuds of relatives. In short, they'd lived with the closeness and harm of family in ways that had allowed them to come importantly together again now.

She listened as Felicia told her, "You know what—nothing's ever going to be the way it was before her hands got all over me in Miami." She told Jeanette she felt raw, that she needed somehow to heal, to toughen and cure, to be able for the next thing to happen, whatever it might be.

Jeanette opened her purse and placed her credit card on the table next to the bill. She heard her cousin say something about the woman's last words being "You're my sorrow, all those years when I couldn't find you . . . you were my sorrow." Then Felicia said tersely, "I'm nobody's sorrow."

Jeanette didn't blame her cousin for wanting to be more than a sorrow. But she knew that when you got to the bottom of most troubles, sorrow figured into it. She herself had just passed in one side of sorrow and out the other.

The smell of freshly baked bread made her think to order a loaf for her mother. While they waited, Felicia allowed as how she expected to have to deal with Bernadine "the rest of my life."

"Surely not that long," Jeanette said. Then they were laughing, almost like old times, only different—laughter with a halo of sadness around it.

Felicia reached across the table and took the credit card from beside the check and stuffed it back into Jeanette's purse. Jeanette tried to pull the card to the surface, but the waitress suddenly stepped to the table and took the cash from Felicia.

As they left the restaurant and moved toward their cars, their arms fell naturally around each other's waists.

They were back to the comforting gestures of their girlhoods. Still, a strangeness accompanied their closeness, as if an irresolvable pain had unexpectedly made a bridge for them to cross back toward each other.

Jeanette made a mental note to mention to her mother that Felicia had paid for lunch. That way her mother would know, without her having to say a word, that everything between them was again okay.

The Poetry Baron

He signed all mandates "The Poetry Baron." Or, if he wanted to particularly sweeten his way with Mary Beth—the department secretary since the first brick laid at the university—he would obsequiously pen, "The Little Baron" or "The Baronette."

He used a red ink pad and purchased a Chinese seal with a character on it, which he later discovered meant something like "Two Dead Oars." But if anyone asked, he told them it meant "Long Life and Happiness." What was important was having a civilization behind him as old as the Chinese.

ᴔ

In his poetry workshops the Baron liked to maintain the feel of a democratic organism reaching consensus, much as amoebic entities in distant committee rooms arrive at fresh terms like "the mentally challenged" or "the temporarily abled" or the "legally pernicious." The Baron often applied the latter to a new and rising class of welfare recipients who profitably aligned themselves with lawyers to form practically unbeatable teams. They had nothing to lose but time. When it came to forcing settlements out of entities as diverse as Safeway, the NRA, and Planned Parenthood, not to mention any well-heeled relatives of those on welfare, this team was wickedly effective.

He especially knew a lot about welfare mothers, since the eldest of his two daughters had been one for twenty-odd years, with the exception of a three-month hiatus when she'd opened a little hot-dog stand down at the ferry dock. All her letters began: "Dear Dad, I could sure use some money to buy . . ." And ended: "Remember, Dad, there are steps I can take if you can't find it in your heart to help me."

~

When the Baron gazed at the cherubic faces of his female students, he often thought tenderly of his daughter at eighteen, already pregnant with the child of a car thief.

One aspiring young poet, Betina Kibs, particularly appealed to him. She drew a black outline around her lips before painting them a scalding red so that the lips seemed to lift from the face and float toward him. All her poems were about getting dumped by her boyfriends, a succession of Cro-Magnons who debased and dismantled the empire of this defense-less tangle of black hair, blond lashes, golden nose rings, and chartreuse fingernails.

~

The Baron always spoke last, after his students had sufficiently mauled the poem under discussion. Once they'd shaken out its entrails and begun to feign affection for certain turns of phrase, a "good image" or a "muscular verb," he would frame his response with such circumspect benevolence they would be shamed into submission. If anyone began to jump rope with the entrails he interceded, uttering something that was, on the surface, neutral, but which carried sufficient admonitory undertow to bring the little cretins to a standstill. Something like: "You cannot prick with straw—nor pierce with scimitar." They could mull that.

~

In an effort to correct what he considered an egregious and continu-ing neglect of female art, despite critical pretenses to the contrary, he would quote only women poets; yet he scorned anthologies that iso-lated the sex as "ghettoization." In order to demonstrate graphically the inequality of the canon, he commanded his students to rip from the as-

signed anthology all poems except those by women. The binding was
so debilitated, as a result, that he passed out yarn and darning needles so
the students could sew the few remaining pages together again.

Pages and pages, entire sheaves of male poetry wafted in the breeze
created by their excited frenzy of tearing and yanking. Next, the Baron
suggested the young poets pretend they were Russians living in the time
of Anna Akhmatova under Stalin. They could turn off the heat in their
student garrets, sit around in their greatcoats drinking watered-down
tea, and memorize the male poets they were about to discard—the easy
ones, like Walt Whitman, Robinson Jeffers, or, say, Wallace Stevens's
"The Idea of Order at Key West." *They,* the Baron's beloved outposts of
the future, would be the repositories, the last living, breathing archives
of these about-to-be-transmogrified verbal megalomaniacs.

ᴄ

The students were thrilled with the stringency of this assignment.
They were all women, except for one blond chunky male student named
Alfred Greenhill, who wore mulberry-colored socks and printed all his
poems in block letters on cream-colored vellum paper his father sup-
plied from England. Greenhill's father was an English novelist who
went through paper the way elephants crush forests in Africa. Excesses
of this sort caused strange linkages in the Baron's mind—Napoleon's
memoirs scribbled onto the faces of playing cards for lack of paper on
Saint Helena.

ᴄ

The Baron's attention focused often on Greenhill. Why was he always
smiling? What drug was he taking to get that impermeable glazed-over
look? The Baron felt an inexplicable strain of cruelty in his veins when
he read Greenhill's poems. They reminded him of himself at that age—
stinking with "mossy fronds," able oracularly to "gaze across continents,"
not to mention an Audenesque penchant for admonishing "the odious
public." Napoleon would gladly have squandered this over-inflated Bambi

with Marshal Ney's Third Corps, blasted by musket fire, cut to pieces by Russian cannonballs.

The Baron thought history, like literature, provided an integrative stimulus to daily life. Both history and literature, he believed, were capable of spontaneously regenerating the collective memory as an evolving organism. Napoleon, consequently, was never far from his thoughts.

The Poetry Baron, a recovering alcoholic, drank only cranberry juice. Occasionally he energized it with a jounce of seltzer. But only occasionally. If he'd been asked how he'd managed his miraculous recovery, he would have lowered his voice to its most humble register and intoned, "Grace." But nobody asked. As a recovering drunk he was as unspectacularly sober as he'd been spectacular when to breathe was to drink.

Mary Beth left him a nonfat carob cupcake in his mailbox. On it, in gold, was a capital *B* with a little crown over it. She *did* understand.

He listened to the students recite passages by the male poets they'd memorized from the disassembled anthology. After each recitation he would ask if there were lines or images that stuck in their minds. They should write those down. Then the Baron would say, "Memory is imagination. Simply forget all *except* those shreds and tatters. After all, that's what poetry must be—memorable. If it isn't, well then it's just a load of turkey whack."

The students stared at him in wide-eyed adulation. "The significant is always incorporated into the present. If it's important, it will reassert itself. Now, go back to your garrets and burn those torn-out pages. Make a hefty little bonfire and warm your sweet tushes over it." He was sure, he added, that something deep and enduring about the nature of art-through-time would occur to them. He silently reflected on an image from an account of Napoleon, disguised as a Monsieur de Rayneval, lifting his coattails above his famous white breeches to warm his bum before a spitting greenwood fire in Warsaw.

ꙍ

Another letter had arrived from his welfare daughter, Trina. He thought it had the sweet-sour, ready-to-poison-your-picnic smell of rancid mayonnaise. Over the years she had engendered four children, each by a different man. The car thief appeared intermittently to "sponge off her," as she put it, and to babysit the two youngest, who were still at home but verging on becoming teenagers. The other three men came into focus from time to time.

Her "nest" would soon be empty, she wrote. She had recently conceived the idea she might adopt a Chinese baby girl, since children seemed to be her thing. Would he, her one and only, next-to-God father, consider signing papers declaring she had an inheritance coming? He might mention the bad hearts of his prematurely deceased father and grandfather. (Here the Baron paused and placed his right hand on his own chest.) Could he, in addition, verify that he intended to leave her substantial royalties to his fifteen books of poetry? (How, he wondered, should he break it to her that all but two of the books were out of print and that even these had netted a paltry eight hundred dollars?)

Her letter continued: could he possibly have his agent run spreadsheets of earnings for the past twenty years so future earnings could be projected? (Spreadsheets, agent, indeed!) And, if it wouldn't be too much trouble, could she charge her round-trip plane ticket to Beijing on his credit card? The baby would, she was glad to say, travel home free. While Trina was in China ransacking orphanages for just the right baby, his ex-wife would be looking after two of Trina's "four little lambs," as his daughter persisted in referring to her collective offspring.

The Baron hated how "four" rhymed with "poor." He stopped himself there.

ꙍ

Betina Kibs was waiting outside the Baron's office when he arrived. She had baked a batch of chocolate-chip cookies and handed over a dozen, tied in her muffler. The Baron was touched. He recalled Napoleon's Polish mistress, Marie Walewska, described as "beautiful but brainless." Betina put her to shame—she was beautiful in a ruined sort of way, which was the fashion. He felt drawn to her stylistic savvy, her way of affecting an engagingly repellent veneer of a future ripe before its time.

He unlocked his office door, invited the young woman inside to a chair near his desk, and unwrapped the cookies. They were fuzzed with blue nubs of wool. He picked out one that was unaffected and began to munch. Betina suddenly started to sob uncontrollably. The Baron felt concerned and protective, yet he knew it would be a mistake to leap up from his desk and throw his arms around her, as he had been wont to do with female students in his drunken pre-Baron days. He simply bowed his head and began to recite from Dorothy Wordsworth:

> *And when the storm comes from the North*
> *It lingers near that pastoral spot,*
> *And piping through the mossy walls*
> *It seems delighted with its lot.*

Betina appeared to take heart from the incantational rhythms of his recitation. Whatever had been oppressing her dissipated as suddenly as it had descended. The Baron ate another cookie. It was partly crumbled, as if she had carried it over a long and circuitous journey by horseback. Betina began exuberantly to recount Charlotte Brontë's portrayal of merry days at Thornfield Hall. She volunteered she'd been "devouring Brontë" for another class.

The Baron was pleased. He'd performed a kindly act. He had ratified the healing properties of literature. He had also eaten chocolate-chip cookies and managed to keep his hands to himself. After showing Ms. Kibs out, he opened his desk drawer and took a refreshing swig of cranberry juice. Ah, but where was his Caulaincourt to make him swerve off this sweet detour? Order through fluctuation, he reasoned, had carried him through many unsung campaigns. Why stop now?

ᴐ

"Greenhill," the Baron said, jerking the despondent and melancholy souls of the entire roomful of young female poets to attention. "What's the meaning of this drivel?!"

ᴐ

The Baron disliked committees. When he did serve, he opted for high visibility but little real responsibility and insisted on being chair. He'd recently consented to head a committee to design a memorial garden, the money to be donated by a bereft family whose son had thrown himself out a tenth-story window after being rejected by his first love.

The Baron generally fought all things nostalgic, but he conceived the idea of a modest waterfall and defended the proposal as if his Divine Majority must prevail. After their third meeting, he telephoned one recalcitrant committee member to reiterate the necessity of meditational alcoves in contemporary life. How else could the young be expected to accomplish that most important transfer of energy between the dead and the living? Between the so-called real and the possible? When his colleague disagreed with him about the waterfall, the Baron slammed the phone down on him. Anger management indeed! Blast the miserable curs with all you've got, then scrape the dead away from the gates and enter!

ᴐ

One evening his students could barely conceal their wry smiles as he entered the seminar room. (All his classes were held after dark, since he believed poetry survived best when inferior forms of light, those lacking modulation and artifice, were at a minimum. He would have conducted class by candlelight had fire codes permitted.) The students continued to titter until he demanded to know what so amused them.

"Your mouth," Greenhill volunteered. "There's a lavender rim around your lips. Like you've been drinking wine."

The Baron raised himself slowly from his comfortable chair at the head of the long table and began to pace the room with great empire-crushing strides. Finally, when he knew their hearts in their young poet-breasts must be quaking, he stared at them as the Russian Field Marshal Kutuzov had stared down the French near the Nara River. "Cranberry juice," he said. Then strode toward the forest.

∽

The Baron read his mail. Again he had not received a Guggenheim. He dropped the puny pamphlet of winners to the floor and stomped on it. This was the fourteenth year he had applied. Perhaps his courier had been waylaid. He was certain he had enemies. He felt like the beast slouching toward coal-besmutted Glasgow when he considered the ill these traitors-against-posterity contemptuously bore him. He might have shaken them off in his usual meditational stroll at dusk along the Erie Canal, but it was mid-afternoon. He did a few vehement turns around his rose garden, trying to calm himself. He threatened inwardly to migrate to Oregon and took pleasure imagining the missives of entreaty from students and colleagues that would clog his departmental mailbox. Oregon. Hiking and blueberries. Perhaps he could set up shop adjoining a casino run by Native Americans along the Columbia. He would subsist on grants to pen a verse epic on the multicultural aspects of casino life.

Gradually the roses tamed his adventurous spirit with silence. He sang a few verses of an Irish air, about Napoleon trouncing the English. The refrain cheered him: *The bonny bunch of roses, oh!*

At last, benevolence was restored. He resolved to turn his resentment into nobility of spirit. He would write a pantoum using the names of all the poets who had ever won Guggenheims.

∽

He studied himself in the mirror. A cranberry stain had inked itself imperfectly onto his upper lip, with a break at the apex. He thought he looked faintly Chinese, as in Charlie Chan, sans spats. He rubbed the stain with Irish Spring soap. But it would not come off. Like a workman, he now kept a thermos of cranberry juice with him at all times, even in the classroom. He learned to drink from it in such a way that a roseate circle formed around his lips.

The students had come to consider his mouth-ring an eccentricity, though some of the more devout claimed it was, like the stigmata, a sign of divine inclusion. At the end of a seminar on free verse he passed out packets of cherry Kool-Aid. "It's easy to love people for their strengths," he said. "But to love them for their weaknesses, now there rests true enlightenment. Human wisdom—*that* is the secret of poetry." A very silly look passed across Greenhill's face. No doubt he had spent the night roasting horseflesh on his saber point at some bivouac fire in the interminable falling snow. The tip of his nose was red.

ဟ

Trina had written to say the Chinese baby girl was at her bosom. "Thanks, Dad, for helping me save her from that terrible rat hole of an orphanage. I know she's in good health because they don't even make it to the orphanages if they're in bad health. They die, some at the hands of their own parents, and are buried in some godforsaken unmarked place." The Baron considered Napoleon's vacant tomb on Saint Helena, shorn not only of its occupant, but of the cherished willows from which the soldiers stripped souvenir branches on the day of his burial. He felt like a stripped willow himself.

The rest of Trina's letter went on to explain that, despite his recent generosity, neither of her youngest "lambs" had winter coats, not to mention that the bristles on their toothbrushes were worn to the nubs. They were down to biscuits and porridge. Her son and daughter, out on their own, weren't making it either. She could use some cash. If he didn't "pony up" she would be sure to point out to her lawyer friend that it was *his* idea for her to adopt the Chinese girl, inflicting emotional guilt and further financial burdens on her. In any dispute it would be his word against hers. All his correspondence would instantly become legal documents, simply by virtue of her accusation. If he had anything he wanted to hide, well, it would just be too bad. He would be one dead poet.

The Baron refolded the letter and wrote "Ode to House Dust."

ꕥ

He had begun to obsess about Betina. He thought he could smell chocolate-chip cookies everywhere. He hoped fervently to find her positioned outside his office door. Instead, the air seemed permeated by the giddy odor of horseflesh, no doubt roasted to feed the starving rabble. He stepped over bodies like cordwood, just to enter his humble retreat.

ꕥ

One of the more acerbic female students reported having singed the plastic shower curtains in her apartment while burning white male poetry in her bathtub. The plastic stench had alarmed other tenants. The fire department had been called. She was about to be evicted. Did anyone need a roommate?

The Baron remarked that the price of great art was that the artist be misapprehended, publicly disparaged, and ultimately exiled. Greenhill invited the homeless student into exile with him and five male students majoring in engineering.

ꕥ

The Baron took a long solitary walk by the Erie Canal at dusk. The pale oval face of Betina was seldom out of his mind now. His current wife simply thought his distracted air meant he was generating a new epic poem. He was. The heroine was mature and blond, to throw his wife off the scent. The outlines of limestone mountains appeared in misty passages at intervals, as on ancient Chinese scrolls. The poem would bear the enigmatic dedication "To My Beloved."

ꕥ

Mary Beth left a memo in his box. The committee for the memorial garden had been peremptorily dissolved. The parents of the dead student
had withdrawn funding. The Baron mused sadly on the unrecorded de-
mise of a waterfall. He made a notation in his notebook. Later that day
a snapshot of a double waterfall, labeled simply "Burney Falls," mysteriously appeared in his mailbox.

ꙅ

As in a Chekhov story, the Baron's eyes "grew oily and rapacious" when
he looked at Betina. Finally he seized a moment after class one night,
while escorting her to a rendezvous with yet another of her dolty boyfriends. He asked her to have lunch so he could suggest strategies for getting her out of a certain rut regarding her subject matter. She accepted.
The Baron went back to his office and, as if to raise a triumphal hunting horn or to sound an advance, lifted his thermos of cranberry juice
to his lips.

ꙅ

"Greenhill," the Baron roared. "You wouldn't know slant rhyme from
a banana peel if you slipped on one!"

ꙅ

Trina wrote to say her lawyer friend had informed her about something
called Renewal Rights. According to federal law, the Baron's "works"
written prior to 1978 belonged partly to her. It appeared, she wrote,
that one-fourth, or maybe as much as one-third, of any proceeds from
anthology and reprint rights, et cetera, should be coming to her. She
would naturally keep this under her bonnet, since, if her younger sister were to find out, she could conceivably claim her own share. Trina
wrote that his "legacy" was very important to her and to her lambs.
She was glad the government was making sure she "participated" in his
legacy, whether or not he intended it. This law, she pointed out, would
countermand anything he might write into his will to exclude her. She

was especially happy she would now benefit from his legacy, both after his death and now, while she was still young enough to enjoy spending the proceeds.

The Baron made a note to seek advice from his own lawyer friend.

∽

The Poetry Baron sent his students out over the weekend to feed the hungry at an inner-city soup kitchen. They needed to learn social responsibility. It should seep into their poems osmotically, he told them, not simply be barnacled on. Many of them, unlike the Chinese, had never had to share a meal dipped from the communal pot. How would they have stood up to an evening in retreat with Marshal Victor at twenty-seven below: "Frozen birds, frozen horseflesh, frozen tears."

∽

His lawyer friend had gone to Florida for an extended holiday. The Baron was left in the dark about Renewal Rights, although a voice on the telephone at the Writers' Defense League told him they could only apply *after* his death. He wrote Trina this with some trepidation. He confessed he didn't have the time or "psychic surplus" to get into a dispute with her. He had to beat out a lot of recently retired poets who could now write full-time and were, therefore, a serious threat to his hopes for the Pulitzer. Encumbered as he was with the crippled syntax of post-adolescent, hormone-driven poetry aspirants, not to mention his potentially bad heart, he was lucky to crank out an occasional chapbook. Could he buy back her supposed rights to one-fourth of his literary empire? If so, how much would she take?

∽

The Baron felt beleaguered, persecuted, invaded by malignant and remorseless spirits. Yet, as he surveyed his motley troops, he felt oddly companioned. A courier, looking much like Greenhill, his feet bound with woolen mufflers, approached to present the news: 32,765 cadavers of horses burning on the fields of Borodino. He had counted every one, so great was his disbelief. This apparition was followed swiftly by a late image of Napoleon astride the little horse named Hope trotting gallantly along the goat paths of Saint Helena. The Emperor had just arrived on the island and rescue still loomed falsely.

"The Soul has Bandaged Moments," the Baron mused mysteriously to his students.

ꙮ

He drove Betina to the airport restaurant for lunch. It was attached to a mostly vacant, but, he'd been assured, comfortable hotel. They sat in a booth overlooking a vast flat tract of industrial properties bounded by high chain-link fencing. They regarded this succession of window-less warehouses, the contents of which would remain an eternal secret, as others might have surveyed the holdings of a great and prosperous estate. They dined sumptuously, but quickly. Then he led her down the carpeted corridor off the restaurant to Room 111 and turned the key. *He knew no haste,* he thought, as he arranged her on the flowered coverlet. *Slowly, slowly up Mount Fujiyama.*

ꙮ

"Greenhill!" the Baron thundered. "Would you ever stop writing like some third sex to some fourth sex and just get down to it, son!"—for he'd felt very tender of late toward his only male student, no matter that he still grinned like an altitude-starved initiate of the Furies. He took Greenhill aside after class and slipped him a box of ribbed, gold-colored condoms: "Greenhill, get out there and tumble."

ꙮ

Betina's poems had begun to devise configurations in which her fe-male voices bested their arrogant male persecutors. She wrote mythi-cally, powerfully. A disquieting but compliant hero appeared whose aroma was of "cypress and coffee," and who, "like a spoiled horse, fresh from the stable," kept carrying her *to bed. To bed.*

↶

The Baron would likely have reigned on happily forever had it not been for Greenhill's spiking his cranberry juice at a student-faculty party. The Baron became a wild man. Imitating the dog in Ferlinghetti's poem trotting "freely thru the street," he got down on all fours and sloshed cranberry juice obscenely onto the ankles of the very colleague who'd put down his waterfall. Burney Falls indeed! He then stood on the hostess's sofa and recited the penultimate lines of Anne Sexton's "Consorting with Angels" in a strident, apocalyptic voice:

> *I'm all one skin like a fish.*
> *I'm no more a woman than*
> *Christ was a man.*

Next, as if to exalt by example, the Baron began to strip off his clothes before the horrified gathering. Only Betina, rushing forward with her raincoat, saved him from complete and utter ruin at the hands of the ungrateful mob.

"Greenhill!" he shouted, lunging unsuccessfully for the boy. "Become a medical doctor. Consult livers and spleens. Go into sanitation. Catalogue rare fungi in the rain forest. But leave poetry, for God's sake, to the passionate and inspired, you lusterless bog of inertia!" In this last plea he heard his own voice rebound like a runaway droshky, heading straight for him.

With that, the Baron passed out and had to be carried from the house, an immense personage borne away on the shoulders of his obscure and unworthy subjects.

↶

The next morning his wife's tearstained face seemed inordinately magnified by his feeling of having been bodily occupied by unholy forces who had squandered him in some cruel and futile campaign. It was painful to lift his eyelids. He smelled as if he'd been rubbed head to foot in *Eau de Cologne of Whiskey*. And what of his legacy? What of his one and only voice among the many?

Just like the French, not to bury their dead until the stench compelled them. But here he was, above ground and seemingly alive. True, his standard had been trampled. The Queen of Beauty had retreated through a sea of slippery mud in her closed carriage. Now a turbaned emir in the form of his dear wife approached his bedside with what he took for a sign of treaty, or was it *entreaty?*

"Whose raincoat is this?" he heard the Baroness inquire. The Great Amnesiac raised himself painfully to his elbow and stared at the strange limp artifact. Could this be the dark blue cloak of Marengo, still damp with sprinkles of holy water? Staring at it, he reflected that it was eminently unfair that the already-bloodied horses of the Polish lancers would yet again have to swim through "knife-edged slabs of ice" to save Napoleon's bacon. And poor Empress Marie Louise—the affront of Marie Walewska's blue-eyed child sired by the Emperor—it was beyond disheartening. Life and history were, he conceded, fraught with intimate betrayals, despotic interludes, impoverished duchies, evacuations by night, twinkling stars over the fugitives, and someone advancing, shouting, "The Cossacks! The Cossacks!"

The Baron reached out and touched the hem of the raincoat. His fingertips reverberated with the current of his unremembered actions from the night before. Indeed an entire tracery of misused power and conscienceless defilement coursed through his being. The snowy escarpment of a singular remorse enfolded him. In his heart's eye he saw a few lonely campfires lit at the foot of a hill. Or had the torch been put to the imperial carriages? He thought he could smell the Emperor's table linen burning. No matter, he would call for his sheepskin and go forth on foot to dismantle the shabby impostors who had been wreaking such havoc in his kingdom. When he returned, he would see to it that the horse named King George henceforth would be called *Sheikh*.

He must, if he survived, interrogate the pastry cook about how to make the oranges sweeter.

The Baron hoped, should anything befall him, the little hair he had left would be sufficient to provide ringlets for his beloved family members. His students would be glad for any remaining snippets. Faintly, at the back of his cranium, he could hear the relic seekers at Longwood ripping the Chinese wallpaper away like the frenzied rats who'd enlivened the floorboards under the Emperor's dinner table.

He turned at the door and embraced the Baroness as if he might never see her again, for he did love her dearly. And, at that moment, as he later would distantly recount, "huge tears began to fall from his eyes."

The Woman Who Prayed

Dotty Lloyd believed herself happily married to a rural mail-man named Del—until she came across a cache of love letters from Hilda Queener. It so happened, only the day before, Hilda's overexcited poodle had piddled all over the waiting-room couch at the Lady Fox Pet Boutique where Dotty worked.

The instant Dotty discovered Hilda had penned the hidden letters, a memory of a distasteful childhood encounter sprang to mind. Hilda, the daughter of a dentist, had carried herself in junior high with the cool poise of a giraffe at a kite convention. She smelled of Jergens lotion and she was fond of cherry-flavored Life Savers, which she shared with her friends. Dotty's father owned and operated the only pest-control service in the town. She gave off the pungent odor of chemicals designed to eradicate.

Nearly thirty years had passed since the two had tangled in eighth grade over Roger Gillwater. Hilda, with great gusto, had slapped Dotty's face in front of their class because Roger had dared to walk Dotty home. In Hilda's mind, Roger was reserved. Luckily for him, after high school he'd migrated to Hawaii, where he married a part owner of a beachside hotel. He had appeared the previous year at their twenty-fifth class reunion wearing leis of lavender orchids and had twice excused himself from his wife to dance with Dotty. On their second foray onto the dance floor, Hilda floated by on a slow number with a grade school principal, and reached over playfully to pick a blossom from one of the leis around Roger's neck. Then the principal's shoulder carried away her knowing smile.

As Dotty now turned one of the letters in her hands, Hilda's jealous slap lashed her cheek across time and space. There in the garage, the stunned faces of her adolescent classmates came back to her. They seemed to lean with her over her unfortunate find. The letters had been mailed to Del at PO Box 1422. "Queenie," they were signed. "Love, Queenie." Dotty began to check their postmarks to determine the extent and timing of her husband's betrayal. She assumed this was the feared midlife crisis that caused a man in his forties to veer off in search of the "absolute cheese," as one of her customers had put it.

It was scalding in those initial moments to note that the letters had been carefully arranged in the order Del had received them. She saw with chagrin that the top one was dated only three days earlier. Furthermore, the correspondence spanned an entire year and each month's bundle was secured with a wide rubber band, the kind Del used on his mail route. Clearly the letters had been treasured.

She might never have come across them if she hadn't made that foray into the garage. Dotty had decided to resurrect a scuffed ivory purse for the spring wedding of a niece, and the cardboard box marked "Smoke Detector" had attracted her attention.

Her initial shock was followed quickly by outrage. She fell upon the contents like a lioness onto the carcass of an antelope on the wide Serengeti. She carried the box into the bicycle shed at the back of the house and plugged in an electric heater to ward off the spring damp. After securing the foot stand on her bicycle, she climbed onto the seat to be closer to the lightbulb. There she began to read. Her eyes and heart moved through the pages—hours and days of events of which she'd known nothing.

"My darling, Del,"—the letters often began. Dotty never addressed Del as her "darling." It was a word she considered definitely over the mark. Though they'd been passionate in their twenties, they'd developed a kindly, affectionate intimacy over the years. Sweetie, she called him, and Sugar. He called her Pumpkin.

She pored through the letters. The light of the bare electric bulb emphasized the surreptitious nature of her inquiry. "Oh Del, I can hardly bear to know you are so close, yet so far." The expressions, though sickeningly pitched at the level of soap opera, still had the power to wring her heart. Weren't these the very things illicit lovers *always* said?

After the ache died back, though, Hilda's spasmodically expressed longing for Del strangely began to relieve Dotty. She considered it evidence of her husband's care in not meeting her childhood rival too often. He clearly did not want to arouse suspicion and bring on the collapse of their marriage. Or was she grasping at straws? No sooner had she been able to shore herself up than she would read from Hilda: "Your letters are a great comfort to me." Just to imagine love letters from Del, nestled among lingerie from Frederick's of Hollywood in Hilda's bureau across town, made Dotty fairly steam. She and Del had courted beginning in high school, so they hadn't needed love letters. She felt retroactively robbed! She wanted to drive to Hilda's with a box of matches and a barrel of kerosene.

Instead, she took the letters from the box, hid them under a sack of birdseed, and unplugged the heater. Then she returned the box to the garage shelf and made straight for the beach down the hill. It was Wednesday, her one afternoon off. She needed to get hold of herself before Del came home at five.

Like the ocean before her, Dotty's mind began to move in and out over her dilemma. She noticed that the ocean no longer consoled her. It instead presented itself as a huge methodical system, which mulled and combed and splashed itself from time to time. It simply claimed, then retracted; mulled, then recoiled. With the tide frothing toward the white logs marooned on the beach, she made the decision not to confront Del with what she'd found, until she was ready.

Somehow she got through the evening without bursting into tears or saying anything sharp or insinuating to Del. They watched a program on an archaeological dig somewhere in the Middle East, had a snack of cantaloupe, and went to bed. Lying next to Del, knowing about the letters, caused her to feel more alone than she could recall. She turned away from him, drawing her knees up inside her gown. Just as she dropped into sleep, Hilda Queener whirled past with one of Roger Gillwater's leis garlanding her long neck.

At her job next morning, a feeling of counterfeit normalcy returned. She ran shears over Bucky, a black cocker spaniel, and considered how to bring up the subject of the letters to Del. She feared she would accuse, berate, and condemn. And why not? He had to answer for what he was doing. Yet even to speak of this would involve such a departure from the safe shore of their mutual respect and kindliness that the prospect overwhelmed her. She knew that once she told Del of her discovery, Hilda would take center stage. As long as Dotty kept things to herself, in a way the betrayal hadn't quite happened. The secret of her discovery matched the secret of the affair.

It seemed prophetic that she was working on Bucky as she addressed her quandary. The dog, named after Buckminster Fuller, lay on his side, the plaintive whites of his eyes showing. Bucky had been saved by an architect just prior to his scheduled execution at the pound. Dotty ran the electric clippers carefully along one black velvet ear cradled over her palm. When she stared into those brown eyes she thought she glimpsed a kindred soul. The animal seemed to beseech, to ask perpetually to be spared. She wanted as much.

That night after dinner their church fellowship group arrived at the house for their scheduled "visiting night." After reading and discussing Scripture together, it was customary, at the end of such visits, to ask the householders if they would like to discuss any personal trouble. Dotty felt herself trembling when Ms. Carriveau, the feisty group leader, asked, "Now, is there anything we can do for *you?*" Dotty looked toward Del, but his head was already bowed in preparation for the closing words. They all joined hands and Ginger Carriveau gave a blanket, all-purpose prayer. Dotty was grateful to shut her eyes and bow her own head, not to have to look at Del, who showed not a trace of remorse or guilt.

Inside the calm space of prayer, Dotty felt comforted. She'd always prayed at the usual times and places. But this time the benevolent, concentrated force she'd been closing her eyes toward since childhood seemed to have been patiently awaiting her. As she prayed now, in the secret pain of her discovery, the letters seemed to shed some of their power, to recede from the infectious claim they'd begun to make on her life.

"May you, Del and Dotty, trust in each other, and in God's will. Let His guidance come into your hearts. Amen," Ginger said confidently, as if, by expressing this aloud, it was sure to happen. They continued in silence for a few moments, as was their custom, offering their private prayers. Del's palm clasped Dotty's in seemingly perfect agreement to their life together. How dear he was, despite all. It was hard to believe he could be apart from her, straying with the twice-divorced Hilda Queener.

After the members of the fellowship group shook hands and headed to their cars, Dotty turned and gazed at Del. He had the untarnished look of a pilgrim in frontier portraits of the first Thanksgiving. His mild blue eyes, set deeply below his high forehead, belied her recent discovery.

During the rest of the evening they were tender with each other and she had the strong impulse to reveal that she'd found the letters. But the urge gave way to wanting to visit the letters once again, alone. Inside the prayer, Dotty had been able to feel *she,* not the letters, held the power. The fact that she could let this trouble drift offshore for a time, without addressing it, gave her hope that her relationship with Del was durable, resilient enough to withstand whatever might come. There was no reason to hurry. That had been the lasting message of the waves as she'd walked the day before.

Later that night, while Del was showering, she decided to make a trip to the bicycle shed. She picked up a box of wooden matches from the counter and took a saucepan from the cupboard. Once inside the shed, she put the pan and matches down, took up one of the recent letters, and climbed, like a schoolgirl, onto the unsteady perch of her bicycle. She read the letter in its entirety. Hilda Queener provided the sorts of details she could not banish—that she wore Del's flannel shirt to bed, a shirt he'd left with her for that purpose. Hilda wrote she was "putting aside a little spare cash" for them "to take a cozy holiday together." Dotty nearly flew apart at the word "cozy." The last holiday she and Del had taken, the previous summer, they'd pulled their camper near LaPush, sixty miles west, and parked in a clear-cut overlooking the ocean. Dotty read on, bracing herself. Hilda said she was keeping the money in a jar under the sink. "When can you get away?" she asked—as if Del were held prisoner in his own home!

Dotty stepped down from the bicycle and picked up the box of matches. She took one out and ran it along the pebbled side of the box until the head snapped and darted into flame. As she knelt over the saucepan, she took up the letter and held the match to it. In the relative darkness of the windowless shed the letter, with Hilda's handwriting across its pages, caught fire and seemed to rush upward, assuming heat and power in the small space. The eagerness of the love letter to burn caused her to open her mouth like a child before summer bonfires at the beach. Was she imagining it, or did the pages seem more free, more ardent as they burned? She held page after page of the letter as it lifted into the dark. She hated the letter's agreement to its destruction, its lack of shame. "The hussy!" she murmured, and heard her mother's voice echo inside her own, as she'd castigated women who "shacked up" rather than marry.

The final bits of paper, tinged with blue, dropped into the saucepan where they smoldered and blackened. She felt mixed about what she'd done. It seemed entirely within her rights, yet, at the same time, she knew it was a weakness to have gone so far. She recalled a story from one of her customers, the owner of a German shepherd with hip trouble. This woman had discovered a single love letter hidden in her husband's fishing-tackle box, next to a Blue Devil lure. She'd waited until he was in the shower to confront him. Then she'd insisted he stay buck naked, water trickling down his body like sweat, and burn the letter over the toilet, in front of her, to prove that, as he insisted, the woman meant nothing to him. *This,* Dotty had felt, was going too far.

She glanced at the remaining packets. They defied her to consign them to ashes and, for the time being, won a reprieve. She picked up the saucepan and matches and started to the house, pausing to knock the ashes into the brambles.

It was quiet in the house as she entered. She turned the deadbolt and saw that the lights were off in the den. Del had evidently gone to bed. She sat down in the darkened living room and gazed into the yard, lit only by their neighbor's house lights. She had come a long way from the relief and comfort of the prayer earlier that evening. She smelled of smoke, of hidden love, of secrets and betrayal.

The next morning after Del left for the post office she walked out into their yard in her bathrobe. She was working afternoons the rest of the week and she was glad for time alone. At the base of the apple tree she noticed the faint green-yellow buds of daffodils pursed on the verge of opening. A wren was splashing in the hanging birdbath of the Japanese plum. The scene was guileless, bathed in sunlight. Like a stranger to her own life, she stood in their yard with bounty all around her, and allowed herself a strange impulse. She bowed her head. After a few moments with her eyes closed she felt outside time. Her spirit reeled forth into a vastness that had been there all along, but which she approached now out of her own direct need. Her attention seemed sturdy and calculated to let any attending powers know she appreciated all she'd been given, despite this recent trouble. She gave thanks for the assurance beauty itself was in the world—its vibrant stir of aliveness of which she was a part, however small.

When she opened her eyes, she saw her home with Del afresh—the swing set they'd painted together, the mailbox with their names: "Del and Dot Lloyd" lettered in gold and black, the hummingbird feeder wired to a post near the red-currant bush where the birds would be sure to find it when they returned from their winter migration.

Her uplift in spirit caused her to recall something their pastor had said recently in a sermon: "Prayer is a way of spreading God's presence. As Paul said, 'Pray without ceasing.'" So, perhaps it followed that the more a person prayed, the more God would indeed exist in the world. And the more of God there was in the world, the more banished would be the likes of Hilda Queener—for she knew from living in the same town all these years that Hilda's amorous exertions had caused more than one marriage to ricochet out of orbit. Prayer or no prayer, she couldn't get Hilda out of the picture.

For the next several nights she burned letters over the saucepan. When the last one had crumbled into a gray ash, she realized she knew something she couldn't have known any other way. She hadn't changed anything between Del and Hilda, or between Del and herself, but she had fruitfully crossed and recrossed the boundary between outright anger and aching dismay. Pain had a way of cauterizing itself, she knew, if you could stand it, or stand up to it.

She began to pray in odd moments during her days at the Lady Fox as she groomed a steady succession of animals. She knew it was wrong to ask for things out of selfish motives, but she brazened away, inwardly, and asked that Hilda Queener suffer some debilitation. Nothing life-threatening, mind you. Only purely cosmetic manifestations, such as the sudden release of foul odors, or perhaps if her gums could show when she laughed, or a craving for raw garlic might overtake her. Then Dotty quickly tried to make up for this by praying for refugees in war-torn corners of the world.

After grooming two paired Pekingese and later an Afghan, she went for a break in the little outside snack area. But the prayers wouldn't stop coming. She bowed her head for Hillary Rodham Clinton. Since she was herself a Democrat and a woman, she doubted God's investment in the current ascendant breed of Republican—though, as with other wayward souls, she assumed the heavenly door might be left ajar for them to repent and be brought into the fold at some later time. She offered these prayers in good faith, knowing they might do no more than ripple the surface of her own soul as they wafted into the universe. But wasn't this the sure good of prayer, that it boomeranged back toward the one who prayed and gave a modicum of hope?

Dotty's boss, Julie, came outside to smoke and found her standing under the maple with her eyes closed.

"Just taking some sun," Dotty said, and did not open her eyes. Julie puffed on her cigarette in silence downwind of Dotty, making curt little snapping noises when her lips left the cigarette. The smoke had a heady, narcotic effect, reminding Dotty of the charred but mentally resilient love letters.

"My hands are itching like crazy," Julie said. "I swear that shampoo leaks right through my rubber gloves!"

"Uh-huh," Dotty said, and kept on with her prayer for the owner of the Afghan, Cara Jensen, who'd just been told she was out of remission on her breast cancer. Cara had long ago told Dotty that her name in Italian meant "dear one." "Take care, dear Lord, of your dear one, Cara," Dotty prayed.

After Julie went inside, Dotty gave a prayer for Julie's red, chemically scalded hands, so like her own. Then she moved quickly to ask for blessings on a dog named Zowie she'd read about in the morning paper. The animal had been shot and killed protecting its master's home from intruders. She didn't want to neglect this innocent, sacrificed in the line of duty. Its homebound fate was somehow very moving to her.

That night Dotty was gazing out the window as Del drove his pickup into the garage. She heard the truck door slam, but he did not enter the house immediately. She thought of the empty box on the shelf and wondered if he was going to it now, intending to add yet another letter from Hilda, but discovering the others missing.

These thoughts accompanied her present endeavor to keep her mind inside a stream of prayerful reverie she'd entered near the end of her shift at the Lady Fox. She had begun to pray with her eyes open. This allowed her continuous access to her prayers. Dotty had offered so many prayers that day that, if her efforts counted for anything, she was convinced God must be more amply present in the world. Certainly she felt deeply infused by her own attentiveness to those for whom she prayed.

When Del came into the house he said nothing to indicate any change, and they set about fixing a little dinner together of spaghetti and fresh salad. He behaved in a very deferential way, as if trying to make something up to her, without revealing what it was. If he had discovered the letters missing, he also had chosen silence.

That night Dotty prayed in the shower and while brushing her teeth—for the sound of running water acted as a natural stimulant to prayer. The longer she kept the secret of the letters, the more the scope of her prayerfulness widened. Virtually every waking moment was spent addressing herself to her prayers. They allowed her to lift away from Del's affair, to bypass it, to ward it off with a genuine and specific concern for others.

As soon as she'd completed one prayer, another suggested itself. She realized how busy the nuns and monks must have been for centuries in their monasteries. She had clearly underestimated them. Each day, when her customers told her of this or that calamity, she set to work. She kept God busy. *She* was busy.

That night in bed, trying to move into sleep, she continued to pray, as if all would be lost if she ceased to perform her repeated pleas. When she tried to regard her effort as possibly hopeless—a silly waste of time—something strong and resilient flared up against her doubt. Del was turned on his side, away from her, but she was aware of his sleeping head on the pillow next to hers. Possibly filled with dreams of Hilda. She couldn't know. For her own part she lay throughout the night in a prayerful drowse that carried her into morning.

When she got out of bed and went downstairs, she saw that Del had already left for work. She was struck by his having gone from the house without waking her. This was unlike him, and unlike her not to have woken. She recalled the moment from past mornings when, after breakfasting together, they kissed good-bye at the door, that island of once harmless departure, which had become so bittersweet of late. She saw that his lunch box was missing and that the mayonnaise had been left with its lid off where he'd made his sandwiches. Why this should have caused her to tremble and move toward tears, she didn't know. When she finally quieted herself, she had the urge to pray for something momentous—for Lebanese refugees, for the bereaved relatives of airline passengers lost in a Florida swamp; for anyone, anywhere betrayed, bereft, and lonely. She lit a votive candle on a side table near the couch in the living room and got down before it on her knees.

In some paralysis of her own needs, she focused on the fate of her marriage and on her love for Del. Treacherous or not, he was still her husband. She closed her eyes and entered a long, narrow corridor of necessity. She was praying for herself. She was unsure, as with the whole idea of prayer, whether or not her effort was wasted. God could fail to hear or to answer. She might lose her husband to Hilda. But there was something worse than losing Del. She might plunge into a life of doubt and bitter inward-gazing while she raked her soul hopelessly across the unbroken silence of God.

The world felt more intimate there on her knees. The candle flickered and dodged across her face in the daylight. After a while she relaxed into her own love letter, a prayer that issued from her as naturally and needfully as breath. It was intoxicating, like the smell of seaweed—tidal and vast, going out across the planet, touching all, pleading for all.

Prayer unceasing kept her on her knees until the dark came down. It was late when Del returned home. She was aware when he parked in the garage and entered the silent house. A door closed as he crossed into the adjoining room on his way to her. Finally he was over her and she felt him lifting her from her knees by one arm. Then his voice, low and halting, from a distance, as he began to try to explain.

Acknowledgments

I wish to thank my friend and former secretary Dorothy Catlett and Greg Simon, who has helped immensely on all of my books for the past twenty years. I also wish to thank my editor Katie Dublinski and all those at Graywolf who have been so attentive to this book. Thanks also to the Irish painter Josie Gray for the use of *Near Kinvara* for my cover.

At the Owl Woman Saloon was first published in 1997 by Simon & Schuster. A paperback edition was published by Scribner in 1999. *The Lover of Horses* was first published in 1982 by Harper & Row, Publishers, Inc. The first paperback edition was published for the Perennial Library by Harper & Row, Publishers, Inc. Graywolf Press published a second paperback edition in 1992.

The stories in this collection, some in different form, originally appeared in the following publications: *Antaeus* ("Turpentine"), *Atlantic Monthly* ("The Poetry Baron"), *Five Points* ("To Dream of Bears"), *Glimmer Train* ("Mr. Woodriff's Neckties"), *Kenyon Review* ("My Gun"), *Michigan Quarterly Review* ("The Mother Thief"), *Ploughshares* ("Bad Company," "Coming and Going," "Creatures," and "A Pair of Glasses"), *Story* ("A Box of Rocks"), *Sycamore Review* ("Rain Flooding Your Campfire"), *Tendril* ("Recourse"), and *ZYZZVA* ("I Got a Guy Once" and "The Lover of Horses"). "King Death" first appeared in the *New Yorker* under the title "A Figure of Speech." The poem "The Man from Kinvara" first appeared in the *New Orleans Review*.

The text of *The Man from Kinvara* has been set in Berkeley Oldstyle, a typeface originally designed under the name of Californian by Frederic W. Goudy in 1938 for the University of California Press in Berkeley. This book was designed by Ann Sudmeier. Composition by BookMobile Design and Publishing Services, Minneapolis, Minnesota. Manufactured by Friesens on acid-free paper.